EVERYWHERE STORIES

EVERYWHERE STORIES

Short Fiction from a Small Planet

Edited by

Clifford Garstang

Press 53

Winston-Salem

Press 53, LLC
PO Box 30314
Winston-Salem, NC 27130

First Edition

Cover design by Kevin Morgan Watson

Cover art, "Old World Map," Copyright © 2009 by Andrey Krasnov, licensed through iStockPhoto.

Printed on acid-free paper
ISBN 978-1-941209-11-0

To the adventurer,
on the road, and on the page.

"We shall not cease from exploration, and the end of all our exploring will be to arrive where we started and know the place for the first time."

— T.S. Eliot

"To travel is to discover that everyone is wrong about other countries."

— Aldous Huxley

"The world is a dangerous place to live; not because of the people who are evil, but because of the people who don't do anything about it."

— Albert Einstein

Acknowledgments

"Au Lieu des Fleurs," by Matthew Pitt, Copyright © 2004 by Matthew Pitt. First published in *Witness*, Vol. XVIII, Number 1, 2004. Reprint by permission of the author.

"The Boy with Fire in His Mouth," by William Kelley Woolfitt, Copyright © 2010 by William Kelley Woolfitt. First published as "Renunciation" in *Riddle Fence*, No. 7 , 2010. Reprint by permission of the author.

"Comfort Me with Apples," by Rochelle Distelheim, Copyright © 2012 by Rochelle Distelheim. First published in *Persimmon Tree*, Summer 2012. Reprint by permission of the author.

"The Ecstatic Cry," by Midge Raymond, Copyright © 2006 by Midge Raymond. First published in *Ontario Review*, 2006. Reprint by permission of the author.

"Eggs," by Susi Wyss, Copyright © 2007 by Susi Wyss. First published in *Bellevue Literary Review*, Fall 2007. Reprint by permission of the author.

"Heathens," by Alden Jones, Copyright © 2003 by Alden Jones. First published in *AGNI*, No. 58, 2003. Reprint by permission of the author.

"A Husband and Wife Are One Satan," by Jeff Fearnside, Copyright © 2009 by Jeff Fearnside. First published in *Potomac Review*, No. 46, Fall 2009. Reprint by permission of the author.

"In the German Garden," by Jay Kauffmann, Copyright © 2014 by Jay Kauffmann. First published in *upstreet*. Reprint by permission of the author.

"The Money Pill," by Tim Weed, Copyright © 2012 by Tim Weed. First published in *Lightship Anthology 2*, 2012, Alma Books. Reprint by permission of the author.

"The Ring," by Marc Nieson, Copyright © 2011 by Marc Nieson. First published in *The Wordstock 10*, 2011. Reprint by permission of the author.

EVERYWHERE STORIES

SHORT FICTION FROM A SMALL PLANET

INTRODUCTION

It's a dangerous world. From rogue militias in war-torn central Africa to roving gangs in Central America, from revenge-seeking bikers in New Zealand to terrorists in Israel, from wild boar in a German forest to the icy waters of Antarctica, from over-zealous mausoleum guards in Beijing to shape-shifters in Zambia, from cancer in St. Petersburg to post-Katrina pestilence in New Orleans, the modern world is fraught with potential disaster. And yet, it's a dazzling world, a complicated world, filled with amazing stories.

When I was a kid, my family lived in Indiana, right in the middle of the United States. Then we moved a couple hundred miles west, to Illinois. We vacationed every summer on nearby lakes. When I went off to college, I didn't go very far, just up the road to Chicago. Until I graduated, that was the extent of my world. Pretty narrow, just like most Americans in those days.

And then my world changed. After college, I joined the Peace Corps and was assigned to teach English in South Korea, a country about which I knew next to nothing except what I'd learned from *M*A*S*H*. I spent two years there—in a provincial capital, not in Seoul—and afterward traveled throughout the region, visiting Japan, Taiwan, Hong Kong, China, Thailand, Malaysia, Singapore, and Indonesia. My eyes were opened, and I was hooked. When I returned to the U.S., I started law school, angling for a career in international law, which eventually took me to places I never dreamed I'd visit and more long stints in Asia. I became a citizen of the world. Not bad for a kid from Indiana.

Eventually, after leaving my legal career, I turned my attention to writing fiction, and because all of my professional experience was international, it should come as no surprise that I tended to write multi-cultural stories in international settings. Those are the stories and novels I like to read, too. Many of my writer friends, even those who haven't traveled widely, have told me that they also like international fiction. That's what gave me the idea for this anthology: a collection of short stories set all over the world. There are more than

200 countries, though, and that would make for a very large book. So we're starting with twenty stories set in twenty countries, and maybe, someday, if we can justify publishing additional volumes in an *Everywhere Stories* series, we'll cover the whole world.

It has been an exciting project from the start. In the fall of 2013, I put out a call for submissions and was thrilled to receive more than 650 responses. That exceeded my wildest expectations, and it also meant that I could be selective about what I chose to include in the book. Because I could only take one story per country, and because I was aiming for some balance among the continents, I had to turn down many fine stories. And although I wasn't initially looking for stories with a particular theme, one eventually emerged. The result is an amazingly diverse collection of stories by writers who have lived and worked around the globe or traveled extensively. Their connection to these places isn't casual. The stories go beneath the surface, the way all great fictions do.

Travel invigorates and enlightens, and so does reading. You don't have to go to the Congo to gain an understanding of the challenges women face there. You don't have to go to Costa Rica to learn about resentment toward fly-by evangelism. You don't have to go to Iran to sample Persian culture and anguish. When it's done right—as the stories in this anthology are—fiction can transport you and show you the essential details, the soul of a place. A fiction writer is like an archaeologist in that way, digging, brushing away what doesn't belong and revealing what a casual observer—a tourist—might miss.

Read the book. Explore the globe. But remember, it's a dangerous world.

Clifford Garstang
Editor, *Everywhere Stories*
June 2014

AFRICA: *Central African Republic*

EGGS

Susi Wyss

Grace and her friend Solange pick their way by moonlight down the dirt paths of their Bangui neighborhood, wandering toward the main road where streetlamps will light their way to the Bar Etoile. Other than the steady singing of crickets and the sporadic bark of a dog, the neighborhood is quiet, houses closed up for the night, faint slits of orange light from a kerosene lamp seeping through an occasional crack in a shutter. The humid night air sticks against her skin, and Grace tries to remember not to lick off the lipstick that Solange applied to her lips.

Solange is uncharacteristically silent, although she did mention at the start of their walk that Alexi might come to the Bar Etoile tonight—information that made Grace's stomach contract into a knot. She can't tell whether she's nervous about seeing him or if she's just hungry—she hasn't eaten since midday, when she bought a stick of fermented cassava at the market where she sells dried fish.

Despite her hunger, Grace feels lucky. She finally has a place to live and a new friend in Solange. Although it's only been a year since her mother died, she's almost forgotten wandering with her two younger sisters from their village for several days to reach the capital of the Central African Republic. A distant aunt took in her sisters, but insisted that Grace, who was almost thirteen at the time, was old enough to fend for herself. So she slept outdoors and picked up odd jobs around the market, carrying loads for merchants, until she was able to get a market stand of her own and, finally, a place to sleep—a one-room mud hut with a thatched roof that leaks when it rains.

Yes, her luck has finally changed. And the next step—if her good fortune holds—is to find a man with the means to live in a solid, concrete house with a tin roof, more than one room, and a latrine that's not communal. A place that's big enough for her sisters to finally come live with her.

This is where Solange comes in. She, too, has plans to meet the right man, and has expressed clear ideas how to go about it. Two years older than Grace, Solange already has a baby who is being cared for by the mother of the baby's father. Grace—who has never "made fun" with a man, as Solange puts it—is grateful not only for Solange's friendship but also for her advice.

As they approach the main road, the din of voices and clamor of an animated Congolese song fills the air. People are either walking briskly, hanging around idly, or hawking wares. Several boys brush past them, carrying wooden trays of cigarettes, chewing gum or kola nuts. Two women sell *kangoya* out of large jugs on tables, their clients seated on benches, drinking the milky palm wine from tin cans. Solange, too, runs a *kangoya* stand that Grace passes on her way home from the market. Two months ago, Solange called her over, cracked a joke, and chatted with her; now Grace stops to talk with her every day. When Solange suggested she come out with her tonight, she didn't hesitate to say yes; Solange always knows how to make people laugh, and Grace wants to laugh. Besides, she feels grown up around her older friend, and Grace is eager to finally become an adult, to shed her childhood like a snake molting its useless skin.

A green bus rolls by, honking, and then a taxi. While Solange pauses at a roadside stand, pawing through wares displayed in a propped-up wooden case, Grace stares at a boy nearby, holding a stack of square cardboard egg trays, several layers of boiled eggs arranged in a tall pyramid on the top tray. Eggs were one of the few things that her mother ate toward the end, boiled and mashed up, or scrambled and fried. Grace brought her the food as she lay on a dirty foam mattress. A *pagne* cloth had been spread over the bed, but the ends were too short to stay tucked under the mattress and it kept bunching up beneath her. By then her mother was so thin that Grace feared her bones would tear through her skin.

Solange's laughter pierces Grace's thoughts. "It's always good to be prepared," she's telling the vendor, then adds with a wink: "It's too late to dig a well when the house is already on fire." He laughs, making an abrupt, cough-like sound. Though she doesn't understand what her friend is talking about, Grace is used to Solange spouting proverbs, most of them borrowed from her late father, a preacher who had three wives.

Solange gives the vendor two coins and he hands her a small cardboard box, which she opens, pulling out a strip of three condom packets. Grace recognizes what they are—when she went to the hospital a few months ago for a twisted ankle, she had to sit through an informational session where a nurse waved a condom in front of the crowd of waiting patients. Tearing off one of the packets, Solange offers it to Grace, who hesitates.

"Don't be silly, Grace," Solange insists. Embarrassed that the people around them might notice what she's holding out to her, Grace grabs the condom and tucks it into the *pagne* cloth tied around her waist.

As they continue their walk to the Bar Etoile, Solange is apparently energized by the bustle of the nighttime crowds, because she finally slips into her usual chattiness. "I'll bet you anything the Rabbit will show up, looking for you," she says. "I told him we'd be there."

Solange has dubbed Alexi, one of her regular customers at the *kangoya* stand, "the Rabbit" because of his oversized front teeth. The first time Grace saw him, she pretended to ignore him—after all, he was clearly much older than she was—even though he stared at her the whole time she talked with Solange. Since then, he has started to joke with her, and his drinking friends play along and call her his wife. Two days ago, he took her to the *mishwi* stand to eat grilled meat. They sat side-by-side, chewing and talking, hands touching as they reached for chunks of meat and dipped them into spicy red powder before popping them into their mouths. It made her feel grown-up to have a mature man seated next to her paying for her food, as if she really were his wife, as if they belonged together. And although she can't imagine making fun with him just yet, she's decided that she likes his toothy smile.

"You could do a lot worse than him, you know," Solange continues. "He makes good money from his taxi, and he'll treat you well."

Grace knows that Solange wants to meet someone who will take care of her and her baby, maybe someone like Alexi with a regular source of income. On more than one occasion, Solange has said that when she gets married, she'll take her baby back from its grandmother.

In the three months that Grace has known her, Solange has had two boyfriends who bought her things and promised they would live together one day, but they have both disappeared.

Looking at her friend, dressed in multicolored pants and a flowing top, her hair in long, thin braids, Grace thinks how beautiful she looks, how effortlessly she attracts attention, fluttering around like a bright butterfly. Despite herself, she looks down at her own outfit—made of cloth with a pattern of tiny, dark-blue flowers against a white background—and wonders if anyone will even notice her next to her vivacious friend.

"You're so pretty," Grace tells Solange, "you'll find someone even better than Alexi."

"Of course I will," Solange answers. "Stop looking so serious when you say that—it's very unattractive. Trust me, no man likes a serious girl." As if to demonstrate, Solange lets loose a boisterous laugh, just as the Bar Etoile appears ahead, its walls painted midnight blue with large, silver stars.

Next to the entrance, the usual boys in dirty shorts and T-shirts are selling wares. Grace watches one of them carry a pyramid of eggs, looking much like the egg-boy she saw earlier. A second boy laughs and jostles him, making one of the boiled eggs fall to the ground, breaking its shell. The egg-boy looks at it for a second, places the tray on the ground, and gives the other boy a swift kick to the stomach. Two others throw themselves into the fray, either to pull them apart or to join in, but Grace barely notices the commotion. Instead, she gapes at the fallen egg, its brown shell shattered into a crackled pattern as intricate as a spider web. A piece of shell has split off one end, exposing the glistening surface of white underneath, speckled by flecks of red dirt. A deep gash reveals a tantalizing glimpse of the golden yolk inside. Grace remembers her mother's words that if she ate an egg a day she would grow into a *ngangou wali*, a strong woman, and her stomach rumbles. She wonders if she could reach out and snatch the shattered egg without being noticed; she imagines picking off the dirt and bits of broken shell to resurrect a meal. But before she can act on her impulse, Solange grabs her by the arm and yanks her into the club.

The inside of the Bar Etoile is crowded with people dressed in their well-ironed, best clothes, seated on chairs at low wooden tables or dancing on the teeming dance floor. The concrete floor seems to vibrate from the booming music. Grace is startled by the bar's lighting—not because of the dimness, which she'd expected, but because the white clothes worn by various patrons are glowing a luminous blue-white color. As she and Solange weave through the sweaty crowd, taking a full tour around the dance floor, Grace tries to imitate her friend's stroll—head held up high and hips swaying to the thumping music. They find a few empty chairs in the back and sit down.

"No one will see us back here," Solange complains. Grace can barely hear her over the music, has just had time to understand what she said, when Solange nudges her, shouting into her ear, "The Rabbit's coming."

Grace looks up to see Alexi pushing his way through the crowd toward them, another man trailing behind. Even though he has an average build, he seems short next to his friend, who is at least a head taller. He introduces the tall man, yelling over the noise, "This is Alphonse."

Maybe it's the loud music, maybe she's lightheaded from hunger, but for a moment as she gazes at Alphonse's tall figure, Grace thinks of her father. Although he died a year before her mother, four years after her parents had stopped living together, she remembers him as a vague, tall presence in the first eight years of her life, a shadow that slipped in and out of the house, usually coming home just for meals. As Alphonse bends his frame to sit next to Solange, Grace peers at him more closely, realizing that except for his height, he actually looks nothing like her father. Still, the fleeting moment of familiarity has reminded her of a time when her mother was still healthy, her family intact, and for a moment she is confused by the clamor and bustle of the club.

Alexi has found a chair and is sitting next to Grace. "After a long day of work," he says to her, "it's nice to look at something that looks as good as you. I've been spending so much time in my taxi I may as well live in it. Would you like to live with me in my taxi, Grace?" he asks with a wink.

Distracted by the lingering memory of her father, Grace isn't sure how to respond. Instead, Solange leans across Grace to shout at Alexi, "Your old taxi isn't a place for a nice girl like Grace. A diamond doesn't belong in a dung pile. Besides," she adds, her voice rising an octave into what Grace recognizes as her teasing voice, "where would she cook your meals—in the trunk?"

Alexi laughs as Solange settles back into her chair. "Talking about cooking is giving me an appetite," he says, looking around the club. "Isn't there something to eat around here?" He makes a loud hissing noise to grab the attention of the egg-boy who has brought his cardboard trays inside.

"Give us four, and add some hot pepper," Alexi tells the boy, who places the trays on the table and grabs one of the beige ovals from the top of the pyramid. The boy taps it with a spoon and then carefully peels the shell off, leaving some on the bottom to hold it without touching the actual egg. Splicing the top with a knife, he inserts hot pepper powder into the opening before handing the egg to Alexi and then starting on the next one. Alexi passes the egg to Grace, who takes the offering with both hands, staring down at it, forgetting for a moment the earlier hunger that gnawed at her insides.

Her mother had always been a deeply religious person, so Grace was not surprised that in her final days she called out not to her children, but to God, asking Him, "What have I done to deserve this? Who will take care of my children when I die?" By then she'd wasted away—despite Grace's best efforts to feed her—into a skin-cloaked skeleton. When her mother refused the eggs she brought her, Grace ate them instead. Since her mother's death she has not touched a single egg, as if by avoiding them she'll be able to forget her mother's illness and its aftermath.

"Aren't you going to eat it?" Alexi shouts over the music. He's holding another egg in his hand, his eyes and teeth glowing intensely in the bar's strange lights. Solange and Alphonse are eating theirs, leaning into each other and laughing at a shared joke. Grace eats her egg in three bites, swallowing it without tasting it. She feels a sudden surge of her mother's presence, her mother's exhortation for her to grow up, to become a strong woman. Alexi offers her the egg he's been holding and she grabs it, eager to finally fill the emptiness in her belly.

Later, only a few hours before the sun will rise again, Grace and Alexi are watching their two friends dance to a slow song. Their hips are glued together in an undulating rhythm, their eyes closed, Solange's left arm reaching up to Alphonse's shoulder, her other arm falling loosely to her side. Only a few couples are left on the dance floor, each locked together in a private dance. Leaning toward Grace, Alexi shouts,

"It's too loud in here. I want to talk to you outside." He has to repeat himself, because she can barely hear him over the music. When she understands him the second time, she nods her head.

Outside, the air is much cooler. The egg-boy is standing in front of the club, sharing a cigarette with the boy he'd fought earlier, their brawl apparently forgotten. Only a few eggs remain on his stack of cardboard trays. Grace follows Alexi as he passes the boys, around the wall to the side of the club, stopping at the back corner. Other than the throbbing of the music through the wall, they are undisturbed. She feels him staring at her, as if he is deliberating about what he wants to say.

"Look," he says, "I like you. I can be nice to you and help you, but you have to be nice to me, too. I work hard all day and at night I get lonely."

He hasn't touched her, and Grace thinks that he almost looks sad. She wants to tell him that she likes him, too, but she can't seem to contort her tongue to form the words—her tongue feels as if it has suddenly grown too big for her mouth. Afraid that she might be appearing childish, she scrambles to think what Solange would do, then pulls the condom from the waist of her *pagne*, slipping it gently into his palm.

She watches Alexi hopefully as he opens his hand to look at her offering. His eyes seem to focus on it for a second before he jerks back his arm, dropping the condom as if it were a glowing ember that burned his hand. He takes a step backward, obscuring his face in the shadows.

"I don't wear those. There's no point if it's not meat against meat," he says, using the expression "*nyama na nyama*," a line from a song that was popular when her mother was still alive.

Grace, too, takes a step back, surprised by the vehemence in his tone. Until now, she has never heard him raise his voice. He grabs her upper arm and pulls her to him, his voice quieter but laced with urgency: "Are you telling me I'm not clean? I thought you trusted me."

Not wanting to upset him further, Grace remains quiet and avoids eye contact. He finally relaxes the grip on her arm and drops his hand.

"I'm sorry, Grace," he says. "But it hurts me that you think I'm not clean. If you want me to be your friend, you have to trust me. I'm older than you; I know what I'm doing." While he's talking to her, he takes her hand and places it on the front of his pants, rubbing the palm of her hand against the hardness behind his zipper. She lets him move her hand there and doesn't say anything. Leaning into her, his beer-scented breath hot against her cheek, he whispers into her ear: "Don't worry, Grace, I know how to take care of you." Then he pushes her hand away and unzips his pants.

Even as he crushes her against the wall, she knows that she could call out for help and that the egg-boy and his friend might come and stop this from happening. But she remembers Solange's words, *he'll treat you well,* and she doesn't make a sound. She lets him mash his closed lips into hers while he raises her *pagne* and fumbles with the front of his pants. She feels the rough cement wall pressing against her back through her blouse, the vibrations from the bass of the music inside pounding through her, and the sharp, tiny rips as he pushes his way inside her. Letting her body go limp, she stares out over his shoulder at the splatter of stars in the dark sky. She feels as if her body is a separate part of her, as if she is floating away from her bones and flesh and skin, drifting up into the night air, the darkness folding softly around her like the wings of a great, blue-black butterfly.

Her mother had made it sound so easy, this process of growing up and growing strong, of navigating the precarious river to adulthood—a mere matter of eating a daily egg. Now that Grace knows the truth, now that she has an inkling of the dangers she will have to face, she can only wonder why she was in such a hurry to become the strong woman she will now have to be.

AFRICA: *Democratic Republic of the Congo*

INTERNATIONAL WOMEN'S DAY

Jennifer Lucy Martin

Like its sister villages throughout eastern Congo, Shamwana opens International Women's Day festivities with a parade. Women and girls of all ages march together along the dirt road to the football field for their annual game, their arms interlocked, their heads held high, their voices united in song. Ladies at the front hold their Women's Day banners aloft so the crowd of cheering men and boys can applaud the truth and merit of the banners' words. This year's proclamations are painted in sparkles of red, blue and yellow, the colors of the Congolese flag. *Le huit Mars est le jour pour les femmes congolaises et toutes les femmes du monde! Nous sommes la force de notre pays et nous sommes aimés par nos frères! Aujourd'hui nous célébrons le jour de la femme!* The mid-morning sun—a diamond in the azure sky above—bounces off the sparkling words, at times blinding the onlookers. Some of the men and boys blink, some block the sun with their hands in order to read the banners, some turn away. They all cheer.

More and more women join the procession as it nears the football field. Many of them are dressed as men, on this one day wearing trousers instead of dresses, shirts with or without vests, their hair tucked up inside caps. They hold the stubs of cigars between their teeth or chew tobacco, spitting gobs of brown juice at feet in flipflops in the dancing crowd moving alongside them. They clutch empty whiskey bottles and pretend to swig from them. To the delight of the crowd, one of the women near the front stumbles along, hiding a smile as she shouts curses and gestures outrageously at everyone like a drunkard. Some of the men are dressed as women, wearing wigs and long dresses, holding pestles or water buckets or straw brooms. Today, the men will cook. They will pound millet and gather firewood and cook fu-fu while their older children smile and their younger children look on in confusion.

The parade of women and girls passes the Médecins Sans Frontières clinic and the small, square church, its wooden door painted turquoise, and the covered well and the crowded cemetery and the new mudbrick walls and UN-donated tin roof of the rebuilt school. Perhaps this one will not be so easy to burn.

Eleven-year-old Carine, dressed in her brother's shorts and striped T-shirt, marches alongside her mother. She has been chosen to be one of the goalies. Yesterday, the men pointed at her. Yesterday, they selected her.

Carine sees Pierre le vieux standing in front of his small kiosk. Pierre and his son, Pierre le jeune, escaped Rwanda's genocide many years ago, settling in Shamwana with their cousins and baking bread. As she passes close to the kiosk, she smells the heady aroma of freshly baked baguettes. Le vieux smiles at her and she smiles back, wondering as she often does what became of his wife and daughters. Her nose tells her le jeune is nearby as well. His stink of stale sweat and cigarettes and beer creeps into the air like Carine's half-remembered nightmare crept into her sleep last night. As far as anyone in the village knows, le vieux and his son, though Hutu like most Shamwanans, were never Rwandan soldiers or Interahamwe. As far as anyone knows, they didn't take part in the slaughter of their Tutsi neighbors. But the cousins whisper in the dark about a terrible night in Rwanda long ago when le jeune was away with boyhood friends, when le vieux was home with his wife and daughters, when the Interahamwe swept through their village, forcing Hutu fathers to kill the children of their Tutsi friends or watch their own children be killed, sometimes both. Shamwana hears these whispers, Carine hears these whispers, but no one knows if they are true and le vieux never speaks his wife's name, or his daughters' names.

As the parade reaches the football field, the surrounding mountains tower over the women. The scent of freshly cut grass replaces the stench of le jeune in Carine's nose. She helped to cut the grass yesterday afternoon and early this morning, swinging her sharpened machete high into the air and down again over and over along with the other men and women and older children. Dozens of machetes lie scattered across the sidelines of the field now. Though the mountains block some of the sun, enough light slices through to create a cavalcade of brilliant machete mirrors up and down the field. Fractured, skinny images like jumbled puzzle pieces, upside down and rightside up, of men and women—or men dressed as women and women dressed as men—follow Carine as she passes by, they wait for her ahead, they surround her as she stands with her team at center field.

The entire village is here. Not everyone will play—only the younger women and older girls—but everyone will watch and cheer. The American missionaries, gone home for holidays for a few weeks, have sent Shamwana a soccer ball to replace the usual rag ball. Its firmness and bounce is a great improvement. Carine's team's captain, Esperance, wearing jeans and a yellow tie and with an ace of hearts sticking out of her too-long shirtsleeve, proposes their strategy and all agree.

As Carine begins to walk to her goal, she feels a hand on her shoulder. Her body knows her mother's touch, the firmness of her palm, the wedding ring, the calloused fingers, all softened by the light caress of one little finger against her neck.

Her mother walks alongside her. "Do you feel ready today, Carine? We will win, yes? You will do your best, yes?" Her mother smiles, but her eyes falter and look away.

"Of course, Mama." She tries to smile back, tries not to look at the machete mirrors, tries not to remember the men moving and panting above her mother on the ground beside the tree last week, tries to see and feel only her mother's hand, to smell only her mother's faint scent of millet, to hear only the laughter of the growing crowd.

The referee trots by them to centerfield, whistle in one hand, soccer ball in the other. He will time the game—he has a working watch—and they will play for one hour with no breaks. Antonio has been the referee every year since Carine can remember. He is the best football player in the village, of course, since he is Angolan. It is said he deserted from the Angolan army after Angola invaded Congo to support the government along with Zimbabwe, Namibia, and Chad just after Rwanda and Uganda invaded to support the Mai-Mai rebels. Carine knows Shamwana is right in the middle of Katanga, right in the middle of the region the UN calls the Triangle of Death. The rebels burn and rape and loot villages and then run into the forest so the government soldiers can have their turn. It is said the Rwandans want Congo's copper, the Angolans want the gold, the Namibians want the diamonds and everyone wants the coltan because the muzungus in the States and Europe need it for their cell phones. It is said Antonio grew tired of the suffering and the killing and hid beneath a mound of mosquito nets in the back of a UN cargo plane bound for the airstrip near Shamwana. It is said he carried a grenade in his pocket, ready to kill one more time if he needed to. These things are said at night around the fire, but during the day, Antonio's play on the football field is unsurpassed in Shamwana. He has the grace and speed and strength of a leopard.

Carine and her mother reach the goal. The crowd is swelling. She can't be sure who are men and who are women.

Her mother bends down and looks into her eyes. "It will be all right, Carine. You are a wonderful goalie. That is why you were chosen."

She nods as her mother jogs away. That is why she was chosen. They selected her for goalie only yesterday. It was last week that the two men in fatigues selected her first.

Sylvie is the other team's goalie. She is a few years older than Carine. Despite the football field between them, Carine can see, or thinks she can see, Sylvie's grin as the bigger girl points at her, points and trots a few meters toward her. Carine's toes grind into the grass, pulling up newly macheted lumps, the side of her foot brushing against one of the rocks used as goal posts. Sylvie's arm stays straight in the air, her finger like a gun aiming at Carine, until the soccer ball drops to the ground in the middle of the field and the game begins.

She tries to concentrate. The winning team will be celebrated, the winning goalie will be hoisted on shoulders, will be presented large plates of fu-fu and cups of tea with many cubes of sugar to drink, will be asked to make a speech. She does not play nearly as much football as her brothers, but she plays whenever there is no school and her work is finished. Carine is known in Shamwana as a strong player and especially a strong goalie even though she is only eleven years old.

"Please. She is only eleven years old."

Her mother's voice has never sounded so small. It is last week and she and Carine have gone to collect firewood in the forest. They are only a half a kilometer or so from Shamwana. Carine can see the road behind the two men who wear fatigues and carry machetes, but are they Mai-Mai or government? Or even UN? They look Congolese, but Rwandan Hutu are short, too. Carine and her mother haven't spotted the men in time to hide. The men are walking toward them quickly, their machetes swinging in their hands, not smiling, not greeting. One of them points at Carine with a quick flick of his finger.

"Please. She is only eleven years old. She is too young."

The men are so close now Carine can smell their sour sweat and beer-breath. She knows what sex is. Her brothers have told her and now she is afraid to look at the men, afraid to look into their eyes and at their bodies. One of them drops his hand onto her shoulder and it doesn't feel like her mother's hand. It feels like the jaws of the dog that bit her last summer, the one that wouldn't let go.

"Please. She is only eleven years old. She is too young. I will make you happy."

The men are looking between Carine and her mother now, their red-rimmed eyes flickering down and up again. The man with his hand on her shoulder nods and shoves Carine away. She falls to the ground and her mother says to her, "It will be all right" before she tries to pull the men further away so her daughter will not see, but Carine does see, and she hears and she smells.

Now the crowd is shouting and the soccer ball is flying toward her. Women and girls run toward her, too, as she scoops the ball up. She feels her fingers tremble against it. Men yell encouragement from the sidelines—"Tu es la sportive!"

The ball is already grass-stained green like the back of her mother's dress last week. Just as Carine is about to throw it to one of the players upfield, the whistle blows. A woman from the opposing team sits on the ground at midfield cupping her ankle in her hands. Fellow team members bend over her as her captain and Antonio examine her foot. Was she tripped? Players from Carine's team watch and walk back and forth, shaking their heads and tsking, tsking. Finally, two men—perhaps one is the lady's husband—help the injured woman off the field.

Who will replace her? Carine watches as the other team gathers to discuss. Heads nod, heads shake, voices grow loud. Sylvie remains at her goal, staring at Carine. Finally, the captain points into the crowd behind the distant goal and a figure in a bright purple dress runs forward. The new player is far enough away that Carine can't be sure she isn't a man.

The game begins again as the crowd roars. The ball flies back and forth, up and down the field. Women and girls on both teams chase it, pass it, run up and down the field kicking it to each other. The purple dress plays defense. Shots are made on both goals, but Sylvie and Carine both play well. All shots are repulsed. Another woman, this one older and on Carine's team, stops and holds her hand against her heart. She must rest. This time, Antonio does not allow a team conference so Esperance quickly picks someone from the crowd to replace her.

As the match progresses, the game remains tied at zero. Neither side is able to score a goal. With no breaks, women and girls are becoming winded, are running slower, stumbling at times. Some are falling down. Not all get up. Carine sees a girl she knows on the other team—whose parents are from Namibia—crawl off the field. Without invitation, someone from the crowd takes her place, someone in a long dress. The game continues—no one seems to have noticed the new player—and suddenly the ball is kicked directly into Esperance's face from only a few meters away. It is an accident, of course. The other team ensures Antonio that no one *intended* to hurt Esperance even though perhaps their teammate was tripped earlier. Still, Carine can see blood pouring from her captain's nose, bright red and glistening in the sunlight. Esperance stands at the side of the field holding her head back, but still the blood flows, dripping onto the machete at her feet.

Carine wishes she had a watch, wishes she knew how many minutes are left in the match. It seems to be happening so quickly and so slowly at the same time, like the nightmares that started last week, her dreams of hordes of eyeless men clenching knives in their teeth and crawling onto her bedmat. Will the game ever end?

Carine's mother replaces Esperance as captain, but her calls to her players are drowned out by the increasing roar of the crowd. Carine looks behind her and sees the crowd is now surrounding the entire football field, pushing up into the hills, rippling like the bag of snakes her brother bought in the market last month. She can see men and women and maybe men and maybe women and machetes and Rwandans and Burundi and Congolese and the looming mountains behind them all. She sees people handing francs back and forth, making bets, making money, losing money, gesturing, laughing, punching each other's shoulders, their eyes manic, their loud voices indistinguishable from one another. The air is alive. The sun has turned blood-red. Another woman trips and falls, hurting her arm. It is bent at a strange angle—is it broken? Was she pushed? She leaves the field and is quickly replaced by two more. Three more. Four. Still no one has scored.

Two men—not in dresses—stand behind the goal, so close Carine can smell the beer, the rancid sweat, the cigarettes. She wishes she were not wearing shorts. She can feel their eyes moving up and down her body. She can see their jagged, smirking reflections in the machetes lying near the goal-rock. Is one of them moving his hand toward her? Can she feel the shadow of it dancing above her shoulder? Where is her mother?

She wipes sweat from her eyes, tries to shade them from the scarlet sun with her hand. She looks upfield, squinting. The teams have grown much larger. There are dozens, maybe hundreds, of people running around the field now. Blurs of dresses and trousers whirl and spin in front of her and flash across the cage of machete mirrors encircling the field at the crowd's feet. The machetes are all stained red with blood now. Antonio blows his whistle again and again, but no one listens. No one stops.

The crowd surges forward as, on the sidelines, men begin to hack at the Women's Day banners with the red machetes.

The purple dress kicks the ball forward. Players sprint toward Carine, their arms pumping, their legs thrusting. They wear dresses. They wear trousers. Are they men or women? Are they Congolese? The crowd rushes forward again and now everyone is on the field except for the injured.

Carine cannot see her mother. She recognizes no one. She cannot breathe. She cannot move. The players all race toward her, kicking the ball ahead of them, their wigs falling off, their hands wielding red machetes and bits of banner as they shout her name, as they celebrate, as the game goes on.

AFRICA: *Uganda*

THE BOY WITH FIRE IN HIS MOUTH

William Kelley Woolfitt

My father called to say that my mother had died in her sleep, unexpectedly but peaceably, and that now he could eat, drink, and make merry. He manufactured security gates that trucks of bandits could not ram through.

He said my mother had died holding one hand over her eye, the other arm held out, three fingers extended. *Tell me if you see the letter E.* An optometrist's gestures. She had crusaded against river blindness, the plague of groundnut and plantain farmers who lived near rivers, where bred the tiny flies that deposit larvae in human tissue, causing lizard skin, leopard skin, and at last, irreversible scarring of the cornea.

I hung up the phone. I wished that I could have seen my mother again, given her a final chance to tell me if there was anything I could do to make her happy, anything that was within my powers. Though she didn't believe she should be made happy, or that I had any useful skills. She considered me a selfish middle-aged nobody, no wife, no child, no spine, no guts.

I flew to the country of my childhood with a suitcase of eyeglasses.

My father kissed my cheek at the airport. He drove recklessly, overtaking trucks on blind curves, veering around bicyclists, pedestrians, and stray goats. He ate a different meat at a different restaurant every night for a week. He drank so much waragi and banana wine he could barely walk. "Maybe you should take it easy," I said. On the seventh night, he collapsed while dancing at a disco on the roof of a hotel, wracked with spasms, coughing up blood. There was nothing peaceable about his death from food poisoning.

I had him cremated. I opened the can of my mother's ashes, poured his ashes on top. I turned to comforting myself. My father would have recommended excess; my mother would have prescribed stripping away.

In the market, I walked among piles of bananas, shoes, and sweet potatoes. Children asked me to buy sodas, batiks, live grasshoppers to snack on.

A small crowd gathered around a performer. He was a beautiful boy, tall, slender, with arms that moved like birds, perfect teeth, scabby hands and blistered lips. He put a torch into his mouth, pulled it out, and the fire was gone. A meat vendor brought him a coal from her brazier. He pretended to swallow it, rubbed his throat, patted his stomach.

When he spat out the coal, his tongue looked black and swollen.

After his performance, the boy went to a booth of jerrycans. I followed him. He traded places with the man working there. I continued to watch. He seemed ordinary now. He did not toss a jerrycan to make it spin through the air before landing in a customer's hands, or juggle the change, or sing the virtues of his wares.

I left the market at dusk, passed a procession of children. Girls in pastel orange dresses, boys in pink button-down shirts and khaki shorts. Too many to count, and one more on the hip of the woman at the back, a scrawny boy with stick-legs and stick-arms that swung as she walked. She gave me a paper slip with an address printed on it, said that her children made greeting cards from recycled paper, I should stop by. I decided I would attempt to communicate. I said, what a big family you have. Or at least I tried to; I was still rusty with her language. She said that the children had been orphans and street beggars, they slept in a church basement now. Her name was Ruth. I asked if I could carry the boy on her hip. She said that he would attack a stranger, and I said, with what, and she said, with his teeth, he was a biter.

I mailed postcards. I read any novels I could get my hands on. I bought strange vegetables, choosing them for bright colors or unique textures, chopped and threw them into a skillet of peanut oil, and dined on stir-fry.

My father would have bought ice cream for Ruth's children, and yoyos, jacks, and rubber balls. My mother would have organized donations, provided them with vaccines, vitamins, mosquito netting, ink pens, and writing tablets.

I went by minibus to the Kasubi Tombs, took off my shoes, and entered the round wattle-house roofed by a great dome of thatch. The granddaughters of the royal kabakas were old women now, and they were sitting on mats and animal skins, weaving baskets from grasses. They were lingering near their familial dead, buried just beyond the red barkcloth curtains. I heard a whispering tour guide say that the bodies of the kabakas had been dehydrated on drying racks, and that the curtains concealed not just another part of the house, but a great forest, the home of the spirits.

My mother had said that if a thief broke into her house, she would give him her rings and fix him a meal. She shaved her head, wore sack dresses, cooked matoke that was bland as paste.

She said she had been given a treasure, the knowledge of how to let everything go.

I walked into the yard of my parents' house. The high wall around their property was topped with barbed wire and busted bottles, jagged-side-up. I thought that if I looked carefully enough, if I listened long enough, then surely I would be spoken to. The clouds were so pale I almost could not see them. The sky was blue as a whisper.

At the market, I looked for the fire-eater. I had been thinking about the sores on his lips. I had no words for "petroleum jelly," but I could hold up the tube I had bought, and the bottled water, and I could say, can I give these to you.

I wanted to take his picture, to drop coins in his cup.

AFRICA: *Zambia*

FOLLOWING THE ENCANTADO

Brandy Abraham

They continued on, farther down the shoreline, passing women throwing nets into the water and gathering reed moss from the shallows. He thought they would be naked. He subscribed to *National Geographic.* He thought their breasts would be like round rocks against their bodies. But they were wearing tunics that went past their knees. He felt himself being pulled toward them and he leaned out, pressing the side of the boat deeper into the water.

He noticed how they did not speak back to him. But he called out anyway.

The sea was not shocking to them.

They waded out. The bottoms of their tunics were sheer. The moss from the bottom had been dyed and the kimono color bled in ribbons across the current.

He bowed the boat deeper into the water, whispering. He could hear something ancient. Leaning his ear closer, nearly dipping it in, he heard it again. A low voice that sounded like fish scales being rubbed from raw skin.

Jacob, the boat driver, warned him that a piranha could jump out and grab him by the throat. But still he listened.

"There is music under the water," he gasped.

"There is nothing but fish," Jacob said back.

He rowed them away from the women. From the shore where a girl waved, her arms laced with strings and pebble beads, her tunic soaked to her navel. She had hair that melted into the water. He believed it looked like black glass. As if her eyes were all that illuminated and he was running into the night sky.

A DIFFICULT THING, A BEAUTIFUL COMFORT

Richard A. Ballou

It was a difficult thing. For most, it would always be a difficult thing. One day Marion was there and the next he was gone. Somewhere between 10:23 p.m. Tuesday and 11:00 a.m. Thursday he disappeared. Señor Guarino was the last person to see him. He confirmed that he had spotted Marion walking up the stairs outside his apartment on Tuesday evening. He knew it was the young man in question because the street lamp is right next to the landing, and he could not mistake the tall, slender figure with the gray English driving cap. No other Porteño, he said, wore a hat like that. There was no reason not to trust Ed Guarino. He was long retired and had nothing better to do each evening than to consult his watch and observe the goings and comings of the neighborhood from his living room window. He could have told the police the exact hour any number of people came home that night. Old as he was, he still possessed quite an acute eye.

Marion was a night owl. He was the last to arrive at work each morning, generally between 9:30 and 10:30, but never sooner. The others were all there no later than 9:00. Marion was the only exception, because Señor Concerta admired his work and his intelligence and his devotion. Besides, Marion lingered well into the evening each day and frequented the office on weekends as well. He put in more than enough hours to make up for his late starts. More than more than enough. Señor Concerta's small firm was like a second home to him.

There was something about Marion that people naturally liked. But not the kind of affection that led to friendships. It was hard to get to know him, and he was not particularly outgoing. In fact, almost painfully private. But he was such an honest and genuine young man. And there was an aura of tenuous hope about him. As if he were at once what was most promising about the future and also the most fragile. Like a precise cutting from a vintage vine native to a foreign land. During import across the Atlantic, it had to be carefully tended and protected; upon arrival, planted in just the right sun and slope and soil. But if it survived, one day it would reap the finest wine, a distinctive Malbec, say, from Mendoza: unusual yet uncommonly rewarding to nose and palate, equally intense and intricate, possessing a deep but delicately fading plum color and lingering finish well beyond its years.

An unusual wine for sure, for there was also the matter of Marion's unusual ways. A habitual late starter, it seemed he was also a perfectionist. At times, he would take a whole afternoon to complete what others typically wrapped up in an hour. It was as if he looked upon the task as a labor of art. On occasion, it seemed he got stuck on the simplest of things. Repeating and redoing and retesting the obvious. As if punishing himself with unnecessary detail. But such compulsiveness never applied to the more difficult endeavors. Those Marion accomplished with an amazing celerity and grace. Like a virtuoso he seemed to rise to the occasion, and like a master the most challenging work was invariably sent his way.

Señor Concerta was not the first to overlook Marion's eccentricities. From grade school through six years of college, teachers and even fellow classmates had always been willing to afford him wider latitudes. He never took advantage of such leniencies, however. He was forever paying them back, and with interest.

When Marion did not arrive at work by 11 a.m. Thursday, the second day of his absence, a tremor of mild concern rippled through the office: he must be ill. Marion was not a person to miss work with any kind of frequency. But now and then he got one of his migraines and was out for days at a time. No one liked to think of him lying in such pain, all by himself in that small apartment. Not that they preferred he work indisposed, but the office was not quite right without his presence. He was as much a fixture as the antique grandfather clock in the entrance. It had its idiosyncrasies too: failing occasionally to toll the noon hour or running weeks on end keeping the most perfect time only suddenly to lose, and for no apparent cause, five or even ten whole minutes.

But Marion was missed also because in a pinch he could handle so many different jobs. And if there were a question on how to perform some arcane task or how a more common one had once been done or where to find this document or that rendering, then you could go to Marion for the answer. If Señor Concerta was the heart, then Marion was the soul of the establishment.

Señora Tutorra de Rivero, the office administrator, called Marion's apartment at 11:00 and then again at noon. At 1:30 a co-worker, Davide, who was closest in age to Marion at the firm, was sent after his lunch break to check on him. Since Marion did not own a car and walked the nine city blocks to work, there was no way to tell if he was at home. And so, reluctantly, Davide mounted the stairs to the second floor and knocked on his door. He knocked several times, he said. He thought to try the doorknob, but he felt that would be intrusive. He reported to Señor Concerta that apparently Marion wasn't inside. Although a man of considerable emotion, Señor Concerta was not by nature an alarmist. It was unusual for Marion to fail to call in, but then perhaps he had become absorbed in something important. A sudden inspiration that had taken him to the library or to another city for some field research. Perhaps, and this gave Señor Concerta a shudder kindled equally by joy and apprehension, Marion had at last found a girl.

In not displaying further visible concern, Señor Concerta was simply affording Marion the usual liberties. But still, he had Señora Tutorra de Rivero call again the middle of that afternoon and once more before she left for the day. He half expected that Marion, perhaps a bit embarrassed at his irresponsible behavior, would come in well after closing hours when everyone would have left; and so Señor Concerta stayed late. He called Marion's apartment himself at 8:30 and then went home to his wife and three daughters.

Señor Concerta later said he dreamt about Marion that evening. That he was visiting the city aquarium and there suspended in one of the large tanks was the young man. He was several feet below the surface and yet had no trouble breathing. Every few seconds his chest would gently rise and fall. Otherwise, Marion was motionless, his arms and legs stretched out like a body pinioned to a wheel, his wide open eyes staring not to the world beyond the glass but off to the side into the far reaches of the water. Señor Concerta said he tapped on the glass to get his attention, but Marion apparently could not hear him. He confided that in the dream he was not afraid for Marion. But he thought that he might be entangled in something, something behind him that he could not see; and that was the reason Marion couldn't move about freely. Señor Concerta tried to locate one of the attendants, but there was no one in sight. He wandered all about the building to no avail. And then he could not find his way back to Marion's tank. He walked up and down every aisle. Yet the more he searched the farther and farther away he seemed to find himself and the longer and lonelier the aquarium's halls seemed to grow.

Señor Concerta said that he panicked in his dream. He wanted to get back to Marion, but at the same time was afraid he would never find his way out of the building. Soon there was water on the floor and trickling down the walls; a tank was leaking somewhere above. He awoke to find every inch of his body in a cold sweat.

The next morning when there was again no answer at Marion's phone, Señor Concerta called each of the three nearest hospitals. He himself went by and asked the landlord to open Marion's door. The bed was made, the kitchen counters and sink clean, the small, studio apartment generally immaculate. There was nothing askew, nothing out of order, no evidence to indicate a sudden illness or departure or foul play. Marion's sleek, ten-speed bicycle was leaning against the wall just inside the door, his portable television and stereo nestled in the homemade shelving that also housed his collection of books—an equal mix of professional reference volumes, familiar literary classics, and modern titles totally foreign to Señor Concerta. Tucked into a corner nook was a small, built-in desk barely wide or deep enough to write on. Its pale mahogany surface was clear except for a cup of drawing pencils and a straightedge. In the tidy closet Señor Concerta noticed hanging the young man's blazer, his two suits, and both the gray and navy linen slacks he wore to work on the weekends, all neatly hung and freshly pressed. On the floor of the closet Marion's slim, leather portfolio case leaned against two well-traveled pieces of luggage.

Señor Concerta then reported Marion missing to the police. He never forgave himself for not having reported it earlier.

Marion's mother, Aleta, caught the first flight out of Washington, D.C. It made a stop in Dallas, a four hour and forty minute layover, before an overnighter to Buenos Aires. Eighteen and a half hours in all, it was a grueling trip under any circumstances. She did not get more than an hour's sleep on the plane. Nor did she go to bed on her arrival. After visiting with Señor Concerta and the local authorities, she divided her time that first day between walking the streets near Marion's apartment and sitting in her son's reading chair waiting for his return. While there, she did not read or listen to music. She did not write in her journal. She didn't even make a single phone call, for who knew when news of Marion would come across the line. Nor did she nod off. Instead, she sat and alternately stared out the second floor window at the street below or at the door.

The door had been painted and repainted many times over. There were several places where the enamel had dimpled and peeled, and even from across the room she could discern the various layers. White, a marine blue, forest green, and the present, gunmetal gray. There were probably other colors as well, but she couldn't make them out from this distance. It was a thick and oversized door, much too large for such a small apartment. Over the course of the afternoon she had memorized its every detail, at least those discernible from the chair: eyes closed, she could delineate the precise length and width of the six panels, the location and size of each and every bubble and crack, even the shifting pattern of shadows cast across its flawed surface as the summer sun declined. At some point Marion had gone out that door. Despite the lack of evidence, she just knew that her son would walk back through it at any time.

And Marion would immediately apologize, despite the circumstances, whether it was his fault or not, even if he had been in some kind of danger. He would quickly deflect all concern back upon her and the others. Until everyone had largely forgotten that he was once even missing. He was so like his father that way, God rest his soul. Aleta had remarried five years after Marion's father passed. Even as close as he was to his father, the young man had not taken issue. He seemed to genuinely want her to be happy and to move on. She had hoped that it would help Marion move on as well.

Not that he hadn't adapted to the loss in good time, better in fact than she had expected. Perhaps too well. There was something unspoken lingering there, something she could not quite put her finger on, as if Marion were constantly drifting, ever so slightly, in and out of focus away from her, pulled by some invisible, redoubtable force out to sea. Like that time when he was only six and his father had placed him in the rowboat on the side of the dock, and before he could get in himself the line somehow came untethered and the boy and the boat floated out of his reach. Aleta shrieked, but the father only laughed and said the current would bring it back. And it did soon enough. Marion had not panicked. There had always been a calmness about him, and he trusted his father to a fault. The two needed only to exchange a glance or a nod to communicate. There had been no further mention of the incident that day or even later, but Aleta had disturbing dreams about it for months.

Like her first, her second husband was not a native. An American citizen, he worked in the U.S. State Department at the embassy, and after their marriage his job soon took him back to Washington, D.C. The promotion afforded him the opportunity to entertain foreign guests from time to time in their new home. She handled the dinners, at her insistence. Planned the meals and purchased the foods and did most of the cooking. Although somewhat timid and retiring, she was an energetic and gracious hostess. That she typically spoke their language put her guests at ease, and she was always up to date on current events in their homelands. The preparation and execution of such dinners occupied her on average perhaps two days a week. The other three she did research and wrote. The research was for a professor of Latin American history. Her double masters in history and linguistics along with her fluency in Spanish, Portuguese, Italian, and English made her a perfect fit for the translation tasks. Some of it was even challenging.

She was writing a novel that incorporated her research. It revolved around three families: that of a conquistador, a missionary, and an Incan of noble rank. Both during the time of the Spanish conquests and for a hundred years thereafter. There was romance and intrigue, murder and sorrow. Interspersed was carefully placed historical detail. But she was most interested in the conflicts and confluences among the three cultures, on the ever sliding and graying borders between them. She was halfway finished. Though she had never written a novel before, the book was actually quite engaging. Perhaps because she was well read.

Aleta could have brought her writing along as well as some of the historical tracts she was translating. But it would have done her no good. She could not stop thinking about her son. When she was not searching to recall his voice and his smile and the things he had talked about on their last phone conversation, she concentrated on shutting everything out of her mind in the hopes that some clue would come forward from her subconscious, a faint yet reassuring suggestion of his whereabouts. It was the only way she could cope.

For the three weeks of her stay, she kept religiously to her vigil and her routine. Checking first thing in the morning with the authorities, walking the streets and showing people she passed various photographs of her son, studying the newspapers over lunch on the remote chance that a stray lead would present itself. Then retreating to his apartment in the hot afternoons waiting for Marion to walk through that thick, heavy door. Again, she alternately gazed out the window or watched the door, making periodic attempts to shut it all out of her mind. Over those three weeks she gradually lost that ability. And with it her hope eroded as well. There would always be a thread of it, a thin umbilical that would forever affirm her son was still alive. But she would never again have any sense of completion.

In the years that followed, Aleta continued translating, and yet the novel went unfinished and she had lost the talent to entertain. And there was no place that felt like home. She made half a dozen trips back to Argentina, sometimes for extended stays. She separated from her husband, returned to him, and left him again for good. She was like a tiny bird with no territory, constantly flitting about.

Meanwhile that nightmare of Marion drifting away in the rowboat had come back to her, only now she could not see him because the sea was covered in a dense fog. None of this would have happened, she thought, all of this could have been avoided. If only Marion's father were still here.

For his part Davide always regretted never having tested that door. What if, he agonized, Marion had been in the room at that very moment? Perhaps he could have gotten in front of whatever sequence of events that had led to his disappearance. Just one small intervention at the right time would have meant all the difference.

Davide had always been jealous of Marion, the special attentions he was afforded. He, too, was a young, rising star. At twenty-six, even younger and hence perhaps more promising. But so opposite from

Marion. Davide was one of the first to arrive and the first out the door. He prided himself on being so efficient and productive and not overdoing things as his counterpart did. He was forever ahead of schedule, and his work was indeed top notch. He thought Marion not only odd but his mystique largely false.

Now the memory of that mystique would forever haunt him. As would his former doubt of his rival's legitimacy. Davide openly divulged his regrets to his fiancée, perhaps his first sign of weakness in her presence. Supportive partner that she was, she helped him by diverting his attention forward to their wedding and their promising future. And she convinced him it was best to leave Señor Concerta's employ. Not just because of the memories but since her soon-to-be husband was ready to move on to bigger things. A larger, more prestigious firm with instant name recognition, national or even continental rather than merely local or regional in scope, where that quaint, family atmosphere would be replaced by a more professional and dignified environment worthy of his many talents. Oh no, she was not questioning the challenge of the projects he had been assigned to nor Concerta's reputation for only the finest work. But there was more to a career, she said, than the work itself: with a bigger firm, think of the people they could meet and the continuing opportunity—Davide had management, even executive, potential in her eyes.

Bigger and bigger things came as she expected, but with each for Davide the satisfaction grew less and less. Despite his success, he knew there was something missing from his work, something invisible yet lasting and essential that Marion always invested in his.

Señora Tutorra de Rivero never voiced her regrets to a soul. Nor her deep feelings for Marion. No one would know how she secretly cared and how close she was to inviting him to dinner, just the two of them. How she sensed she could help with his troubles. Although it went unspoken, everyone was convinced that Marion was troubled somehow. He was just too different not to be. But in the señora's mind, no one except she had the ability to penetrate the walls about him. She knew the age difference between them would work to both their favors. At thirty-eight, Eva Tutorra was recently estranged from her husband of twenty one years. Señor Concerta knew that. Maybe one or two others at the office, Marion included. She was so close to inviting him to dinner. Perhaps that very Wednesday night.

In the first, long weeks that followed his disappearance, Eva was beside herself. There was no one she could confide in. She was all but certain that, although silent, her affections were not only sensed by Marion but entirely mutual. After all, she still had her looks and her figure, and Marion, though shy, always glanced in her direction when she passed; and there was the way his attentive, blue-gray eyes lingered when they spoke. For weeks, she came back to the office in the evenings and waited for him, under the theory that whatever darkness had driven his sensitive spirit away would eventually lure him back after hours. And that she would be there to welcome him and smooth his return. The first few nights she carefully examined the contents of his desk and his files, discreetly searching by the tightly focused beam of a swing arm lamp for a diary or daily log or notes to himself of some kind, and then poring over each and every draft and sketch for some indication of his unknown designs. As office administrator she had copies of all the keys. And when she finally was resigned to the fact there was nothing, for a series of nights Eva slipped in and just sat there in a fine evening dress and her best stockings and heels, alternating between her desk and his. Then one day she no longer came.

A year later Señora Tutorra returned to her husband, who indeed welcomed her back, throwing a surprise party to commemorate their reconciliation at a grand old hotel on the plaza nearby. She tried her best to learn to love him again.

In the years that followed, Señor Concerta would never forget his dream. It recurred from time to time, but each instance he was quicker to wake. Sometimes he never saw Marion at all. He himself was simply lost in the tenebrous halls of the aquarium. There were days, however, especially in the late afternoon, that he thought he saw Marion at a distance in the street. A young man, head slightly above all the rest, angling his way through the crowd. Such is common, he was told, in cases of disappearance. The mind in its quest to make things whole, to return things to a former normalcy, fills in the inexplicable void. At a restaurant Marion's mother went so far as to tap a young man on the shoulder, from behind she was so sure it was her son. Señora de Rivero and Davide had similar experiences.

Señor Guarino never expected to see Marion again. As much as he watched the streets, he made no double takes at tall, lanky passers-by who might have resembled his former neighbor. Not even should they be wearing a gray English driving cap. He felt no remorse at Marion's disappearance. For sure, he found him likable just as everyone found him likable. And he, too, sensed that same delicacy of hope about the young man. But he hardly knew Marion other than in passing, and what could he have done, sedentary old codger that he was?

There was, however, more to his seeming indifference. Sure, it was a sprawling and dangerous city. And certainly with a person as private as Marion, it would be next to impossible to uncover the clues. "But there are times," Ed Guarino told the detective assigned to the case, "that Porteños are simply consumed. They do not run away or do themselves in, they are not kidnapped or murdered, they don't by meaningless accident fall off a breakwall into the sea. Their bodies never turn up because their source has reclaimed them, through some unfathomable wound that swallows them whole."

The detective had no hopes of solving the disappearance. His investigation was just a formality. He was overworked and the department had more pressing matters in a metropolis where the violent crime rate had doubled in the last six years. There were seven murders a day, a kidnapping every thirty-six hours. Yet even though he would soon drop any active pursuit of the case, and as much as he would have liked to believe Señor Guarino's odd notion so he could completely close the file, to the detective such words were still nonsense. As they would have been to those who only casually knew Marion or had simply heard or read that he had vanished.

But to his mother and Eva Tutorra de Rivero, to people like Señor Concerta and even Davide, the possibility would have been welcomed as a most beautiful comfort.

RUE RACHEL

David Ebenbach

When she woke up on the train, lying across two seats under her mink coat, her turquoise sneakers poking out into the aisle, Rachel for a minute didn't know where she was. Dizzy from the sleep and the pills, she lifted up on an elbow and looked out the window at fields of snow. "My *god*," she said. She was supposed to be in a class, Psychology or Econ, depending what time it was, but instead she was on her way to Montreal. Rachel let her head fall back down, her long dark hair spreading around her.

The only reason she was going to see Adrien was because she was worried about him and what was happening to him up there. It wasn't like she was *with* him, though she had mentioned him significantly to that guy on the train who had helped her with her bag, just so there was no mistake about her being interested in anything.

"My boyfriend should be here helping me," she had said, popping a gum pop at her helper. "But he's in Montreal, at McGill. That's why I'm going."

The man lifting her bag, red-headed and scruffy and with paint on his clothes, said, "Great," like he meant that it was really great.

"Yeah," she said. "He needs me." She knew Adrien was hanging out with guys who were heavy into clubbing and other things. Even after a month, when he came back down to visit, he was all skinny and distracted.

Rachel hated the train. She went back to sleep and slept as much as she could, and in between naps she woke up with itchy skin and a sense of everything happening slowly. She knew about side effects. Her father was a doctor. Twice she found the scruffy red-headed man, who was reading some book, and she sat down across the aisle and told him things about herself.

"I'm from Manhasset," she said. "On Long Island. I don't know any French." And she stared at the light brown bowls of his eyes and saw patterns in his facial hair, and she scratched her thighs. The man seemed like he didn't have much to say.

When the Customs woman came through the car, Rachel said she had nothing to declare, even though actually she was bringing three cartons of Camel Lights to Adrien. You couldn't get them in Montreal. The woman asked her basically the same question again and again. "You didn't bring any gifts?" she said. "You're visiting someone without gifts?" Rachel hated her. The woman was like Adrien's mother, who she also hated. Like she owned the world.

Then, after all the blank whiteness of upstate New York, the lights of Montreal finally made their little show outside the window.

Adrien met her at the station. It was not like Penn Station; it was too empty. Adrien, skinny and tall, stood in the middle of it like a stop sign. She handed him her suitcase to roll.

"I can't believe I came here," she said. "Where am I?" He had been trying to hug her when she started talking. Now he said, "Okay. Let's go." She could hear the accent. He was born in France, and sometimes she could hear it. Rachel had been to France. It was no big thing to go there.

As they walked to the doors to get to the taxis in all the snow, she saw the red-headed man walking toward the Metro sign. Everyone talked about the Metro in Montreal. She didn't understand what was supposed to be so great about it.

Instead of going back to his apartment first, to drop off the suitcase, Adrien took her straight to this restaurant that served crepes, on a street called Rue Rachel. When the taxi dropped them off at the snow-clogged intersection, Adrien pointed up at the sign. *Rue Rachel.* "See that?" he said.

She did see that. It was kind of nice. Unexpected. "Is it a long street?" she said.

He nodded. "It runs all the way Northeast—" he pointed "—from the Parc Mont Royal." She was staring at him. She still felt sleepy from the pills and the train. "It's very long," he said.

"That's nice," she said, and she leaned against him, her fur coat on his wool one. Then she straightened up. "My back hurts. We should go to the restaurant and you can rub my back."

Inside, she squirmed against her seat while he ordered for them in French. The language sounded deceptive to her. Then he noticed her squirming and he reached out to squeeze the muscle in her shoulder. Just then, though, she didn't want him to do that. His dark curly hair had been made funny by his winter hat, and it needed to be cut. Also, the restaurant was full of old people eating themselves to death.

"Are we going to a club tonight?" she said.

"Sure," he said.

"Thank god." She bent her arm to pinch that same muscle in her shoulder. Her other hand dropped the fork. "I have the drops," she said. A lot of times she got that way during classes, when the pills would make it hard to hold on to her pencils or pens, and her friends would tease her. They were pretty fun friends, except maybe Jen. It'd be nice to have them around tonight. "What?" she said. Adrien had said something that she'd missed.

"I asked if you were on those pills again."

Rachel looked at him with her chin in her hand. She wished they could have gone back to his place first so she could have changed clothes, but maybe it was better this way. Once, she was at his apartment in New York, and she was in the shower, pretty sleepy from stuff, and she fell and landed on her back on the edge of the bathtub. And Adrien had run in, but when he saw her, he just started laughing. Then he took her to bed so she could rest, and in a few minutes they were having sex, with her hair still wet and her back hurting.

"You haven't said anything sweet to me yet," she said now in the restaurant. "I was on the train all day to come here."

"I didn't?" he said, reaching across for her hand. She let him hold it. He started to say something, but she interrupted.

"I mean, do you love me? Not like that, I mean, but do you?"

He pulled his hand off and opened his mouth.

"Don't talk to me about pills," she said in a flash of anger. "At least I don't take crystal meth."

He looked around, nervous. "Jesus," he said.

She rolled her eyes. It wasn't like she had said it in French.

They went back to his apartment to change clothes. It was cold, but bigger than the apartment he used to have in Manhattan. That was something.

"Well, so what *do* you want to do tonight?" Adrien said at one point while she was getting ready, his long arms up in the air. Rachel had just been saying some things about not wanting to hang out with his friends, and before that had just pushed Adrien's hands off her tits. She had been sitting in front of the mirror and he came up from behind and put his hands on her tits. Then they were both in the mirror, him with his arms in the air, and her holding a hairbrush.

Then they met up with a couple of Adrien's friends, both of them Quebecois, both excited about the Camel Lights. Everybody was in these winter coats and hats, and you couldn't see what anybody really looked like. But right away she got the idea that she didn't like Martin, whose name was pronounced Mar*tan*, and who seemed like he was all superior and condescending or something. He definitely had an accent. The other guy, Patrick, she couldn't tell.

Now they walked together down some sidewalk covered in unshoveled snow toward a club that played hip-hop. She had her fur coat on, but she was still cold.

"Maybe you should eat more," Martin said when she complained. "Grow bigger and warmer." Adrien was walking with Patrick, the two of them smoking.

She sneered at him. *Fuck you*, she thought. *At least I'm not on crystal meth.*

The club was crowded and the music was thundering. Adrien shouted that it was supposed to be the biggest dance floor in Canada, and pulled her onto it right away. It was definitely big. Rachel felt unsteady but settled into some easy movements with her hips while Adrien bumped up into her, and when he did, she could feel his dick in his pants. Every time she moved she was going between that and all the other bodies. All these people in Montreal, she could tell, were really impressed with themselves. After a while she went and sat down and Adrien followed her to the table. Patrick had ordered everybody mojitos and the glasses were already sitting on the table.

"I'm sorry," she said, loud, over the bass. "I can't drink that."

"What?" Patrick said.

Adrien rolled his eyes. "She has to watch her drink every minute now."

Rachel looked at him and hated him. She would never marry a guy who would be like that. She turned to Patrick and said, shouting, "I have this crazy girlfriend who carries around a Snapple bottle of GHB."

"Of what?" Patrick said. He wore glasses, in a good-looking way.

Adrien laughed. "Date-rape drug," he said.

Patrick seemed stunned. "She carries a bottle of date-rape drug?"

"I know," Rachel said. "My god. She takes it herself. She likes the way it feels." Martin showed up now and sat down.

Patrick's eyes and mouth were wide open. "She gives *herself* the date-rape drug?"

"*And* me, one time," Rachel said. She remembered that feeling, slipping away, slipping down and away. "She secretly put some in my drink so I'd be, like, on her level. She does that all the time to people. She's crazy. So now I have to watch to make sure nobody does that to me again."

"But what happened next with your girlfriend?" Martin said, smiling and licking his lips in a dirty way.

Rachel gave him another sneer. "We did it *all night*," she said, making sure the sarcasm was really obvious.

Martin stood up. "Well, I have to go jerk off in the bathroom now," he said, smiling lopsided. And he looked at Adrien, said, "You want to come?" Rachel glared at everybody. Martin was secretly talking about going to get some drugs.

Adrien looked at her, and she said, "Whatever," not really loud enough to be heard over the music, and looked around for a waitress so she could get her own drink. She remembered she was here to save Adrien, but couldn't make herself deal with that now. He shrugged and got up and went off with Martin.

Rachel herself drew the line between prescription drugs and illegal ones. She looked over at Patrick, who was staring at her. The music was really deafening.

"Why would anybody move to Montreal?" she said, even louder than she needed to be. "My god."

Patrick blinked, surprised. "I was born in Quebec," he said.

"Oh," she said. "I'm sorry." She paused a minute. "So tell me what's so great about it."

He frowned like he was really thinking hard. "I like all of it," he said, watching her face, trying to come up with a good answer. She could tell he was a decent kind of guy. "Okay," he said. "Have you been to Parc la Fontaine?"

She shook her head.

"Well, it's got a very shallow lake in it," he said. He really didn't have a big accent. "And it freezes in the winter, and the families all come there to skate, and the college students, and you have couples holding hands and skating, and... I mean, there are these frozen ponds all over Canada, but, I don't know, it's different somehow in this one place. It's like that Breughel painting. You know?" He was talking fast. "And I remember these two little children in big puffy jackets once just falling all over the ice like little pillows, orange and blue, and all around them these students and businessmen skating, and soon they'll all go off to a café and talk, and—"

The waitress came then and got a drink order from Rachel, and she seemed really happy to be a waitress. Rachel turned back and saw Patrick looking kind of like afraid of something.

"Wow," she said. "Huh." She didn't know what he was talking about.

"I'm not explaining what I mean," Patrick said.

"It's okay," Rachel said, picking up her mojito glass and putting it down again.

After a few hours, they all ended up walking around outside, even though it was freezing, because Adrien and Martin were full of energy.

"I want you to see the city," Adrien said to her.

"I'm cold."

"C'mon. You're going to see how great it is."

They walked up St. Laurent and over to Rue Rachel again, with Adrien really making a big show about that, and down St. Denis, and across Ste. Catherine, and Rachel's feet got colder and colder. It was hard to walk on the snow in her shoes, and mostly she looked down to make sure she didn't fall. Adrien and Martin told her to look at all the ethnic restaurants, all the bars, all the clubs, the shops, the people walking the same sidewalks despite the temperature, which was even more ridiculous than before. Patrick, who was mostly quiet now and who split off from them before long, had pointed out the stairs that wound up from the street to the houses' front doors. Rachel didn't understand any of it. She wanted to ask where the mountain was. There was supposed to be a mountain here. But it couldn't be that tall anyway, if she couldn't already see it.

It was late when they got back to Adrien's place. He kissed her when they were inside, and he smelled like the alcohol and the smoke and everything else he'd done.

When they were in bed, Rachel just moved down the bed and pulled down his pants and underpants to put his dick in her mouth, because it was the easiest thing. But first she held it in her hand and then she squeezed it once, hard.

"Jesus! Rach!" he said.

Then she put his dick in her mouth. This part was easy.

When she was a little girl, Rachel had gone ice skating a lot. She could skate backward and spin, and liked the way she imagined she looked in a pink coat, spinning. She made a picture of that in her head when Adrien finally fell asleep, and held onto it for a while. In her mind, she turned and turned in that pink coat, and she could see herself from all sides.

She looked over at Adrien's face. His eyes were closed and his mouth was open. She hated him. She was going to get on a train early in the morning and leave him here with all his problems and his friends. It didn't matter to her whether he was in trouble or not. She could never marry a man like that.

Even in the bed Rachel was cold. She wondered where her clothes were. And then she wondered what Montreal was like in the summer, if it was better when there wasn't so much snow and cold. And then she thought of Patrick's pond melting and nobody able to skate on it. Something about that made her want to cry. Earlier that night Adrien had said that Rue Rachel ran right up alongside a park—maybe it was the one Patrick had been talking about. She started to cry, not sure whether to wish for warm weather or not. All she knew was that somewhere in this city was a man who, no matter what, would just be looking forward to winter again.

HEATHENS

Alden Jones

Molly, *muñeca*, my doll. I watch you flirting with Rudolfo, just across the road, and you pronounce his name the gringo way: Rude-all-foe. I've sent you over to the *pulpería* to buy me a Ginger Ale but it was only an excuse to get you over to where Rudolfo was, and you knew it. I simply wanted to observe. You come back without my Ginger Ale, all taken over with laughter because you don't speak any Spanish, and he doesn't speak any English, and all you've done is stand there smiling at each other like idiots. "He has lice," I tell you. "Oh my God," you say, face broken, and start raking your fingers through your hair. Rudolfo doesn't have lice but for some reason you believe everything I say. Rudolfo's over at the *pulpería* still periodically pursing his lips in your direction, but now you see him as nothing more than the peasant you first considered him to be.

"Do they all have lice?" you ask me.

"A lot of them do."

"Have you gotten it yet?" You look under your nails for bugs.

"No, I keep my hair pulled back and I don't get too close to them." Maybe this will keep you from picking up the kids. Maybe you'll tell the other gringos and they'll all keep their distance now.

"I got lice one year at camp," you say. "It was awful. My mother made me cut off all my hair." Those golden locks. Slippery as silk from corn, or from the bowels of worms.

You've been here for a week now, living with the other gringos in the minister's house. I don't know why you came *here*; I don't ask. I'm the one you all come running to for the answers, the gringa who actually, God forbid, lives here. You and the other girls came wearing long skirts and long sleeves and carrying Café Rica tote bags on your arms, designer coffee to bring home as a souvenir. One of the boys wore a T-shirt that said "I'm so glad I voted for Bush!" I saw you as I was on my way to school, a clot of gringos in the middle of the road, as if you'd just descended from a tour bus in order to see some monument. But there's no monument here, only a road, a school, a *pulpería* that serves Coca-Cola out of plastic bags. And of course a church, though the wrong kind for you. Your kind has no official house; the *evangelicos* here—their converts multiplying by the month—carry their cults from house to house each week, something certain Americans, your Americans, would like to see rectified.

I kept going, walking to school, hoping that none of you would see me. But you, Molly, saw me and thought I was a friend. Pale skin, blond hair, a dress from the bargain rack of Filene's Basement—all things you recognized. You ran over and stuck out your hand and when you withdrew it, it went to the gold cross around your neck.

"I hope you don't wear that while you're in San José," I told you.

"Why not?" you asked.

"It'll get ripped right off your neck. By the *chapulines.*"

That, at least, was true. The *chapulines* rip gold necklaces off of people's necks all the time, especially gringo necks. Some of the facts I pass to you are actually useful. And when you come running to me for knowledge, I give it to you. Don't flush your toilet paper, it will clog the plumbing. Put it in the waste basket. Rice and beans are good for you and you will offend your hosts if you refuse it. Don't flirt too much with the boys or you'll be sorry.

As soon as I tell Jorge about you, he's interested. "Another gringa in town? In our humble little town?"

He picks up the end of my braid and fondles it. I squirm in the heat. The sweat has dampened my dress and my legs seem glued to the vinyl couch.

"A whole lot of gringas. But they're all Evangelical."

"Oh," he says. He drops my braid, then picks it back up off my shoulder and yanks it hard.

"Ow, *cabrón,*" I say. He picks up my hand, kisses it, and afterwards, smiles.

Jorge's mother comes over from the kitchen and sets down a plate of Bredy with thick slabs of white, salty cheese. I pick at the corner of one piece of bread to be polite. I'm more interested in the coffee she brings on her next trip—it's purest black, and as I swallow that first, bitter sip, the taste of it erases the smell of Jorge's house from the back of my throat.

Jorge's house always has this smell, the stench of mold and urine. I imagine the way your nose would wrinkle the moment you stepped through the door, Molly. You wouldn't think of stopping yourself.

I drink the coffee and in the background I hear you and your friends start to sing. "*Jesus loves me this I know...*" You sing in English.

"That's them," I tell Jorge and his mother. They look interested, but they can't understand the words you are singing. "*For the Bible tells me so...*"

"Oh, how pretty," Jorge's mother says. Then, "Teacher, do you like beef stew?"

"Ah, yes," I say, careful not to be too enthusiastic, because I don't want her to serve me any. Jorge's mother, she's like that. It's not what you're used to. No one makes it easy for you to say no.

"*Ves,* Jorge?" she says, throwing up her arms. "Teacher likes beef stew! Listen, Teacher, I make beef stew for Jorge and he refuses to eat it. He says he doesn't like it. But it's good, right Teacher? Don't you see, Jorge?"

"At my house," I say, helping her to make her point, "it's nothing but rice and beans, rice and beans, rice and beans." I smile at Jorge. He scowls. He doesn't like me siding with his mother, so he'll punish me for it, give me the silent treatment for a while. As if that will upset me like it upsets other girls.

"See? Jorge?" Jorge's mother grunts loudly in annoyance, then mutters something to herself. She goes back to the stove to stir something. Beef stew, I presume.

Before I leave, Jorge stops scowling long enough to tell me he wants to meet you. He hasn't laid eyes on you yet, so it has nothing to do with your beauty; he's trying to piss me off. That's the only reason he requests this introduction. He thinks he can make me jealous. Jorge hasn't sensed my claustrophobia, the way I start to fidget when he suggests we go camp out in Jacó, just the two of us in a tent—he doesn't know that I'm glad he'll have you to distract him from me.

I bring him with me the next day to the church you're building. It's down the road from Cristián's house, at the very end, past the two new cement houses and the ten dilapidated shacks, the insides of which you will probably never see. Here's what's inside: living rooms, bedrooms, kitchens, bathrooms; families, *chunches*, photographs. Not so different from your house, and maybe even cleaner. Have you seen the way the women wax their floors? They are obsessed.

When Jorge sees you, he's impressed. You are prettier than I am. You know it, Molly. I'm not sad about that either. More catcalls for you, less for me. There is a balance in this town. Now you can be the beauty queen, and I'll just be the Teacher. For that, I am grateful.

I beckon. I introduce you to him and him to you, a Spanish accent on his name, an English one on yours. Jorge puts on his suave act. Then I leave the two of you together. I'm not about to hang around and translate for you, and besides, I think it will be interesting to see what happens when you try to communicate in your high school Spanish, which is atrocious, and Jorge's high school English, which is merely bad.

I turn to watch as I walk away, and you seem to be doing just fine. Your chin is bending toward your shoulder already. He's staring at your hair. As yellow as the sun and twice as bright. Hard to look away from.

Forty minutes later you run to the house where I live, and instead of knocking you shout "*Upe!*" You've learned! I'm so proud of you Molly, that I feel the glow of pride come over me as I walk to the door. I feel like I do when one of my third graders picks up an English word I haven't taught yet, like when Andrés told me, "Teacher, I love you."

Anita's out of the house so we don't have to go through introductions, coffee, crackers, and polite chatter. I let you in and your smile is so big I notice for the first time how absolutely straight and small your teeth are.

"Oh my God, oh my God, oh my God," you say, the speed of your words reminding me how young you are: seventeen.

"Taking the Lord's name in vain?" I tease, but I'm actually surprised.

Your lips pucker. A dimple appears, deep in your cheek. "I'm not like that, Lana. I'm not all religious; I just wanted a vacation and my church was going to Costa Rica."

"And you heard it was beautiful?" You tell me yes, that's what you had heard. That's what people hear in the States, that Costa Rica is beautiful, and safe.

"So do you think it's beautiful here?" I ask, and you think for a second.

"Sort of." Your eyes wander; you pick up a piece of hair and begin to twirl it around a finger. "I guess it's not what I expected." I ask you what you mean; I'm truly curious. A year before, when I'd arrived, it hadn't been what I expected either. You say you expected the poverty and all, but why don't they try to make things just a *little* prettier? Like, why do they have to throw all their trash on the street? And would it kill them to paint their houses, so they're not all that same putty nothing color?

"Maybe they want to spend their money on something other than paint," I suggest, but to be honest, I've sometimes wondered the same things. A little color wouldn't hurt this town. And if I see a student throw a candy wrapper on the ground, I make the kid pick it up and put it in the trash can.

"Like food?" you ask, with pity in your eyes.

"No, like DVD players and coffee makers and washing machines." I think about explaining this further, but then consider the effort it will take, and so I go back to your subject. "So, you like Jorge?"

"He is so cute, Lana. He wants to take me to the Mirador in Juan Viñas."

Jorge used to take me there; he would drink Ginger Ale, I would drink Pilsen beer. "Are you going to go?"

"I'll have to see what Ursula says." Ursula is your monitor. You probably had to get permission from her to go as far as my house. She watches all of you, but mostly the girls, and especially you. She can smell it on you, Molly, just like I can. That dangerous curiosity. And that's why Ursula and I are looking out for you.

You might wonder, then. If I seem to dislike you so much, why would I want to look out for you?

I would like to address this question in your presence, but I can't. If you can look at me and think I am your friend, how can I explain to you that you are the enemy? How can you miss it, Molly—that look in my eyes when you say you feel sorry for the people here because they kill their own chickens? Your failed attempts at Spanish, and the way you roll your eyes, because you know you don't have to learn it? And the way you flaunt your money, Molly. It's simply obscene, taking cabs with your friends to the city, when you could take the bus like everyone else.

It's your church, your mission, your reason for being here, that bothers me more. You don't question the fact that your church bribes people into converting, actually pays them money. You don't see the irony when you come to my school, handing out bracelets and superballs and stickers that say "I love Jesus," in English, to the kids that don't know what that means, telling them they're gifts from God. That's how American you are—you express your faith materially.

I'm here to give you one last chance, Molly. You're young enough for me to forgive you because I know you can change. I know you want more than what you were spoonfed. I see the way you look at the boys, the way you want to flirt with them. I know what you want from them, even if you don't. When I hear those hymns floating toward me in the schoolyard, your voice stands out, I hear it and I think: That's Molly. You are different from them, the ones who look at me with such shock when I tell them, "As far as I can see it, Jesus doesn't love me. Jesus doesn't even know me."

You're the only one who looks at me with eyes that sparkle.

But I can't just tell you this. If I am going to get you before you're gone, I can't just reach into the water and pull you out—you'll swim away. I have to bait you right, and I have to wait. This is all okay. I've learned, since I've been in Costa Rica, how to be very, very patient.

Your monitor won't let you go to the Mirador with Jorge, so I go with him instead. He sits over his Ginger Ale and sulks.

I sip at my Pilsen and say, "Don't worry, Jorge. We'll find a way."

He's taken off his school uniform and changed into jeans and a T-shirt. When I first met him, he lied to me and told me he was twenty. I wondered why he was still in high school, but a lot of kids repeat grades. I worried that he wasn't very smart. But his little sister is one of my students and she told me his real age: eighteen.

He dug his own hole with that one. You should never tell lies that are that easy to expose. Tico boys do it all the time, they lie without consequences. But Jorge learned a lesson; I told him that because he lied to me, I didn't trust him anymore.

"You know why I did it, Lana," he said, looking slightly outraged. "I knew you wouldn't go out with me if you knew I was only eighteen."

I told him, "I might have gone out with you if you were an eighteen-year-old who wasn't a *liar*."

They lie, Molly, even the good ones. They will lie to you and not even care if you know they are lying. The only way to punish them for this is to stand your ground.

I've stood my ground, but Jorge hasn't given up. He finishes his Ginger Ale, I finish my beer, and Jorge motions to the waiter for another round. He repeats for the tenth time today: "You know, Lana, that if you would be my girlfriend, I wouldn't be interested in Molly."

For the tenth time I say, "*Salado*." If nothing else, Jorge's constant hounding gives me ample opportunity to use this, my favorite tico expression. *Too bad for you.* The other one I like is "*suave*," which means stop or slow down. If you ever took the bus, you'd hear that, Molly, and you'd smile like me at the cleverness of such a small, solitary word.

Jorge shrugs. "I'll keep trying, Lana."

"Okay," I say. "Go ahead, Jorge; keep trying. I guess you're not too concerned about how that would look, La Teacher going out with a high school boy."

For a second he looks perturbed, and he says, "Lana, why are you talking *paja*. You're not that much older than I am, and anyway, I like mature women." It's always about him, see.

"So why do you like Molly? She's younger than you are, Jorge. She acts even younger than she is."

Jorge smiles at me brazenly. "She has something. *Un toque*. I don't know what it is."

I promise Jorge that I will help him.

"What if you acted as her monitor?" he suggests. "Would Ursula trust you to look after Molly?"

"Maybe she would..." I touch my index finger to my forehead and press on my skull. Inside my skull, my brain is reeling. I'm reeling you in. "Maybe I could take her on a little day-trip," I suggest.

Jorge and I come up with a plan. We are going to take you to San José, Molly. We're going to get you there.

You've been outside the town before, of course. You've been to the places the gringos go. The butterfly farm. You walked on the plowed-over trails in the rain forest, screaming and giggling with your friends, scaring all the birds away. You got sunburned on the beach—on the Pacific side, of course; they would never take you to the Caribbean side, where those two gringas picked up the wrong hitchhiker and got themselves murdered.

You've been to San José already. You stayed in the Gran Hotel on Avenida Segunda, just steps away from the Plaza Central, where you and your Evangelical band gave your obligatory performance.

Here's what it looked like:

You walked to the center of the Plaza in a herd, looking suspiciously at the long-haired men around you. This is a target area for robberies. There are always so many gringos here.

You stood in a line with ten other girls. Behind you, the boys made up their own line. They always stand behind you, right? Yeah, right. You tried not to look bored as your minister picked up the microphone and began his speech. You'd heard it a million times.

"You are suffering," the gringo minister told the crowd. "Things are not always good in your life."

He handed the microphone to a tico man, some recent convert, who translated this. People stopped to listen. Yes, they thought. *I suffer.* They wanted to know how they could make that suffering stop.

You pulled at your skirt, it was hot outside, and the boys were beginning to sweat in their oxfords, making half-moon wet spots under their arms.

The minister told the crowd, "You feel a lack inside. This lack you feel is a hole. A God-shaped hole." The tico man stuttered, trying to translate this.

"God can fill the hole," the minister said. "Let God fill the hole."

Then you sang while one member of your group walked around and passed out pamphlets. You crossed your arms to better bear the weight of your bags full of souvenirs. The bags said Café Rica. El Mall San Pedro. *You came all the way to Costa Rica to go to the mall.*

How do I know this? I see it every month. Days in San José when we happen to be around the Plaza, my friend Lisa and I sit on the steps and watch you, snickering and yelling things and cracking ourselves up. Lisa once stood up in the middle of a translation, looked behind the line of gringos, put her hands to her cheeks and yelled, "Look! Howler monkeys!" and those idiots turned around and looked. Another time,

Anita had given me a napkin full of biscochos, fresh from the frying pan, as I'd left for San José. Lisa and I each took one, still greasy, and chucked them at the singing gringos. Lisa hit a tall boy on the arm. He looked around, his expression somewhere between scared and curious. I aimed mine, Molly, at a girl who could have been your twin. Her waist was small; her eyes were so blue I could see them from twenty meters away. She was comfortable in her skin in a way that only girls who look like you can be. She was giggling her way through the chorus of some song that I didn't know the words to because I was raised a heathen.

I aimed my biscocho at her head, but I was too far away. It hit her on the skirt, leaving a small grease mark near the hem. She shrieked and turned around, ran behind one of the boys, and grabbed his shoulders, using him as her shield. Everyone watched her as she gasped in air, wheezing through a laugh.

She was used to commanding attention. Even while she pretended to act scared, you could see how delighted she was, that everyone was looking at her. She did exactly what you would have done, Molly.

I didn't even know you yet. Yet I did.

I've known girls like you all my life. Summers I worked tickets and snack bar at Six Flags, and girls like you would come to my register and order Diet Cokes and nachos. They drove convertibles and there were always boys with them. When these boys were alone, they would come up to the counter, ask me for ice cream in coy tones. Sometimes I would agree to go on dates with them and they would take me to the movies, or to play mini-golf in the sweltering July heat. Sometimes we parked. I wouldn't have sex with them; there was only so much I was willing to risk. There was more than enough for me in fingers and tongues, in a boy's breath on my neck, and with certain boys, allowing them to bear witness to my pleasure was ample compensation for their efforts. But I got them off anyway. It was fair, and I liked being able to watch desire give way to satisfaction, how it registered, differently, *real*, on every boy's face.

I did this because I wanted to, but afterwards, some boys would look at me as if they'd gotten away with something. The next time they came into the snack bar they would pretend not to know me, or they would be with girls like you, and point at me and say something to them. The girls like you would turn away from their game of Ms. Pac-Man and glance at me, though they were usually polite enough to not stare too long. I wasn't hurt as much as I was perplexed.

I hated the way they giggled, these girls. I hated the way they wanted the boys around, but squirmed away from them when they were. I wanted to see one of them cry. I wanted evidence that just one of them was familiar with pain. Once, I did see one of them pink-eyed and weeping. A red-haired girl in a purple bikini ran into the snack bar, tears streaming down her face, and my heart swelled and dropped into my stomach. I had to know what had happened to her. I dropped my ice cream scoop into the cloudy water. She was looking around for someone to help her, it seemed, and I wanted it to be me.

But before I got to her, one of the lifeguards from the Louge next to the snack bar did. He swallowed a bite of his hot dog and took her by the arm.

She breathed in, seeming relieved. "I lost my tennis bracelet. It must have come off when I was going down the waterslide. It probably went down the *drain*!"

He was a hero, John, the lifeguard. He waded into the Louge landing pool, dodging kids coming off of slides, and their heavier, more dangerous parents, as they plunged into the pool. He could have gotten a foot in the face at ten miles an hour, but John dove, and when he finally climbed up the steps, he had a string of diamonds in his hand.

That girl had stopped crying the minute John took her arm. After this, I would watch him and the other male lifeguards do this over and over again, dive for lockets, for earrings, even for a cheap beaded friendship bracelet, to make a girl feel grateful. And when he handed her the bracelet, she hugged him, pressed her bare stomach against his, and went back to her friends, laughing, relieved that everything was in its place.

There were always the girls like you, Molly, and there were always the boys who liked them. I thought when we all got older things would change.

I came to Costa Rica to get away from people like you. I went as far away from you as I could get, and here you are.

You start coming over to my house every day, at my invitation. I don't let Jorge come over too often; I don't want to give Ursula anything to wonder or worry about. I serve you *fresco* from the fridge, made with boiled water and the store-bought mix that Anita gets from the *super* in Turrialba.

"I love this stuff," you say, swallowing it down.

"It's just sugar, chemicals, and food coloring," I tell you.

"Ew," you say, then you change your mind. "Well, who cares. I'll have some more." I never drink Anita's *fresco*, except when she offers it to me directly. I drink coffee, black.

I pour you more *fresco*. It's supposed to be the color of star-fruit. It's as green as a crayon.

"So you're almost done with the church?" I ask, and you shrug and say "Yah." I ask you what's next.

"We're going on a river rafting trip, then we're going home," you say. "I have to start applying to college. My mom really wants me to go to Tulane. It's like her dream. But I think I'd rather go to UK." I pause for a moment, then realize you mean the University of Kentucky, and not the United Kingdom.

"Will you be sad to leave this town?" I ask.

"No," you laugh. "I haven't had a hot shower in two weeks. And Rudolfo won't leave me alone, he keeps coming by with Ginger Ale. I don't even like Ginger Ale. It looks like he peed into a plastic bag and stuck a straw in it. Ursula's beginning to get a little annoyed with him, too. And I'm really, really sick of rice and beans." You stop, suddenly seeming less sure of yourself. "Oh, but I loved meeting you, Lana. I'm so glad you were here. I don't know what I would have done if you hadn't been here."

"And Jorge?" I ask.

Your eyes roll back in your head. "He is so beautiful, Lana. He's the one reason, aside from you of course, that I wish I could stay here longer."

I'm priming you, Molly. I move from my spot on the stool and sit down next to you on the sofa. My thigh is touching yours.

"Tell me Molly," I say. "I know your church is opposed to premarital sex, but what would they have to say about good old-fashioned fooling around?"

You bat your eyes at me, as if to prove your innocence. "You mean like kissing and stuff?" I drum my fingers on my knee and smile.

"Cut the crap, Molly," I say. "You know what I mean."

"You can't tell anyone that I'm telling you this," you say. I realize I can feel my own pulse. You look over at the wall as if your history is being projected there. "The first time I ever fooled around with a guy was on a church retreat."

"A church retreat?" I repeat dumbly. I can't even imagine what that is.

"They're so clueless! They think that because we're so innocent and obedient they can put the girls and the boys right next to each other. What do they *think* will happen? The boys sneak into the girls' rooms, of course."

"The girls never sneak into the boys' rooms?" I ask.

You're biting the rim of your glass, now empty. You exhale loudly through your nose and mouth and your breath fogs up the inside of the glass. How can your every action be so charming?

"No," you say. "The boys always come to us."

Just as you say this, I hear footsteps outside. Then Jorge's voice, a curt "*úpe*."

I let him inside. He sits down on the couch and takes my place.

"*Voy a pasear*," I say, and leave, winking at Jorge. I cross the road, pick a rock, and sit on it, staring across at the house. I watch for Anita. She's playing bingo at the church—the real church. She shouldn't be back for a while but I keep my eye out just in case. Across the street, two of my students are playing in the gutter, poking sticks into the water. One of them spots me.

"Teacher!" he yells. It's Juan Carlos. He and his brother, Ernesto, shout out "Hello!" in unison, then go back to digging in the water. They're wearing those little rubber boots I love.

A tractor chugs up the road toward me, spilling sugar cane onto the road. There are sugary mud puddles on the road, and smashed cane everywhere. Flies hover over the bigger puddles. If you grab a piece of cane before it gets run over, you can suck the sweetness out of it.

The tractor passes. The three men sitting in the front seat turn to stare at me. The door opens with the tractor still moving, and one of the cane-cutters jumps out onto the road. He's wearing a T-shirt on his head and the same rubber boots that Juan Carlos and Ernesto wear. It's Gemelo, the father of five of my favorite students.

"*Hola*, Teacher!" he calls as he approaches me. "What a beautiful day. It's like summer. No rain for days. True?"

"True," I say. His smile is huge; it always warms my heart. He kisses my cheek. Gemelo loves me and his love is platonic. He loves me because he knows I adore his kids.

"I see all your gringo friends are building a church down by Cristián's house," he says. "I see them around, but I can't talk to them, because I don't speak English!" He laughs. I wish he would say *because they don't speak Spanish.* "I tell Aida Carolina to talk to them in English, but she says she can't."

"We've only just started," I try to explain. "It took me ten years to learn Spanish. In ten years, Aida will talk like a gringa."

"They sang some songs," he says. "It's the work of God, Lana, all you gringos coming here to help our children."

Gemelo is *evangelico* too. Once I sat in his house as he made each of his kids recite the books of the Bible from *Génesis* to *Apocalipsis.* When the carnival came to the city nearby, his kids were not allowed to go. None of the *evangelicos* were. I asked Aida why she couldn't go, and she shrugged. I couldn't tell if she was sad or not.

I know why Gemelo converted; he told me the first day I met him. "I had vices, Teacher," he said that day. "I threw all my money away on liquor and cigarettes. Now that I'm with Christ, my money goes to my family."

That was the most common explanation I'd heard in this town from those who had converted. It was about family, and it was about money. But when people look at you, Molly, you and your friends, it's only about money.

I'd almost forgotten about you. "I'm going home," I say to Gemelo, and he slaps my arm a couple times. I kiss him on the cheek. "Come to the house sometime," he says, and I promise him that I will. I walk back across the street, avoiding puddles, tip-toe up to the door, and push it open.

Jorge's leaning against you with his hand up your shirt. You see me and start to giggle, pushing his hand away. Jorge looks at me. We lock eyes. He winks at me, and then I start to giggle too.

Three days before you're ready to leave, you and your friends come over to the school to play with the kids. As soon as I see you, I duck into the lunchroom. I sit on a stool meant for a seven-year-old and bite my nails for a while. The other teachers come in one by one. They drink *fresco* from a vat in the kitchen, dipping plastic blue cups into the sugary pool.

"Teacher, your friends are outside in the schoolyard," one of them says.

"They're not *my* friends," I say, and the teachers explode with laughter. Lorena slaps me on the back.

"We're glad to hear you say that," says Lorena. "We were worried, them being your countrymen and all...but we'd really like to see them get the hell out of here."

"They're worse than Rogelio and Dorian," says Rosa, referring to two of the more zealous converts in the town. "At least Rogelio and Dorian only try to convert people by luring them into their homes, then talking the Bible to death. They don't try to seduce children with candy and toys."

I tell them I agree, and Teresa brings me my own cup of *fresco.* I drink it. My body is used to the *bichos*; I won't get sick, like you would.

When I go back out to the schoolyard, I look for you among the gringos, but you're not there. The kids are decorated with new bracelets and half of them have little round stickers on their foreheads.

"They look like little Indians!" says one of your friends. I recognize him as the one who wears the shirt that says, "It's not a choice, it's a baby!"

"Here," I say, and hand him a fresh glass of *fresco.*

"Is it boiled?" he asks.

"Yah," I say, "drink it." And he does. People are so easy to boss around, Molly. It truly scares me sometimes.

You've been going around from door to door, passing out pamphlets. It's your last deed. The church is done and you're ready to leave town. After your rounds you stop by my house.

"Half the town was converted before we came," you say. "I spent most of the day drinking *fresco* while Father Andrew talked to them about the Bible. People are so *nice* here."

You show me the pamphlet. On the cover there's a picture of a blond woman and her blond child. They're crouched next to a flowery bush, petting a bear. *A bear.* And there is a deer sipping from a lake in the background, and a couple holding hands next to a house, and a pair of birds fluttering by. The caption reads: "Life in a Joyful New World."

"Are you trying to tell me," I ask you, "that if we all became Christians, we could sit around petting bears?"

"I don't know," you say. I open the pamphlet and read it in Spanish. At the end of the pamphlet, after all the promises of happiness, there's a catch. *Of course, there are requirements to be met if we are to live forever in the coming Paradise on earth.* Does it list that you can't drink alcohol? Smoke? Dance at the *discomóvil*? Play Bingo? Wear spandex? Does it tell you to renounce your carnal ways?

Does it tell you that you have to give 10% of your salary to the church until you die? Because, Molly, these are the rules in this town. But it doesn't list them. It just says, *Accept Jesus Christ as your Lord and Savior.* That is the only requirement they tell you about now.

I look over at you. You're fanning yourself with a pamphlet.

"Do you really believe this stuff, Molly?" I ask you.

"Sure, some of it," you say. "Don't you think it would be such a beautiful planet, if only everyone could be *nice*?"

Anita walks through the door with a blue-and-white striped bag full of groceries. You still haven't met her. I open my mouth to introduce you, but you jump up and say "Hola," shake her hand limply, then turn your back on her.

"Gotta go," you say. "I'll ask Ursula if I can go to San José with you, I'm really excited, Lana." And you leave, smiling briefly at Anita on your way out the door. Anita stands there, looking confused. I apologize for you, Molly. I explain to her that customs are different in the States. It doesn't help explain to her why someone who came into her house, drank her *fresco*, and sat on her couch would flee the moment she arrived.

We eat mango to get your taste out of our mouths.

On the last day of your stay here, I am the one the kids come to, crumpled stationery in their hands, pencils poised. They ask me, "Teacher. How do you say in English, Dear Molly can you send me a gold bracelet, a poster of the Power Rangers, and a picture of yourself."

"Why are you asking her for these things?" I asked the first girl who came to me with this request. The first kid. I don't know if you know anything about kids, Molly, but once one of them does something, twenty more will follow.

"Because I *asked* Molly if she would send me these things. She said *sí, sí, sí.* I just want to make sure she doesn't forget."

"But Yeimi, Molly doesn't speak Spanish. If you asked her for these things, I doubt she understood you."

"Then why did she keep saying *sí, sí, sí*?" I'd like to know myself. But there is something else that you're leaving for me, Molly. Little Jenifer makes this known to me, just walks up to me while I'm eating my Chiki cookies during *recreo* and ruins my day.

"*Usted es una gringa,*" she states, looking up at me, innocently. Yes, I say, I am a gringa. I think this is cute and laugh a little. But then little Jenifer says, "*usted es turista,*" and Molly, it's like I've been slapped in the face. She looks shocked that this doesn't win her the same pleased laugh that calling me a gringa had.

"A *tourist*?" I say. Frankly, I'm outraged. I'm outraged by the statement of a seven-year-old. "You think I'm a *tourist*? Jenifer, how long have I lived here?"

"Since last year," she shrugs.

"Why did you call me a tourist?" I ask.

"My mamá told me, gringos are tourists, and tourists are gringos," Jenifer says. I tell her that her mother is wrong. I give her a hug and half of my Chiki cookie but inside I boil and rage. Suddenly, I realize I might cry.

Look, Molly, what you have reduced me to.

I get up Saturday morning and pack my travel bag. A change of underwear, a shirt, my toothbrush and soap. The book I'm reading, my wallet, a notebook, two rollerball pens that my father sent me from the States. Then, Molly, something for you. Three Sheik condoms in a small, square box.

"Where are you going, Lana?" Anita asks me. I tell her San José. "Be careful of the *chapulines,*" she warns. "Don't walk east of the post office." It's endearing, the way she always warns me of the same thing when I leave. The *chapulines* will never get me, Molly. I'm no *turista,* no stupid gringa. I tell her I'll be careful and she gives me a napkin full of biscochos for the road.

On the bus to San José I ask Jorge, "When you think of gringos, what do you think of?"

"You mean, do I like them?"

That's not what I meant, but now I'm curious. I ask, "Do you?"

"Yes," Jorge says. "I like some of them. But they're like everyone else in the world, Lana. Some gringos are good, and some aren't so good. It's like the Nicas. Everyone here in Costa Rica thinks that anyone who comes from Nicaragua is a thief or a murderer. Yes, some Nicas are thieves, but some of them aren't. All over the world. Good people and bad people. It doesn't matter where you are. Just because you're a gringo, it doesn't make you a God."

"That's why I like you, Jorge," I say. Then I think a minute and ask, "Do you think I think I'm a God?"

Jorge smiles and reaches for my hand. "No, Lana. That's why I like *you*." I let him squeeze my hand but then I pull it away.

Jorge continues, "People say things about gringos, there are the stereotypes. They say that all gringas wear loose clothes, but that's not true. Molly wears tight clothes." I don't bother to explain to him that most gringas think they're fat and feel no need to flaunt it. He wouldn't get this; no one does. The kids are always asking me if I'm pregnant because of my loose dresses. But girls like you don't have to worry about this. No worries, no worries, no worries at all.

It's noon when we get to San José. Jorge yells *parada* when we get to Parque Morazán and the bus pulls over to let us off.

You'll meet us here later, at the Turrialba/San José bus station. Ursula is letting you come because I promised her I'd meet you right at the station, and then drop you back at the Gran Hotel by eight o'clock. How predictable, Molly, that your clan is coming all the way back to San José, staying in a five star hotel, getting picked up by some fancy river rafting group, and climbing into a special van that will turn around and take you right back where you came from. The river runs straight through our town.

It was easier than I had imagined, getting Ursula to agree. All I had to do was bat my eyelashes, like you do. I made her think I was nicer, sweeter, and needier than I am. I told her, "Molly just *has* to see the ballet; she told me how much she likes to dance. And Ursula, it's been so long since I've had a friend. I'm all alone here, you know. Let me spend one last afternoon with Molly." I stuck out my lip. She pitied. She stopped just short of patting me on the head and said, "Okay, dear."

I want to do something nice for Jorge so I take him to the Gran Hotel for breakfast. We order pancakes. There's no syrup so I pour honey over mine. We watch the gringos sip at their genuine Costa Rican coffee.

"That's where the ballet is," Jorge says absently, pointing toward the Teatro Nacional, just across the plaza from the Gran Hotel.

"You know, this is where Molly and her friends are staying tonight," I tell him.

"Here?" Jorge's eyebrows rise. "They must be rich. How much does it cost to stay in a place like this?"

I tell him I don't know. I do, though. I read it in my guidebook. It's what I make in a month and a half.

"Well, the place I'm taking her, it's a little less pretty. But it's fine. You will see, Lana. It has everything you need." He smiles at me and I ask for the check. Jorge fights me for it, but in the end I pay.

This place, Molly, is like nothing I've ever seen. You'll pass right by it on the bus but you won't notice it; it's marked by a small blue sign with its name in block letters: HOTEL BRISTOL. Underneath it reads, "Open all night!" If it weren't for the sign there would be no way to know it was a hotel. It looks like any other hole in the wall. We get out of the cab, enter through the open doors, and walk up a few steps.

"How do you know about this place?" I ask Jorge.

"Been here before," he says, feigning nonchalance. He's told me how he had an affair with a married woman whose kids are my students. He won't tell me which woman, but he's given me enough details that I believe him. I want to know who it was, but I refuse to ask.

At the top of the steps is a closed gate. Beyond the gate, I see a room, but it's so dark that I can't tell what it looks like. I hear the TV going.

"*Upe*," says Jorge, and after a moment a teenage boy appears on the other side of the gate. He stares at us blandly and Jorge says, "I'd like to rent a room for a few hours." A few *hours*, Molly!

"How many hours?" asks the boy.

Jorge checks his watch and says, "I suppose six." He takes out his wallet and hands the boy two thousand-colón bills. The boy hands him a five-hundred in return and unlocks the gate for us.

We walk behind him into the lobby, which is completely dark except for the light coming from the TV, and the light coming from a fish tank in the corner. In the fish tank, there are two swollen goldfish, one black, the other gold.

"Take any room you like on the first floor," says the boy. "The ones on the second floor are all taken." He returns to his place in front of the TV. There's a soccer game on. "Do any of them have windows?" I ask. The boy tells me no. Jorge leads me into a room off the lobby that smells suspiciously like his house, though more of mold, and less of urine. There's a bed, of course, and a bathroom. A garbage can in the corner that has some garbage in it—a couple of balled up tissues, an empty packet of Deltas. The mattress is vinyl. When I sit down on it, the sheet pulls away, and I realize that the sheet has literally been thrown over the mattress, not tucked in. Why bother, I suppose.

"It's perfect," I tell Jorge. It's the seediest place I've ever been in. I'm electrified.

"Do you think Molly will like it?"

"Oh, yes," I say. I try to picture you sitting on the bed. Molly, if you want Jorge, I hope, I hope you'll take him. But it will be more likely that you won't. He'll have the condoms, and he has my blessing—but even without these things Jorge might feel he has a right to you. And I'm giving you a chance to take matters into your own hands; this is my gift to you. No one to hide behind, no one to give that cute pout to, Molly. Just you. Deciding what you want, and taking it.

Jorge sits down next to me on the bed. He sighs, pulls at his shirt. "It's hot in here," he says. He's not complaining; he's giving himself an excuse to remove his shirt. He pulls the T-shirt over his head and stretches out on the bed.

"You're hairy," I say, looking at his chest. I'd seen the hair poking up above the collar of his T-shirts from time to time, but I never imagined how ample it would be.

"As hairy as a monkey," he says, smiling. "Come here," he says, now pulling at me. He tugs at my arm, and I think, why not? I'll lie with him. I'm interested in how that chest hair will feel.

"I'll lie with you," I explain, "but that's it, Jorge. *De acuerdo*?" He nods, but he's only pretending to agree. Soon he's trying to kiss me. He's pulling my face so it lines up with his. His fingers make dents in my jaw.

"Jorge," I complain, breathing onto his face. "I told you. Cut it out." I inch further away from him, then lie still. Now he starts to beg,

Molly, he begs like my students do when they want to color in their coloring books. "Ay Lana, *porfa, porfa*, please let me. I want to kiss you. Just a kiss. *Porfa*?"

This is all foreplay to Jorge. Girls here say no, even when they mean yes. They don't want to come off as sluts, see. "Shut up, Jorge," I say, and then I stand up. "Okay. I've seen the room. We can go now. We have to meet Molly in an hour and it'll take us that long to walk."

I have to wait while Jorge pouts on the bed. Pouting can take a long time. I stand near the door, waiting, tapping my foot. I hear human noise coming from above us. Low hums. Monosyllabic male word-grunts. Above us, a couple is reaching their peak, and the walls are thinner than you might expect.

"Listen," Jorge says.

"In the middle of the day?" I ask.

"It's Saturday," Jorge says, as if I've missed something. "Listen," he says again, as the woman's voice grows louder, and louder, until she's almost screaming. Her voice is competing with the noise of the soccer game.

"Lucky her," I say.

"No," Jorge corrects me. "Lucky him."

It's always about him.

Jorge finally gets off the bed, heaves a sigh, and puts his shirt back on. He's doing his best to look depressed. "You know," he says, "that you're the perfect woman for me. The most perfect woman in the world."

How sweet, right Molly? *Right.* I smile in a way that I consider sarcastic and which he will interpret as flattered. I take two steps toward Jorge, put my hands on his shoulders, and kiss him on the mouth. When his mouth opens, I slide my tongue inside. He starts pulling at my hips and I close my mouth to end the kiss.

"One last thing," I say. I reach for my bag and fish out the box of condoms. He takes them from me and the look of lust on his face is replaced by an eagerness, a sense of purpose. God, they're *so* much like dogs.

Jorge tries to take my hand as we walk through San Pedro, but I keep it to myself. "I'm old enough to be your...teacher," I say, and we both laugh. We pass the mall. Teenagers hang off the balconies in spandex and extremely tight acid-washed jeans. Not your Evangelicals, Molly. We turn onto *calle* 14 and walk along in silence for a while. There is little traffic. I listen to the sounds our footsteps make on the sidewalk: Jorge's soft sneaker steps, my click-clocking sandals.

"Be good to Molly," I tell Jorge.

"I will," he says.

"I'm serious," I say. "Listen to her. Give her what she wants. *Listen* to her, Jorge."

We're crossing the street when Jorge suddenly grabs me by the sleeve. "Shit," he says in English. Of course. It was probably the first English word he learned. Jorge starts to run, towing me by my shirt.

"What's going on?" I ask, quickening my pace, but I won't go any faster than a speed-walk. I look around. There's a bunch of teenagers crossing the street behind us. Otherwise, there's no one around.

"Run," Jorge says. "Run!"

"What are we running from?" I start to say. But then I realize that the teenagers behind us have started to run, too. They're running toward us. They're running after us.

"*Chapulines*!" Jorge lets go of me and starts to sprint. I run after him.

I'm panicked, Molly. I don't understand. These kids, they look like the kids at the mall. They're younger than Jorge, maybe younger than you. Half of them are girls. How could they be the *chapulines*? I'm running as fast as I can in my sandals, jumping over potholes, looking for an escape route. Jorge keeps looking back to make sure I'm with him. I'm sure he could run faster, but he doesn't; he's looking out for me. He stays with me, Molly. He stays with me until they close in on us and one of the boys grabs me by the back of my shirt, almost knocking me down. He could have kept running, but he stopped.

"Let go of her," Jorge says, and I say "Get your fucking hands off of me." I struggle until I see that the boy has a knife in his hand. We're surrounded by twenty kids in fashionable jeans, cut-off shirts, and lipstick. A girl in a hot pink leotard stands in front of Jorge. She's got a knife, too.

"Here," Jorge says, and offers his wallet.

"Everything," the boy says, and we give him everything. My bag, my watch, and Jorge's leather belt. The girl in the hot pink leotard wants my earrings. I give them up. The boy with the knife goes through Jorge's pockets. When he finds the condoms, he holds them up, and they all start to cheer.

"You like to fuck the gringas, eh?" Those are his last words. He spits in my direction but misses; his saliva hits the street. The *chapulines* take off running. Jorge and I run the other way.

I cry, Molly. I hate myself for it, but I cry. I'm not upset about losing my things, except for the rollerball pens and the money. It's other stuff that bothers me. The things I should have known.

Jorge sits with me on the sidewalk. He's pissed, Molly—he loved that belt. And now he'll never have you. His chance is gone, and soon you will be too.

I push the tears off of my face and turn toward him. "I'm sorry," I tell him.

"Not your fault," he says.

"I didn't know that *chapulines* looked like that."

"What did you *think* they looked like?" he asks. I tell him I don't know, but I had my ideas. I thought they looked like the cane-cutters in town, once they'd taken the T-shirts off their heads and put down their machetes. I thought they were men in their twenties or thirties with dirt caught in their wrinkled skin. I thought they walked alone. I don't know why I thought any of this, other than the fact that those were always the people harassing me in the town, hissing *gringuita machita venga pa'ca.*

"I'm sorry it won't work out with Molly," I say.

"Well, we still have the room."

I look at him, confused. "But the condoms are gone, and we don't have any money to buy more. We can't exactly ask *her* to buy them."

Jorge shrugs. "It's not like I have anything to worry about. She told me she was a virgin." I watch him play with the laces on his sneakers. "People have sex without condoms," he explains. And right there, Molly. That's where it ends.

"Not you and Molly," I say. I say this in my Teacher voice and Jorge knows I'm serious. I get up and start to walk toward the Turrialba/San José bus station. We're late. You must be waiting. Jorge and I walk together in silence and while we walk I look at him and think, you just don't know who your enemies are. And your enemies are so often your friends, Molly. It will always be like this, I fear.

You're glad to see us. The Turrialba/San José bus station is not in a nice neighborhood; you were nervous to stand there all by yourself, no one but you and the ticket-seller. But nothing bad happened to you, Molly. Nothing bad has happened.

You give Jorge the money to take the bus back to town. He kisses you on the mouth, gently. You seem sad to see him go. I pull you away from the station, giving Jorge a nod. I'll see him tomorrow.

"How much cash do you have?" I ask you.

"About two hundred bucks," you say. "I haven't spent much since I've been here. There's not much to buy, except coffee."

You don't mind lending me some cash. You feel sorry for me. You ask me why I don't go to the police, and I explain, it happens all the time. It happens all the time. Nobody cares. We have the *chapulines* just like we have the rainy season and trash polluting the street.

"I just want to get to a phone so I can cancel my Mastercard," I say.

"What, you're afraid they're off charging things from the J Crew catalog?" You laugh, Molly, and you make me laugh, too.

"Then you can buy me dinner," I say.

I take you to the Thai place near the bus station, and cancel my Mastercard from the phone there. You eat your first Pad Thai and love it. We split lemony cheesecake for dessert. We order coffee. It's the first meal I've had in weeks that doesn't involve rice *or* beans.

"Where was Jorge going to take me, anyway?" you ask.

"To the ballet," I say, and you smile. Over lemony cheesecake, you and I are both innocent.

At the Gran Hotel you thank me for everything. "I learned so much from you," you say. You hand me two twenty-dollar bills, and your address written on a piece of stationery that one of the kids gave you as a gift. But I won't write you, Molly. I'm done taking care.

You look like you're waiting for me to hug you, your shoulders slumping slightly, as if you're afraid to make the first move. I take your chin in my hand. I kiss you on the lips, and you let me. For two long seconds our lips are pressed together. Then I make a loud smacking sound to let you know it's a joke.

"Okay," you say, laughing nervously.

"*Bueno*," I say. In your eyes I think I see questions I will never answer, but sometimes I only see what I want to see.

On Sunday morning, I'm back in the town, sitting on the grass in Marielos's yard, looking at the highway. I chew on stalks of cane with some of the kids that live in her house. There are about twelve of them in two rooms; I can't figure out if they are all brothers and sisters, or if some of them are cousins. Some of the girls are already composing letters that they want to send to you and your friends in the States.

I help them translate, knowing that you won't send them any gold jewelry. You probably won't write them back. They're about to learn a lesson in disappointment. But that's what I'm here to do: teach.

Around ten o'clock, I see a sleek minivan come over the hill. It's one of those vans that only transports people like you and me—tourists and gringos, gringos and tourists. It's you, Molly, you and your friends.

"Look," I say to the kids, and point toward the van. As it passes I see Ursula in the front seat with the seatbelt pulled across her chest, and then I see you. You're waving. The little girls run to the edge of the highway, waving their arms, saying "Adios, Molly! Adios!" Their new plastic bracelets click on their wrists.

The Money Pill

Tim Weed

Suppose a beautiful woman catches your eye on the street. A complete stranger, you understand, but unbelievably attractive, like Scarlett Johansson or Angelina Jolie. When she has your attention she gives you this smile, a smile meant only for you, and so full of sexual invitation that it stops you in your tracks.

Or maybe she touches you on the arm as you pass on a crowded sidewalk. A little guitar pluck, somewhere between a caress and a grab, and she gives you a little wink as she does it. So again you stop, and you turn to watch the elegant sway of her hips as she walks away into the crowd. But just before you lose sight of her she turns and gives you this mocking look over her shoulder that says, Well? Why aren't you following?

My first Cuban girlfriend was only nineteen, slender and pretty, a student of accounting at the University of Santiago. She caught my eye across a mobbed cathedral terrace overlooking the annual Burning of the Devil in the main square. A few minutes later, magical coincidence, she appeared at my side. We gazed down on the crowd filling the plaza: bare chests and shoulders shaking to the conga, black umbrellas bobbing like voodoo talismans to the rhythm of whistles and drums and old hubcaps. We talked about America, the embargo, politics. She professed to be astonished by the fluency of my Spanish. Her fingers brushed my forearm, then came to rest there, as if we were already lovers.

Down in the plaza they set fire to the effigy. Yellow flames licked delicately around the sides of the horned straw man, tasting it, then leapt explosively, consuming the Devil in a roaring conflagration that illuminated the walls of the square and the faces of the crowd in flickering orange light.

I told the girl I had to go. Her pretty mouth formed a pout. "Truly? You're leaving me?"

I leaned in and raised my voice over the loud drumming that had resumed down in the plaza. "I have a tour group coming in tomorrow. I have to be at the airport first thing. Otherwise, I'd stay."

"I thought we were going to be friends." She appeared deeply crestfallen. I hesitated.

"We *can* be friends. Give me your number."

She didn't have a phone, but she wrote down her name and address in my daybook: Lisbet Romero Morales, Calle Alfred Zamora No. 51, entre 5 y 6, reparto Santa Bárbara. "Ask anyone where is Santa Bárbara," she said, gazing meaningfully into my eyes. "And if you come, don't bring the tour group."

I couldn't get Lisbet out of my thoughts. Why not pay her a visit? I asked myself. What harm could it do?

So two nights after the Burning of the Devil, once the exhausted retirees were tucked in at the hotel, I stuffed a roll of convertible pesos into my pocket and stepped out onto the teeming street. It didn't take me long to locate a '57 Buick to commandeer as a taxi. The driver was a hulking *criollo* with a brushy Joe Stalin moustache. I told him to take me to Santa Bárbara.

"I don't know the address," I lied. "Just take me to the neighborhood and I'll walk."

The driver nodded, gazing at me in the rearview. The fact is he made me feel uncomfortable from the beginning. He kept glancing at me in the rearview, his eyes full of some vaguely unpleasant emotion, sadness or envy or anger.

Through the rolled-down windows the street noise was as jarring as ever, loud salsa music and cracked mufflers and the rattling undercarriages of decrepit trucks and recycled Canadian school buses. Santiago is a hilly city, like a disintegrating San Francisco. French-style colonial townhouses and slumping hardwood bungalows from the city's heyday as a pirate capital mingle with teetering post-1959 cinderblock monstrosities. Soviet tankers rust in a polluted harbor ringed by oil refineries and barren mountains. An old man in a red beret and an olive drab uniform, sweat-stained and threadbare from half a century of wear, hawks newspapers for the equivalent of a penny. The stagnant air smells of diesel and urine and cigar smoke.

The driver let me out on a quiet street. I asked him to wait two hours. He grunted in agreement, watching me with his resentful eyes.

There were no working streetlights in the neighborhood, and it had a menacing flavor at night. Man-shaped shadows prowled the alleyways, and there were no police or soldiers on patrol. I concentrated on making my stride purposeful, unassailable. Images of Lisbet kept appearing in my mind. Long slim fingers. The taut arc of her thigh and buttock pressing against my thigh on the crowded cathedral terrace.

The address written in my daybook matched that of a small wooden bungalow, not, I was relieved to find, one of the crowded cinderblock buildings or subdivided mansions. The pale blue light of a television seeped out through gaps in the ancient hardwood planking.

I climbed the steps to the crooked porch. I hesitated a moment, then knocked.

Lisbet answered the door wearing purple Lycra shorts and a faded military tank top with no bra. Long-legged and barefoot, she appeared both surprised and pleased to see me. Three small children craned their heads around to peer up at me for a moment before returning their gaze to the television. The whole room was bathed in that ghostly blue light.

Lisbet took my hand and led me down the hall to a back room lit by a naked bulb. A younger girl whom I later came to know as her sister was sprawled out on the bed reading a dog-eared novel. Lisbet got the sister up and shooed her out. As she was leaving, the younger girl paused in the doorway to favor me with a very lewd wink.

"Maybe this isn't the best idea," I said when the sister was gone.

Lisbet shook her head, smiling. "*Qué va.* I'm glad you came. I didn't know if you would." She placed her hands on my shoulders and pushed me down onto the lumpy foam rubber mattress. The bed was a sheet of plywood propped up on cinderblocks. I attempted to keep my breath even and slow down my racing heart. You might not believe it, but this was the first time I'd done anything remotely like this.

She knelt on the floor and put a cassette in a paint-spattered boom box that must have been at least twenty years old. A lukewarm breeze came in through the window slats as we both undressed. The cassette was Joni Mitchell.

Don't get me wrong, I'd had girlfriends before. Nothing like this, though. Not a girl I'd met in the street and come to visit for the specific purpose of having sex. But then, I'm not the only foreigner who's behaved differently in Cuba than he would at home.

After it was over, Lisbet and I lounged on the bed in silence. The Joni Mitchell tape ended and down the hall the muffled television blared. At risk of drifting off to sleep, I got up and started getting dressed. Lisbet rolled over to watch me, a teasing smile playing around her lips. "Don't dress. I'm not finished with you."

"I have to get back," I explained. "The tour group, you remember."

She stopped smiling and sat up, not bothering to shield her large inquisitive breasts. "Stay with me. You can get up early. I'll make you a good Cuban breakfast."

"No, I really have to go." I took a roll of twenty peso bills out of my shorts pocket and saw from her dismayed expression that I'd made a mistake. But it was too late to change course. She watched in wide-eyed alarm as I pulled three crisp bills off the roll. I held them out for her to take and she glanced at them in distaste.

"I'm not a prostitute," she said, quietly indignant. "I'm a student of accounting."

I was taken aback. "I *know* you're not a prostitute. But I also know you can use this money. Please, take it, as a gift, for your family."

She shook her head. Her eyes had filled with tears. I sat down beside her on the mattress and put my arm over her naked shoulder. It felt awkward, so I took the arm back. "Look," I said. "I'm sorry. But you *do* need the money, don't you?"

After a moment she nodded, tears flowing, and held out her hand for the twenties.

If you've ever been to Cuba, then you know that the island has a peculiar magic for visitors. It's a gritty time capsule, a rustic communist Never-Neverland. Cubans are handsome, well educated, and literally starving for cash. Doctors and engineers have to skip meals in order to stay afloat. There are food ration coupons from the government, but it's never quite enough. If you're a tourist—if your pockets are filled with dollars or euros—everybody wants to know you. You possess a special kind of magnetism unlike anything you've ever experienced in your home country. It's like one of those amazing dreams where you discover a new superpower. It's as if you've swallowed a pill that has transformed you into Hugh Grant or George Clooney. It's easier than you might think to lose touch with reality.

My second Cuban girlfriend was older than Lisbet, and somewhat less educated. The retirees had gone home, pleased with the sanitized experience of Cuba I'd provided for them, and I had a few independent days before the next group came. I rode out of the city in the same '57 Buick taxi as before, the driver having been pleased enough with the tip I'd given him to lurk constantly outside the hotel as my personal chauffeur. We took the western highway, past rusting tankers, billboards with anti-imperialist slogans, and oil refineries chugging out their clouds of poison. I told the driver to stop at a small beach overlooking a shipwreck. A Cuban tour guide had pointed it out to me several weeks earlier, a Spanish ironclad from 1898 visible as two massive rusted gun turrets jutting out at weird angles from the bright turquoise sea. In college I'd done a term paper on Teddy Roosevelt, and it was my intention to snorkel out and explore the wreck.

Stepping down off the highway onto the pleasantly shaded beach I nearly bumped into Yanita. Lovely Yanita, with bracelets on her wrists and a thick Pocahontas braid teased forward over one nut-brown shoulder. Sexy Yanita, her curvy body only minimally concealed by her threadbare yellow sundress. She sold me a polished conch shell for a peso and offered to watch my duffle bag while I snorkeled. Her availability for other services was clear from the beginning, but I'd come to explore the wreck. Grinning sheepishly, I took my roll of convertible pesos out of the duffle and stowed it in the zip pocket of my swim trunks. The undivided attention of a woman so fetching was making me feel like an awkward teenager.

The water was clear, fading out in all directions to voids of opaque blue. Not far beyond the beach the bottom dropped away, algae-covered rocks slanting down to a distant blue basin of featureless sand. I hate deep water; it makes me feel vulnerable to attack from below. The wreck was farther out than it had looked. Several times I almost panicked and turned back. But the basin slanted up again, and I began to see fragments of the ironclad. Soon I was drifting slowly over the prow of the ship, its well-preserved outlines encrusted by coral. The hull had been split in half by American mortars, but otherwise it was surprisingly intact. Beneath the coral crust I could make out the steam drivers, bunkrooms, a bodega, and of course the bases of the two artillery turrets, one of which I climbed to take a rest. Dripping and pleased with myself, I took off the mask and breathed in the rich tropical air. I gazed at the distant shoreline: the sea grapes and gently swaying palms. I could make out Yanita in her lemon-colored dress, waiting faithfully beside the black speck of my duffle. I waved to her, and she waved back. I decided to head in.

She was waiting in the shade of an old sea grape, leaning against the smooth sweep of the trunk with the duffle on the white pebbles at her feet. She handed me my towel and watched intently as I dried off and put on my T-shirt. Her desire for me was exaggerated, almost slavish, but I believed (and still believe) that it wasn't entirely artificial. I sensed primal forces brewing within Yanita's alluring frame. Deep loneliness combined with a lust willed into being by actual gnawing hunger.

She took me by the hand and led me to a rough wooden shack hidden in the mangroves at the far end of the beach. The shack was empty and there was of course no electric light, but bright slats of sunlight streamed in through gaps in the weathered planks. I could make out the ashes of a small cooking fire, and a military-issue cot with rusting sidebars. Yanita gestured toward the cot and I sat down. She shrugged off the sundress.

There's no point in going into detail about what happened next, other than to note that her hands were callused from manual labor and that she was passionate, beautiful, and quite vocal. There was no formal transaction, though I left a few twenty peso notes tucked discreetly under a skillet on the bare earth next to the fire pit. It pleased me to think that this was probably more money than she would make in an entire year. That she and her children—and I had no doubt there were children—would be well fed for at least a few months.

On the way back into the city in the '57 Buick I sang aloud to an Eliades Ochoa tune I was listening to on my iPod:

Como no tengo dinero, tu cariño es falsedad.
Falsedad, falsedad, tu cariño es falsedad.

The driver turned to me with a look of disgust on his big mustachioed face. "Why you sing that?" he asked in English.

"I don't know," I replied, momentarily caught off-guard. "I just felt like singing, and this is the music I'm listening to."

He turned his attention back to the road. "So you do everything you want?"

"Sure. As long as it's not hurting anybody."

He shook his head and the conversation was over. My mood had soured, and I resented him for it. He seemed to believe that he'd gained some insight into my character that I couldn't see for myself. I decided it was time to find a new driver.

My next Cuban project was Marisleysis, a dancer. She was one of a half-dozen salsa instructors at a rooftop studio adjacent to the main plaza where I'd arranged lessons for a museum group from Chicago. The way she moved her body attracted my attention. She wasn't beautiful per se, but she was striking, with ice-blue eyes and the light freckled complexion Cubans associate with Galician ancestry. Her face had a solemn, serious cast that I found intriguing. When she danced, it was pure magic.

I kept trying to catch her eye, but she refused to take me up on it. So I joined the line to learn the dance step myself. When my turn came up Marisleysis was polite, professionally courteous, and cool. I found her reserve intriguing. I determined to win her over.

The Chicagoans were enthusiastic. They wanted to keep going beyond the two-hour lesson, which would end up costing extra and eating into my profit, but I didn't care. My gaze kept returning to Marisleysis. I loved her self-contained grace as she moved through the flamboyant salsa steps. When my turn came I reveled in the sensation of my hand resting on the tight curve of her dancer's waist.

After the lesson I paid the studio director and gave him a generous tip to distribute among the dancers. I waited by the stairs for Marisleysis. She'd changed into street clothes, jeans and a black T-shirt. She had a book bag slung over her shoulder and wore heavy horn-rimmed glasses, which gave her an irresistibly studious, schoolgirl look. "Can I talk to you a moment?"

"Of course." She nodded, eyeing me coolly from behind the lenses.

"Thank you for the way you interacted with the group. It was impressive. Everyone thoroughly enjoyed it."

"It was nothing," she replied with a modest wave of her hand. "We collaborate. Each one plays a role. I am glad you are satisfied with the class." She glanced toward the stairwell.

I felt myself reddening. "I was wondering if you'd be willing to give me private lessons. I would pay you well. In dollars of course."

She regarded me with a stony expression. "Private lessons for foreigners are against the law in Cuba."

"So are private taxis," I replied, "but they still operate." I glanced at the studio director, who was standing just out of earshot, pretending not to watch us. "Listen, we could keep it between ourselves. No one would have to know."

She turned toward the stairwell. "I am glad the class was successful."

"Think it over," I called out as she vanished down the stairs.

I got her schedule from another dancer, one who was more pragmatic about the power of foreign currency. Three nights after the salsa lesson, with the museum group wrapped up and headed back to Chicago, I walked over to a small theater near the university to attend a performance of what my source had called a "*baile folklórico*."

It was *Carnaval* in Santiago. The streets were filled with lean, sweat-soaked revelers drinking white rum out of plastic water bottles. The mood in the air was tense and watchful, a feeling of repressed violence just beneath the surface. The theater space offered some refuge from the sweating mob outside. A few other tourists had found their way in, possibly feeling equally discomfited by the atmosphere in the streets, sun-bleached Australians or Germans from the look of them. Other than those few, the patrons were entirely Cuban.

The other tourists stood sheepishly against the back wall, but I wanted to get closer to the stage. Some of the other audience members turned to glare at me as I shouldered my way down the center aisle. Their expressions were aggressively contemptuous, reminding me of the look the taxi driver had given me when I started singing to Eliades Ochoa on my iPod. I began to wonder what exactly these people thought they saw in me, but I quickly shoved that thought into the back of my mind. Marisleysis was so beautiful. I had to see her.

The performance began with rattles and bells and a weird low chanting in Yoruba, an African language. At first it seemed predictable enough, with the dancers filing out one by one in costumes representing the Orishas or deities of Santería, an African religion that has been passed down in secret, much like Haitian Voodoo, since the days of slavery. Marisleysis came out in a lacy white wedding gown. There was a veil covering her face, but I recognized her immediately from the way she moved. When all the Orishas were out on stage it became clear that each one was associated with an element, such as fire or water, and some other state of being such as purity, anger, or crippling illness.

Two of the drummers brought out a large slab of rusted steel. It might have been a part from a giant truck or a tractor. It was shaped like a plow, and something about the sight of it caused the hairs on the back of my neck to prickle. The drummers struck it with pipes. It made a sound like a bell, only flatter and more atonal. It was a deathly sound, and it chilled me to the bone. I had to struggle not to get up and leave.

Meanwhile, the dancers launched into a frenzy. Their movements were rapid and mechanical. Their faces had gone blank with an almost sexual ecstasy. One muscular dancer who'd been hobbling around on crutches pretending to be a cripple fell into what looked like an epileptic seizure, clenched and twitching and literally foaming at the mouth. Another, dressed in black, lit three torches and began to juggle. Suddenly the drumming stopped, and the lights in the theater went out. The crowd gasped. The dancer who'd been juggling guzzled a clear liquid from a plastic bottle and then spit out a long tongue of fire that leapt across the crowd, filling the room with a ghastly orange light. The people around me, delighted, touched their hair to see if it had been singed.

I was transfixed by dread. I couldn't escape the fact that the fire dancer's eyes, glinting like coal in the flickering light, were staring directly and accusingly into mine.

After the performance, I was a bit shaken up, a bit disoriented. But I was still determined to talk to Marisleysis, and I found myself following her as she left the theatre. The crowd parted in her wake. She seemed to possess some kind of innate authority that even the drunkest of the revelers instinctively honored. At the door to what I assumed was her apartment, I stepped out of the shadows to make myself known.

"You! What are you doing here?" She was surprised to see me, obviously, and not pleased.

I held up my hands and gave her a reassuring smile. "Don't worry!

I saw your performance, and I thought I'd take the opportunity to check back with you about the private lessons."

"You followed me home?" She was staring at me as if I were a giant cockroach that had just crawled up from the gutter. She was even more beautiful than I remembered, dressed in jeans and a black T-shirt with those library-chic horn-rimmed glasses.

She took out a key and pushed open the door to her apartment. "Goodbye," she said, half-turning. "Please do not follow me again, or I will be forced to call the police."

"I only wanted to talk," I protested.

Inside now, she was about to swing the door closed. Seeing that this was my last chance, I darted through the door before she could shut it, and there I was, inside her small apartment. She lunged for the phone. I grabbed her forearm, which was strong, but not strong enough to escape my grip. "Look, all I ask is that you give me a chance. I could help you out, you know, in a number of ways."

Her face was deeply flushed. She looked angry, but not frightened. Above the phone there was a signed photograph of a young Fidel Castro, a tall bearded youth in a forested landscape with rumpled fatigues and a rifle in his hand. I'd never been able to understand his appeal for Cubans, but now, looking at this picture, I could see how someone like Marisleysis might find him heroic. "You are a pig," she spat. "You and your whole *yuma* country are pigs."

Suddenly ashamed, I let go of her arm. I quickly apologized and let myself out. As I shut the door behind me she was reaching for the phone.

I spent the rest of that night lying awake in my hotel room, bracing for the knock at my door.

The knock never came, and in that respect I suppose I was lucky. The whole incident left me in a depressed, self-loathing mood. I found myself replaying in my mind the events of the previous weeks. I began to wonder what kind of person I'd become. The thing was, I'd always thought of myself as a decent guy, someone worthy of affection and respect. But the look in Marisleysis's eyes—like the taxi driver's, and the people at the theatre—told a different story.

I found my thoughts returning to my first Cuban girlfriend, Lisbet. Her playful friendliness. How she'd asked me to stay for breakfast.

How she'd cried when she took my money. Was I wrong to imagine that she'd actually liked me?

After a few days of indecision, I decided to pay her another visit. That night, as with many nights, there was a widespread blackout in Santiago, and there was no moon, so most of the city was drowned in deep tropical darkness. I sat in the back seat of my new taxi, a blue '58 Oldsmobile, as the driver guided me through the inky night to the Santa Bárbara neighborhood. This time, not relishing the idea of walking alone in this blackness, I gave him the address.

As I stepped up onto the creaky porch my heart pounded with excitement. My intentions are pure, I told myself. I looked forward to seeing Lisbet again, getting to know her for real this time, and letting her get to know me. It almost felt like a homecoming.

The younger sister, Lisbet's lighter-skinned double, answered the door holding a candle. She wore a tank top that glowed yellow in the light of the single flame.

"*Buenas noches*," I said with a brotherly smile. "Is Lisbet at home?"

The girl shook her head. "She went to Havana." I couldn't help noticing that she wasn't wearing a bra; the outlines of her nipples were clearly visible under the threadbare cotton. Behind her the house was dark and silent.

Before I could say anything else she'd taken my hand and pulled me inside. There was candlelight coming from the back bedroom where I'd made love to Lisbet. The girl led me there, and I didn't protest. On the windowsill two guttering candle stubs illuminated the louvered window and a hardcover novel lying spine-up on the bed. The girl had been burning incense as she read.

"I'll return later," I said. "When do you expect her back?"

She was already peeling off the tanktop. Despite myself, I felt stirrings of arousal.

"What's your name?" I asked. The words came out in a whisper. The girl stood in her panties with her arms crossed self-consciously over her chest, gazing at me in the flickering yellow light like some kind of attention-starved wood nymph.

"Hiawatha."

"Hiawatha? Really?" I smiled sadly. Picking up the hardcover, I closed it and squinted at the spine: *Pride and Prejudice*, a well-thumbed Spanish translation. I rested the book on the windowsill.

Slowly, she let her arms drop to her sides and then opened them slightly, as if offering herself for my delectation. She was long-legged and as lithe as a gazelle, little dark-nippled breasts high and budding in the candlelight. I felt dizzy. "How old are you, Hiawatha?"

"Seventeen."

"I don't believe you. How old really?"

She frowned and shrugged. "Fourteen."

"Fourteen?"

"Fourteen." She raised her eyes and took a step toward me. "What does it matter? As you can see, I'm a woman already. And you are a man, no? An American?"

I fled that house like you would flee in one of those nightmares where you've committed a crime, and you don't remember exactly what the crime was, but it doesn't matter because you know it was bad, and the consequences will be bad, and there's nothing you can do to make it better. On my way out I tossed a roll of twenties into a plastic bowl that was resting on the television. It was whatever was in my pocket at the time, maybe a few hundred pesos.

Out on the porch, heart racing, I stopped short. Suddenly I could see myself clearly: The person the taxi driver saw, the person the people in the theater saw, the person Marisleysis saw. I thought about going back to get the money out of the bowl, but it was too late. There was no way to take it back.

DISASTER RELIEF

Peyton Burgess

Thibodeaux stands by a mini charcoal grill flipping some preformed burger patties in the courtyard of our favorite bar. The flames against his hunched frame create a shadow on the water-stained wall behind him, and the shadow dances with Patsy Cline's "Back in Baby's Arms" as the song plays through the one speaker still working in the bar. A couple months ago Thibodeaux was working sous-chef at a damn fine restaurant and making some of the best redfish almondene in the city.

Baby Girl is stuck eating one of the burger patties, but she still does it pretty and clean, manicured pinkies up in casual dainty and a paper towel resting on her brown thighs and the frays of her cut-off jean shorts.

"You could make a turd taste good, Thibodeaux!" she yells. Then she sees me staring at her thighs, and lets me for a moment. When we'd lived at her mom's house, I'd been nervous about looking at her and touching her. Now I look at her every chance I get. She lifts up my chin and stuffs a piece of burger in my mouth.

Our first day back and the tap water's too infested to wash your hands before you eat. We'd been warned that the Sewerage Board was shocking the water supply with high amounts of chlorine to kill bacteria, been warned not to take showers, not to brush teeth, but sometimes you'd forget and out of habit you'd stick your hands under a faucet and then your cuticles would burn and you'd remember. It's a hard thing to get used to, not washing your hands with tap water, which is why Thibodeaux is constantly putting lotion on his ashy hands to soothe the burning. Sanitizer gives some reassurance. It's no good for cleaning actual dirt off your hands, but with all the garbage and stinking refrigerators sitting on the curbs, it's nice to know that there's a giant, pump-dispensing bottle of Purell sitting on the bar next to two pump-dispensing bottles of catsup and mustard. The mayonnaise is in the trashcan.

If things were anything like normal, the courtyard would be full of people, maybe Andrei would ask me to feel the nylon-clad thigh of the young woman next to him. I'd politely decline, but then he'd keep prodding me to do it until I'd submit and touch the girl's thigh. The nylon would feel smooth enough that I'd almost put my head in her lap right then and there, and the girl would smile, or not.

"I didn't know they made 'em this big," I say, pumping some of the Purell on my palm.

"Yeah. Got a bunch of 'em for free from volunteers," Thibodeaux yells from the courtyard.

Last time I'd seen Thibodeaux I was picking him up at a gas station in BR after his car broke down. He had called his girlfriend from the payphone, but she'd refused to accept the collect-call charges and hung up. On the ride back, stuck in traffic, I'd tried convincing him that she'd come around. I'd said something cheesy and useless like, "That's what sucks about love, you become a victim of her stupidity and, worse usually, she becomes a victim of your stupidity."

There was a time—it's hard to imagine it now—when Baby Girl and I had conversations with friends we honestly loved, really loved. Some of these friends we loved were people we never met, or don't remember, but if you were there anytime before, you might understand that foolish sentiment.

When Baby Girl and I came back we drove across the connection and a pungent aroma intensified as we neared the city and exited the interstate under the shadow of what was a coliseum. The warped doors tried to keep us from entering the house we rented and seeing the fallen insulation, the black mold that seemed to heave and wheeze as it spread over our artwork, our couch, and the clothes that we had worn just a couple months ago when we would have danced to anything.

While at Baby Girl's mom's house we didn't have sex because we didn't want to disrespect her mom, or maybe we were just too disoriented to lie still enough together, but even after coming back home we couldn't. "Maybe we should just ignore the fallen ceiling and shingles on our bed," Baby Girl said.

Our clothes, still stuck on the floor and covered in the mold that continues to spread through our home, got drenched in our sweat the week before we had to evacuate. Some trumpeter was busting out some crazy shit, and in between sets he played some local rap off his iPod and kept us all jumping during trips to the bar and back to the dance floor. Baby Girl and I danced; I held her belly as it grew with beans and cake and booze right up until the last song. I'd used so much Tabasco that I couldn't feel her lips when she would kiss me. Those were nights when home was a slow bike ride to a place where my head rested on her bicep and my nose on the top of her breast, where I could smell the sweaty fun she'd had that night. That was it: just fun and sleep.

Whenever she would leave me alone in the city for a while, and I never bothered to ask where she went, I'd find myself comparing things in the city to her: her legs and the long limbs of the live oaks and how their roots upend the sidewalks, the smell of the streetcar braking and the smell of her hair after biking home from work. Eventually, the city and Baby Girl became the same affair.

Now, we're riding a big, dirty wave of great loss and pending opportunity into what seems like a rebirth conceived with no expectations. We *are* sure that our fridge is dead, the chicken, pork and catfish inside it long rotten; maggots dine on what remains and frame the inside of the fridge like cake icing. Tomorrow, we'll have to move the fridge to the curb. Our old Japanese cars, humble transportation to the jobs we took for granted, are encrusted with the stink that regurgitated from the sewers and into the streets. A blue tarp lies on the roof of our house, stretched tight and weighed down with bricks in a pathetic attempt to keep out any future rain.

Thibodeaux comes into the bar from the courtyard and grabs a beer from the ice chest. "Yours will be done in a bit," he says to me. The scars on Thibodeaux's arms and wrists always give me a bit of a chill, but he once got laid by a chick that was into his cooking scars. She was actually turned on by them; she made a point to say that New Orleans cooking scars made her wet. The day after she had bathed Thibodeaux's scars in kisses and bodily fluids, he met me on top of the levee so we could take in the sun and watch the tankers come and go from the refineries.

"Is it the scars she likes, or just the fact that you're a cook?" I asked.

"She said she likes scars from cooking here, this city only. Scars from cooking in other cities don't do a damn thing for her. See that one right there?" Thibodeaux pointed at a welt of skin rising off his wrist like an albino leech. "I got that one from some dumbass fry cook on a cruise ship a couple years ago, he threw some oysters in a fryer all sloppy right as I was walking by and I got hit by some oil. That was a shit job. And that scar did nothing for her. And here's the thing, I never told her it wasn't a New Orleans-cooking scar, but she sensed it somehow. Skipped right over the damn thing when she was kissing my hands and wrists. I even tried to convince her that I got it working at Commander's. She just squinted at it and said 'No,' that it made her 'dry as a desert.' But when she found this one from Delmonico's—I'd gotten a little sloppy when I had to help a line cook rush some prep." He pointed at a large scar on his other wrist. "This one. When she got her lips on it, it was as if all the levees failed at the same time! A great summertime flood, bra!"

If there's an acronym for a fetish in New Orleans-cooking scars, Thibodeaux's *T* would be the first letter. Despite that, he's not much of a romantic, but more of a caretaker, which is why he keeps post back in the courtyard by his shitty little grill, cooking that shitty little burger for me. Baby Girl and I could always get an excellent meal from Thibodeaux. Even during times when you're lucky to get an MRE—constipation—from the Red Cross, I bet Thibodeaux could keep us eating something that still makes food feel like a tradition.

"He looks lonely out there by himself," Baby Girl says.

"I think he looks content."

Thibodeaux stares at the flames, with a frown, poking that cheap patty.

A dull crunching sound comes over the music, and as we dwell on Thibodeaux's decline from sous-chef at one of the best restaurants in the city to grill cook at a French Quarter bar, that water-stained wall behind our lonely cook comes spilling down, flooding the courtyard with rotted wood and knocking over the grill. My burger patty, caked in dust and lead paint chips, sits in the rubble.

"Really?" Thibodeaux yells. "Really! It's okay, it's okay. I'll get you fed, bra!" He points at me, wading through the rubble as he charges back into the bar. He lifts up an ice chest and walks back to the courtyard where he dumps the melting ice all over the coals.

He stands, surrounded by the smoke and the bubbling ash at his feet, and he investigates the fallen wall. "This was bound to happen eventually!" he yells. "But the framing looks fine."

I heard him, but I didn't really think about it. Baby Girl squeezes my thigh. And I know she wants me to get Thibodeaux to stop and just sit with us.

"Thibodeaux, it's okay, man. I'm not that hungry anyway," I say.

"No, bra. You gotta eat."

"I got some peanut butter and bread back in my suitcase. He'll be fine," Baby Girl says. She walks behind the bar and grabs a broom and a dustpan.

Thibodeaux rushes back behind the bar and looks through another ice chest. He picks up a greasy freezer bag filled with brown ground beef and sniffs at it. "Shit stinks." He slams the lid down on the ice chest and moves down, opening another. "Yesterday's meat's no good." He shakes the oily water off his hand.

Baby Girl hands me the dustpan. "Get off your butt," she says.

"Thibodeaux, don't worry about it, man," I say. I get up and follow Baby Girl to the courtyard, dragging a trashcan behind me.

Something beyond what we'd planned will come from all this destruction, that's what Baby Girl and I tell one another, and that's what makes us bike home from Molly's to sleep for the first time since coming back home.

The quarter is quiet, so quiet we hear the hum of our tires on the asphalt. There're no horse-drawn carriages clopping down the street, or drunken tourists yelling with the temporary might from shitty mixed drinks and indigestion from beignets. We pedal down Governor Nichols, swerving down the street to St. Claude Ave. As we slow our approach to Rampart we see two green Humvees crawling toward us up the four-lane street. We continue to cross, until spotlights on top of the military trucks blind us. I shade my eyes.

"They're stopping," Baby Girl says and starts coasting her bike.

I think to myself that I don't understand martial law. I don't know what it allows these people to do to us. Seems to me that law enforcement already has enough power, and all martial law does is just give them more room to fuck up and then not be held accountable, that we can be made to look as if we asked for whatever bad shit happens to us, because we like to dance until the early morning, or because we spend too much time on food, or because we look forward to Lent as long as we can.

We slow our bikes and rest our feet on the pavement, watching as the Humvees cut us off with a half-circle formation. Two soldiers climb out of one of the Humvees and point their guns at our feet. We hold our handlebars.

A voice barks through a loudspeaker, demanding IDs and telling us we're violating curfew. The soldiers don't say a word but continue pointing their guns at our feet. I decide they're National Guard. It's obvious from their double chins and the awkward grasps on their weapons that their monthly training requirements haven't prepared them for what's happening here.

"We're just on our way home," I yell at the tinted windows. "We were hungry and can't cook in our kitchen."

"You need to eat at midnight?" one of the soldiers says.

"It's none of your damned business when I want to eat," I say. I'm pissed and I've had some usual beers, but I never expected that everything would go perfect. But when did time start mattering so much?

"Hun, take it easy," Baby Girl says, shaking her head.

Another soldier, sitting shotgun in the leading Humvee, gets out, unarmed, and walks toward us. "We're here for your protection. There're a lot of stolen guns floating around here. You understand? Lots of people with guns." He says it slowly, with a Midwest accent, as if I don't speak the same language.

"Like you guys?" I say.

"Put a bracelet on him," he says.

One of the soldiers swings his weapon around to his back and grabs my arm. He throws me to the ground with my bike still in between my legs; he pulls my arms behind me and I feel the gravel and dirt grind against my lips, and it all tastes metallic like blood. I scream. I hear Baby Girl beg them to stop. I hear a zip and feel plastic cut tightly into my wrists.

"Up!" the soldier says and pulls at my arms. He throws me into the back of a Humvee and slams the door shut. I yell, ask why I'm under arrest. The eyes of the soldier sitting behind the wheel keep a steady, unblinking gaze on me. "Nobody ever said you were under arrest," he says and laughs.

I see Baby Girl looking at me and I press my forehead against the window, I feel helpless, trying to hear what they're saying to her. The superior walks to the passenger side and gets in. The soldiers outside tighten their circle around Baby Girl; she just keeps staring at me, not saying anything. By the look on her face I can't tell if she's scared or just pissed at me. I don't think she's scared. I can't hear what they're saying to her. And if Baby Girl said something, I wouldn't be able to hear her. I want her to tell me something, and thinking about what she might tell me calms me down. "Hey, son!" the superior says, turning to look at me. "If she was to go back to that wrecked-to-all-hell home by herself tonight, and you couldn't do anything about it, how would that make you feel?" He takes off his cap and rubs his crew cut.

"She'd be okay," I say immediately.

He starts running my name and I know I'm fucked at that point.

"You sure you feel that way? Because with the crazies running around this city and with all that unhealthy filth festering in your home I'd bet you'd worry."

When the warrant for my arrest comes up he puts in a call for somebody to come escort Baby Girl home. I yell as they drive me away.

I sit in an encampment for two weeks before being taken to BR. By the time Thibodeaux gets enough money to bail me out, Baby Girl is nowhere to be found. I heard she was still around but I never saw her again. Thibodeaux didn't say much about her. Even when I'd ask he would just stay quiet as if I was asking questions I already knew the answers to.

But sometimes I think about what it would have been like if I had gone home with her that night. I don't like to think that everything would have been okay.

Under the vigil of St. Augustine's rusted cast iron and concrete steeple standing outside our window, I had watched Baby Girl, wearing shorts only, stand at the window and do a charcoal sketch of that steeple. The rust on the cast iron had run with warm rain down the sides of the steeple, staining the old, painted concrete like eyeliner running down the cheeks of a widow. Baby Girl lightly brushed the charcoal down the drawing with her index finger to show the tears.

If I had gone home with her that night, we would have walked our bikes through the gate in front of our house and rested them on top of each other. I'd climb our stoop and open the front door; she'd lock the bikes together to the small crepe myrtle tree in the yard. Inside our house, the air would be thick with the smell of mold. I'd open the front windows and walk back outside, complaining about the smell.

I'd walk around to the side of the house and reach for the aluminum ladder underneath. I'd try to pull it out but it would get stuck on something so I'd start jerking at it until I'd lose my grip.

I would stand up and for the first time, I'd cry. She'd wrap her arms around me and laugh at me a little bit. And it would feel good to hear her laugh at me and I'd forget that I'm crying.

She'd let go of me and squat down with her hands on her knees, looking at the ladder with no haste. I'd help her pull the ladder out, and I'd stand it against the side of our house.

I'd have a feeling we're Louis Prima and Keely Smith reincarnated. I'd climb up the ladder and grab a corner of the big blue tarp on our roof. Baby Girl would holler as I pull with what strength I have and send the tarp cascading into the front yard. We would agree that we'll make love on our air mattress as the stars shine on us through the holes in our roof, and we'll hear the banana trees in the backyard applaud our performance, and maybe we will.

"Do you want me to tell you it gets better?" Baby Girl would ask.

I'd tell her, No, but she would do it anyway. I'd breathe in the humidity and I swear I would smell the scent of the jasmine vines blooming instead of mold.

ANTARCTICA

THE ECSTATIC CRY

Midge Raymond

One of our gentoo chicks is missing.

I flip through our field notebook to find Thom's chart of the colony, then match nest to nest. According to our records, the chick was two weeks old, but now the rocky nest is empty, the adult penguins gone. I search but find no body; its disappearance must have been the work of a predatory skua. When skuas swoop down to snatch chicks or eggs, they leave little behind.

I move away from the colony and sit on a rock to make some notes. That's when I hear it—a distinctly human yelp, and a thick noise that I have only heard once in my life and never forgotten: the sound of bone hitting something solid.

I stand up and see a man lying in the snow, a red-jacketed tourist from the M/S *Royal Albatross*, which dropped its anchor in our bay this morning. He'd fallen hard, landing on his back and apparently narrowly missing a gentoo, which is now scurrying away. The man doesn't move.

I hold still for a moment, hoping he will get up. When I see a spot of red spreading in the snow underneath his head, I start toward him.

Fifteen other tourists are within thirty yards, yet no one else seems to notice. They're still up the hill, listening to their ship's naturalist, the whirs and blips of their digital cameras obscuring all other sounds on the island.

But my research partner, Thom, must have seen something; he gets to the man first. And now a woman is scrambling guardedly down the same hill, apparently taking care, despite her hurry, to avoid the same fate.

I turn my attention to the man. His blood is an unwelcome sight, bright and thin amid the ubiquitous dark-pink guano of the penguins, and replete with new bacteria, which could be deadly for the birds. I stifle an urge to start cleaning it up.

Thom's voice snatches back my attention. "Deb," he says sharply, glancing up. He'd spent two years in medical school before turning to marine biology, and he looks uncharacteristically nervous. By now, four more tourists in their matching red jackets have gathered around us, and I can see that Thom wants to shield them from what he sees.

I hold out my arms and move forward, forcing the red jackets back a couple of steps. The woman who'd hurried down the hill is trying to see past me. She looks younger than the usual middle-aged passengers who cruise down to Antarctica, the ones who have already been everywhere else, who want to check off their seventh continent. "Are you with him?" I ask her. "Where's your guide?"

"No—I don't know," she stutters. Blond hair trails from under her hat into her eyes, wide with an anxiety I can't place. "He's up there, maybe." She motions toward the gentoo colony. I glance up. The hill has nearly disappeared in fog.

"Someone needs to find him," I say. "And we need the doctor from the boat. Who's he traveling with?"

"His wife, I think," someone answers.

"Get her."

I kneel next to Thom, who's examining the man's head. If we were anywhere but Antarctica, the injury might not seem as critical. But we are at the bottom of the world, days away from the nearest city, even farther from the nearest trauma center. There is, of course, a doctor along on the cruise, and basic medical facilities at Palmer Station, half an hour away by boat—but it's not yet clear whether that will be enough.

The man hasn't moved since he fell. A deep gash on the back of his head has bled through the thick wad of gauze that Thom has applied. Voices approach—the guide, the wife, the doctor. The man's chest suddenly begins heaving, and Thom quickly reaches out and turns his head so he will vomit into the snow. More bacteria.

The man shudders and tries to sit up, then loses consciousness again. Thom presses fresh gauze to his head.

"What happened?" the wife cries.

"He slipped," I tell her.

Thom and I move aside for the doctor.

"How could this happen?" the wife wails. It's no mystery, I want to tell her; her husband is about sixty pounds overweight and can't see his own feet, which are stuffed into cheap boots despite the fact that he paid thousands of dollars for the tour that brought him here. But I silently place a hand on her shoulder as crew members show up with a gurney. "We need to get him to Palmer," the doctor says, her voice low. The man remains still.

Thom helps the crew load him onto the gurney, and they take him to a Zodiac. I get a plastic bag from our camp, then return to the scene and begin scooping up the blood- and vomit-covered snow. Because we're in one of the last pristine environments in the world, we go to great lengths to protect the animals from anything foreign. Visitors sterilize their boots before setting foot on the island, and again when they depart. No one leaves without everything they came with. Yet sometimes, like now, it seems pointless. Injuries like this are unusual, but I've seen tourists drop used tissues and gum wrappers, not knowing or not caring enough to pick them up. I want to chase after them, to show them our data, to tell them how much the fate of penguins has changed as more and more tourists pass through these islands. But Thom and I must be patient with this red-jacketed species—we are employed by the same tour company that brings them here. The company sponsors our research, and in turn it gets a tax break and two more experts to give on-board lectures and slide shows. With government dollars harder and harder to come by, I'm grateful—but we earn it more each season, and our work often takes a backseat to keeping the tourists happy.

Thom returns and stands over me, watching for a moment. Then he says, "They need me to go to Palmer with them."

I look up. "Why?"

"The crew is crazed," he says, "and they need someone to stay with the victim and his wife."

"I guess we're at their mercy." I inspect the ground to make sure there's nothing left in the snow. Thom doesn't have a choice—we're often asked to fill in for the crew—but I know what he is really asking me. We have been partners for three years, and I've never spent a night on this island alone.

I stand up. Thom is short, and I'm tall, so we look each other directly in the eye. "Go ahead. I'll be all right."

"You sure?"

"I'll keep the radio on, just in case. But yeah, I'll be fine. After all this, I'll enjoy the peace."

"I'll be back tomorrow," he says.

We go back to camp, a trio of tents a few yards off the bay. From there we can watch the ships approach and, more important, depart.

Another Zodiac is waiting to take Thom to Palmer. He grabs a few things from his tent and gives my shoulder a squeeze before he leaves. "I'll buzz you later," he says. He smiles, and I feel a sudden, sharp loneliness, like an intake of cold air.

I watch the Zodiac disappear around the outer cliffs of the bay, then turn back to our empty camp.

It's hard to believe on an evening like this, with the air sogged with rain and the penguins splashing in a pool of slush near my tent, that Antarctica is the biggest desert in the world, the driest place on earth. The Dry Valleys have not seen rain for millions of years, and thanks to the cold, nothing rots or decays. Even up here, on the peninsula, I've seen hundred-year-old seal carcasses in perfect condition, and abandoned whaling stations frozen in time. Those that perish in Antarctica—penguins, seals, explorers—are immortalized, the ice preserving life in the moment of death.

But for all that stays the same here, Antarctica is constantly changing. Every year, the continent doubles in size as the ocean freezes around it; the ice shelf shifts; glaciers calve off. Whales once hunted are now protected; krill once ignored are now trawled; land once desolate now sees thousands of tourists a season. But it remains, to me, a place of illusion; when I'm here I still feel comfortably isolated, though increasingly I am not.

I make myself a cold, unappetizing supper of leftover pasta and think of my return, two weeks away. Thom and I will be eating well then, cozily aboard the *Royal Albatross* with its gourmet meals and full bar. And my sense of aloneness will be gone, replaced with lectures and slide shows and endless Q&A sessions.

I finish my supper and clean up, careful not to leave even the smallest crumbs behind. At nearly ten o'clock, it's still bright outside, the sun still hours away from its temporary disappearance. I take a walk, heading up toward the colony that was so heavily trafficked today, the one the man visited before he fell. The empty nest remains deserted. The other penguins are still active, bringing rocks back to fortify their nests, feeding their chicks. Some are sitting on eggs; others are returning from the sea to reunite with their mates, greeting one another with a call of recognition, a high-pitched rattling squawk.

I sit down on a rock, about fifteen feet away from the nearest nest, and watch the birds amble up the trail from the water. They appear to ignore me, but I know this isn't true; I know that their heart rates increase when I walk past, that they move faster when I'm around. Thom and I are studying the two largest penguin colonies here, tracking their numbers and rates of reproduction, to gauge the effects of tourism and human contact. Our island is one of the most frequently visited spots in Antarctica, and our data shows that the birds have noticed. They're experiencing symptoms of stress: lower birth rates, fewer fledging chicks. It's a strange irony that the hands that feed our research are the same hands that guide the boats here every season, and I sometimes wonder what will happen when the results of our study are published.

Often when I watch the penguins, I forget I'm a scientist. I become so mesmerized by the sounds of their purrs and squawks, by the precision of their clumsy waddle, that I forget that I have another life, somewhere else—that I have an apartment in Eugene, that I teach marine biology at the University of Oregon, that I'm forty-two years old and not yet on a tenure track, that I haven't had a real date in three years. I forget that my life now is only as good as my next grant, and that when the money dries up, I'm afraid that I will, too.

I first came to Antarctica when I was thirty, to study the emperor penguins at McMurdo. I've been returning every season I can, to whatever site I can, by whatever means. Thom and I have two seasons left in our study. He's married, with two small kids at home; this will be it for him. I'm still looking for another way to make it back.

What I'd like most is to return to the Ross Sea, to the emperors. This is the species that captivates me—the only Antarctic bird that breeds in winter, right on the ice. Emperors don't build nests; they live entirely on fast ice and in the water, never setting foot on solid land. I love that during breeding season, the female lays her egg, then scoots it over to the male and takes off, traveling a hundred miles across the frozen ocean to open water and swimming away to forage for food. She comes back when she's fat and ready to feed her chick.

My mother, still hopeful about marriage and grandkids for her only daughter, says that this is my problem, that I think like an emperor. I expect a man to sit tight and wait patiently while I disappear across the ice. I don't build nests.

When the female emperor returns, she uses a signature call to find her partner. Reunited, the two move in close and bob their heads toward each other, shoulder to shoulder in an armless hug, raising their beaks in what we call the ecstatic cry. Penguins are romantics. Most mate for life.

In the summer, Antarctic sunsets last forever. They surrender not to darkness but to an overnight dusk, a grayish light that dims around midnight. As I prepare to turn in, I hear the splatter of penguins bathing in their slush, the barely perceptible pat of their webbed feet on the rocks.

Inside my tent, I extinguish my lamp and set a flashlight nearby, turning over a few times to find a comfortable angle. The rocks are ice-cold, the padding under my sleeping bag far too thin. When I finally put my head down, I hear a loud splash. It was clearly made by something much larger than a penguin—yet the ship is long gone. And when you're alone in Antarctica, you are truly alone.

Feeling suddenly uneasy, I turn on my lamp again. I grab my flashlight and a jacket and hurry outside, toward the rocky beach.

I can see a form in the water, but it's bulky and oddly shaped, not smooth and sleek, like a seal. I shine my flashlight on it and see only red.

It's a man, in his cruise-issued parka, submerged in the water up to his waist. He looks into the glare of my flashlight. I stand there, too stunned to move.

Then the man turns away, and he takes another step into the water. *He's crazy,* I think. *Why would he go in deeper?* Sometimes the seasick medication that tourists take causes odd and even troubling behavior, but I've never witnessed anything like this. As I watch him anxiously from the shore, I think of Ernest Shackleton. I think of his choices, the decisions he made at every step to save the lives of his crew. His decision to abandon the *Endurance* in the Weddell Sea, to set out across the frozen water in search of land, to separate his crew from one another, to take a twenty-two-foot rescue boat across eight hundred miles of open sea. I also think of Robert Scott, leading his team to their deaths just as his competitor became the first to reach the South Pole—and of the expedition guides who last year drove a Zodiac underneath the arc of a floating iceberg, only to have the berg calve and flip their boat, drowning the driver. In Antarctica, every decision is weighty, every outcome either a tragedy or a miracle.

Now, it seems, my own moment has come. It would be unthinkable to stand here and watch this man drown, but attempting a rescue could be even more dangerous. I'm alone. I'm wearing socks and a light jacket. The water is freezing or a few degrees above, and though I'm five-nine and strong, this man is big enough to pull me under if he wanted to, or if he panicked.

Perhaps Shackleton only believed he had options. Here, genuine options are few.

As I enter the icy water, my feet numb within seconds. The man is now in up to his chest, and by the time I reach him, he's thoroughly disoriented. He doesn't resist when I clutch his arms, pulling them over my shoulders and turning us toward the shore. In the water he is almost a dead weight, but I feel a slight momentum behind me as I drag him toward the beach. Our progress is slow. Once on land, he's near collapse, and it takes all my strength to heave him up the rocks and into Thom's tent.

He crumples on the tent floor, and I strip off his parka, boots, and socks. Water spills over Thom's sleeping bag and onto his books. "Take off your clothes," I say, turning to rummage through Thom's things. I toss him a pair of sweatpants, the only thing of Thom's that will stretch to fit his tall frame, and two pairs of thick socks. I also find a couple of T-shirts and an oversized sweater. When I turn back to him, the man has put on the sweats and is feebly attempting the socks. His hands are shaking so badly he can hardly command them. Impatiently, I reach over to help, yanking the socks onto his feet.

"What the hell were you thinking?" I demand, not really expecting an answer. I hardly look at him as I take off his shirt and help him squeeze into Thom's sweater. I turn on a battery-powered blanket and unzip Thom's sleeping bag. "Get in," I say. "You need to warm up."

His whole body shudders. He climbs in and pulls the blanket up to cover his shoulders.

"What are you doing here?" I ask. I, too, am shaking from the cold. "What the hell happened?"

He lifts his eyes, briefly. "The boat—it left me behind."

"That's impossible." I stare at him, but he won't look at me. "The *Royal Albatross* always does head counts. They count twice. No one's ever been left behind."

He shrugs. "Until now."

I think about the chaos of earlier that day. It's conceivable that this stranger could have slipped through the cracks. And it would be just my luck.

"I'm calling Palmer. Someone will have to come out to take you back." I rise to my knees, eager to go first to my tent for dry clothes, then to the supply tent, where we keep the radio.

I feel his hand on my arm. "Do you have to do that just yet?" He smiles, awkwardly, his teeth knocking together. "It's just that—I've been here so long already, and I'm not ready to face the ship. It's embarrassing, to be honest with you."

"Don't you have someone who knows you're missing?" I regard him for the first time as a man, rather than an alien in my world. His face is pale and clammy, its lines suggesting he is my age or older, perhaps in his late forties. I glance down to look for a wedding band, but his fingers are bare. Following my gaze, he tucks his hands under the blanket. Then he shakes his head. "I'm traveling alone."

"Have you taken any medication? For seasickness?"

"No," he says. "I was in the Navy. I don't get seasick."

"Well," I say, "your boat's probably miles away by now, and we need to get you on it before it goes any farther."

He looks at me directly for the first time. "Don't," he says.

I'm still kneeling on the floor of the tent. "What do you think?" I ask. "That you can just stay here? That no one will figure out you're missing?"

He doesn't answer. "Look," I tell him, "it was an accident. No one's going to blame you for getting left behind."

"It wasn't an accident," he says. "I saw that other guy fall. I watched everything. I knew that if I stayed they wouldn't notice me missing."

I stand up. "I'll be right back."

He reaches up and grasps my wrist so fast I don't have time to pull away. I'm surprised by how quickly his strength has come back. I ease back down to my knees, and he loosens his grip. He looks at me through tired, heavy eyes—a silent plea. He's not scary, I realize then, but scared.

"In another month," I tell him, as gently as I can manage, "the ocean will freeze solid, and so will everything else, including you."

"What about you?"

"In a couple weeks, I'm leaving, too. Everyone leaves."

"Even the penguins?" The question, spoken through clattering teeth, lends him an innocence that almost makes me forgive his intrusions.

"Yes," I say. "Even they go north."

He doesn't respond, and I stand up. He lets me leave, and I go straight to the radio in our supply tent, hardly thinking about my wet clothes. Just as I'm contacting Palmer, I realize that I don't know his name. I go back and poke my head inside. "Dennis Singleton," he says.

The dispatcher at Palmer tells me that they'll pick up Dennis in the morning, when they bring Thom back. "Unless it's an emergency," he says. "Everything okay?"

I want to tell him it's not okay, that this man might be crazy, dangerous, sick. But I can't exaggerate without risking never being taken seriously again—too big a risk with two more seasons of research here. So I say, "We're fine. Tell Thom we'll see him in the morning."

I return to the tent. Dennis has not moved. He is staring at a spot in the corner, and he barely acknowledges me.

His quietness is unsettling. "What were you doing in the water?" I ask.

"Thought I'd try to catch up to the boat," he says.

"Very funny. I'm serious."

He doesn't reply. A moment later, he asks, "What are *you* doing here?"

"Research, obviously."

"I know," he says. "But why come here, to the end of the earth?"

"What kind of question is that?"

"You know what I mean," he says. "You have to be a real loner, to enjoy being down here." He rubs the fingers of his left hand. Thinking of frostbite, and a change of subject, I grab his hand to examine his fingers. "Where do they hurt?"

"It's not that," he says.

"Then what?"

He hesitates. "I dropped my ring," he says. "My wedding band."

"Where? In the water?"

He nods.

"For God's sake." I duck out of the tent before he can stop me. I hear his voice behind me, asking me where I'm going, and I shout back, "Stay there."

I rush toward the water's edge, shivering in my still-damp clothes. The penguins purr as I go past, and a few of them scatter. I shine my flashlight down to the rocks at the bottom. I can't see much. I follow what I think was his path into the water, sweeping the flashlight back and forth in front of me.

I'm in up to my knees when I see it—a flash of gold against the slate-colored rocks. I reach in, the water up to my shoulder, so cold it feels as if my arm will snap off and sink.

I manage to grasp the ring with fingers that now barely move, then shuffle back to shore on leaden feet. I hobble back to my own tent, where I strip off my clothes and don as many dry things as I can grab. My skin is moist and wrinkled from being wet for so long. I hear a noise and look up to see Dennis, blanket still wrapped around his shoulders, crouched at the opening to my tent.

"What are you staring at?" I snap. Then I look down to what he sees—a thin, faded T-shirt, no bra, my nipples pressing against the fabric, my arm flushed red from the cold. I pull his ring off my thumb, where I'd put it so it wouldn't fall again, and throw it at him.

He picks it up off the floor. He holds it but doesn't put it on. "I wish you'd just left it," he says, almost to himself.

"A penguin could have choked on it," I say. "But no one ever thinks about that. We're all tourists here, you know. This is their home, not ours."

"I'm sorry," he says. "What can I do?"

I shake my head. He can't leave, which is the only thing I want him to do. There's nowhere for him to go.

He comes in and sits down, then pulls the blanket off his shoulders and places it around mine. He finds a fleece pullover in a pile of clothing and wraps it around my reddened arm.

"How cold is that water, anyway?" he asks.

"About thirty-five degrees, give or take." I watch him carefully.

"How long can someone survive in there?"

"A matter of minutes, usually," I say, remembering the expedition guide who'd drowned. He'd been trapped under the flipped Zodiac for only a few moments but had lost consciousness, with rescuers only a hundred yards away. "You go into shock," I explain. "It's too cold to swim, even to breathe."

He unwraps my arm. "Does it feel better?"

"A little." Pain prickles my skin from the inside, somewhere deep down, and I feel an ache stemming from my bones. "You still haven't told me what you were doing out there."

Setting his ring to one side, he reaches over and begins massaging my arm. I'm not sure I want him to, but I know the warmth, the circulation, is good. "Like I said, I lost my ring."

"You were out much farther than where I found your ring."

"I must have missed it." He doesn't look at me as he speaks. I watch his fingers on my arm, and I am reminded of the night before, when only Thom and I were here, and Thom had helped me wash my hair. The feel of his hands on my scalp, on my neck, had run through my entire body, tightening into a coil of desire that never fully vanished. But nothing has ever happened between Thom and me, other than unconsummated rituals, generally toward the end of our stays. After a while, touch becomes necessary, and we begin doing things for each other—he'll braid my long hair; I'll rub his feet.

Suddenly I pull away. I regard the stranger in my tent: his dark hair, streaked with silver; his sad, heavy eyes; his ringless hands, still outstretched.

"What's the matter?" he asks.

"Nothing."

"I was just trying to help." The tent's small lamp casts deep shadows under his eyes. "I'm sorry," he says. "I don't mean to cause you any trouble. I know you don't want me here."

Something in his voice softens the knot in my chest. I sigh. "I'm just not a people person, that's all."

For the first time, he smiles, barely. "I can see why you come here. Talk about getting away from it all."

"At least I leave when I'm supposed to," I say, offering a tiny smile of my own.

He glances down at Thom's clothing, pulled tight across his body. "So when do I have to leave?" he asks.

"They'll be here in the morning."

Then he says, "How's he doing? The guy who fell?"

It takes me a moment to realize what he's talking about. "I don't know," I confess. "I forgot to ask."

He leans forward, then whispers, "I know something about him."

"What's that?"

"He was messing around with that blond woman," he says. "The one who was right there when it happened. I saw you talking to her."

"How do you know?"

"I saw them. They had a rendezvous every night, on the deck, after his wife went to bed. The blond woman was traveling with her sister. They even ate lunch together once, the four of them. The wife had no idea."

This is the type of story I normally can't tolerate, but I find myself intrigued. "Do you think they planned it?" I ask. "Or did they just meet, on the boat?"

"I don't know."

I look away, disappointed. "She seemed too young. For him."

"You didn't see her hands," he says. "My wife taught me that. You always know a woman's age by her hands. She may have had the face of a thirty-five-year-old, but she had the hands of a fifty-year-old."

"If you're married, why are you traveling alone?"

He pauses. "Long story."

"Well, we've got all night," I say.

"She decided not to come," he says.

"Why?"

"She left, a month ago. She's living with someone else."

"Oh." I don't know what more to say. Dennis is quiet, and I make another trip to the supply tent, returning with a six-pack of beer. His tired eyes brighten a bit.

He drinks and hands the bottle back to me before speaking again. "She was seeing him for a long time," he says, "but I think it was this trip that set her off. She didn't want to spend three weeks on a boat with me, or without him."

"I'm sorry." A moment later, I ask, "Do you have kids?"

He nods. "Twin girls, in college. They don't call home much. I don't know if she's told them or not."

"Why did you decide to come anyway?"

"This trip was for our anniversary." He turns his head and gives me a cheerless half-smile. "Pathetic, isn't it?"

I roll the bottle slowly between my hands. "How did you lose the ring?"

"The ring?" He looks startled. "It fell off during the landing, I guess."

"It was thirty degrees today. Weren't you wearing gloves?"

"I guess I wasn't."

I look at him, knowing there is more and that neither of us wants to acknowledge it. And then he lowers his gaze to my arm. "How does it feel?" he asks.

"It's okay."

"Let me work on it some more." He begins to rub my arm again. This time he slips his fingers inside the sleeves of my T-shirt, and the sudden heat on my skin seems to heighten my other senses: I hear the murmur of the penguins, feel the wind rippling the tent. At the same time, it's all drowned out by the feel of his hands.

I lean back and pull him with me until his head hovers just above mine. The lines sculpting his face look deeper in the tent's shadowy light, and his lazy eyelids lift as if to see me more clearly. He blinks, slowly, languidly, as I imagine he might touch me, and in the next moment he does.

I hear a pair of gentoos outside, their rattling voices rising above the night's ambient sound. Inside, Dennis and I move under and around our clothing, our own voices muted, whispered, breathless, and in the sudden humid heat of the tent we've recognized each other in the same way, by instinct, and, as with the birds, it's all we know.

During the Antarctic Night, tens of thousands of male emperors huddle together through a month of total darkness, in temperatures reaching seventy degrees below zero, as they incubate their eggs. By the time the females return to the colony, four months after they left, the males have lost half their body weight. They are near starvation, and yet they wait. It's what they're programmed to do.

Dennis does not wait for me. I wake up alone in my tent, the gray light of dawn nudging my eyelids. When I look at my watch, I see that it's later than I thought.

Outside, I glance around for Dennis, but he's not in camp. I make coffee, washing Thom's cup for him to use. I drink my own coffee without waiting for him; it's the only thing to warm me this morning, with him gone and the sun so well hidden.

I sip slowly, steam rising from my cup, and take in the moonscape around me: the edgy rocks, the mirrored water, ice sculptures rising above the pack ice—I could be on another planet. Yet for the first time in years, I feel as if I've reconnected with the world in some way, as if I am not as lost as I've believed all this time.

I hear the sound of a distant motor and stand up. Then it stops. I listen, hearing agitated voices—it must be Thom, coming from Palmer, having engine trouble. He is still outside the bay, out of sight, so I wait, washing my coffee mug and straightening up. When the engine starts up again, I turn back toward the bay. A few minutes later, Thom comes up from the beach with one of the electricians at Palmer, a young guy named Andy. I wave them over.

They walk hesitantly, and when they get closer, I recognize the look on Thom's face. Even before he opens his mouth, I know, with an icy certainty, where Dennis is.

"We found a body, Deb," he says. "In the bay." He exchanges a glance with Andy. "We just pulled him in."

I stare at their questioning faces. "He was here all night," I say. "I thought he just went for a walk, or—" I stop. Then I start toward the bay.

Thom steps in front of me. He holds both of my arms. "There's no need to do this," he says.

But I have to see for myself. I pull away and run toward the water's edge. The body lies across the rocks. I recognize Thom's sweater, stretched over Dennis's large frame.

I walk over to him; I want to take his pulse, to feel his heartbeat. But then I see his face, a bluish white, frozen in an expression I don't recognize, and I can't go any closer.

I feel Thom come up behind me. "It's him," I say. "I gave him your sweater."

He puts an arm around my shoulder. "What do you think happened?" he asks, but he knows as well as I do. There is no current here, no way to be swept off this beach and pulled out to sea. The Southern Ocean is not violent here, but it is merciless nonetheless.

Antarctica is not a country; it is governed by an international treaty whose rules apply almost solely to the environment. There are no police, no firefighters, no medical examiners. We have to do everything ourselves, and I shrug Thom off when he tries to absolve me from our duties. I help them lift Dennis into the Zodiac, the weight of his body entirely different now. I keep a hand on his chest as we back out of the bay and speed away, as if he might suddenly try to sit up. When we arrive at Palmer, I finally give in, leaving others to the task of packing his body for its long journey home.

They offer me a hot shower and a meal. As Andy walks me down the hall toward the dormitory, he tries in vain to find something to say. I'm silent, not helping him. Eventually he updates me on the injured man. "He's going to be okay," he tells me. "But you know what's strange? He doesn't remember anything about the trip. He knows his wife, knows who the president is, how to add two and two—but he doesn't know how he got here, or why he even came to Antarctica. Spooky, huh?"

He won't remember the woman he was fooling around with, I think. *She will remember him, but for him, she's already gone.*

Back at camp, I watch for the gentoos who lost their chick, but they do not return. Their nest remains abandoned, and other penguins steal their rocks.

Ten days later, Thom and I break camp and ready ourselves for the weeklong journey back. We have been working in a companionable near-silence, which is not entirely unusual. Our weeks together at the bottom of the earth have taught us the rhythms of each other's moods, and we don't always need to talk. We do not talk about Dennis.

Once on the boat, the distractions are many, and the hours and days disappear in seminars and lectures. The next thing I know, we are a day away from the Drake Passage, the last leg of our journey, where the Southern Ocean, the Pacific Ocean, and the Atlantic all meet and toss boats around like toys. The tourists will get sick, the smell of vomit will fill the halls, and I will take as much meclizine as I can stomach and stay in bed.

But today I wander around the ship, walking the halls Dennis walked, sitting where he must have sat, standing where he may have stood. I'm with a new group of passengers now, none of whom would have crossed his path. A sleety rain begins to fall, and I go out to the upper deck. As we float through a labyrinth of icebergs, I play with Dennis's wedding ring, which he'd left on the floor of my tent.

I wear it on my thumb, as I did when I'd first found it, because that's where it fits.

Because of the rain, I'm alone on the deck when I see it—a lone emperor penguin, sitting atop an enormous tabular iceberg. A good field guide would announce this sighting on the PA—the passengers aren't likely to get another chance to see an emperor. But I don't move; I watch her as she preens her feathers, and I imagine that she is feeling leisurely, safe, in a moment of peace she can't comprehend or enjoy.

They aren't aware of it, but the emperors' very survival depends on all but perfect timing. During the breeding season, the female must return from her journey within ten days of her chick's hatching. If she doesn't show, her partner, nearly dead from starvation, has no choice but to abandon their chick. He can't get beyond his own instinctual will to live.

I believe that penguins mourn. I've seen Adelies wander their colonies, searching for mates that never return; I've seen chinstraps sitting dejected on empty nests. And I've seen the emperors grieve. The female returns, searching, her head poised for the ecstatic cry. When her calls go unanswered, she will lower her beak to the icy ground, where she will eventually find her chick, frozen in death, and she will assume the hunched posture of sorrow as she wanders across the ice.

VISITING CHAIRMAN MAO

Jocelyn Cullity

It was a cool day, a good day to visit Tiananmen Square. But Xiao Li did not feel like it was a good day. She'd been in line for over an hour to visit the Chairman Mao Memorial Hall in the Square, and she shouldn't have worn high heels, when she preferred running shoes. Li had also offered to carry the knapsack of her client, Claire, while Claire went for a stroll, and the strap bit into her shoulder.

At least the vendors had left them alone. Such chatter boxes. If they hadn't insisted on mocking Li's Shaanxi dialect, they might have sold more than two postcards to Li and an old Olympics keychain to the tourist, Claire. It would have passed the time to look at their things while the long line inched forward, but Li had ignored their foolish prattle, telling them to go away.

Li adjusted the knapsack and scanned the Square, the kite-flyers and the perambulators, for her client. She shifted her weight from the ball of one foot to the other. From her shirt pocket, she removed the two postcards she'd purchased to send to her family, who lived southwest of Beijing, far from the capital. The faulty English text on the back of the postcard showing the Forbidden City in Beijing was an embarrassment. The other, of busy stores and restaurants in Beijing's Qianmen area, captivated Li. How amazed her grandmother would be. "It's quite chilly," Claire said, suddenly standing beside her in the line with her hands in her sweatshirt pockets. The baggy sweatshirt looked old, the word "peace" on the front almost faded away. She wore a red bandanna, small, circular sunglasses, and her face was covered in freckles, the color of tea leaves. She didn't appear to be rich. Her jeans were ripped, and she sported a white rubber bracelet.

"Thanks for carrying that," Claire said. She took the knapsack from Li and nodded at what was now a shorter queue ahead of them. "It's been what, over an hour? Sure takes long enough to see the guy."

Li couldn't get used to her informality. She pointed to a sign on the concrete building. "That is the handwriting of Mr. Hua Guofeng, who supervised the building of the mausoleum after Chairman Mao's death in 1976."

"Ah, yes," Claire said, adjusting the red bandanna. It was a neat contraption, the cloth tight across her head, tucked behind each ear, the perfectly-folded triangle at the back, down the center of her hair. It was a type of red scarf, but different from the one Li and her classmates had worn during childhood.

"It's a fascinating item you wear," Li said.

"This?" Claire put her hand to her head. "Keeps my hair back. Thanks, I like it, too." She stepped away and whistled at the long line behind them, mostly Chinese families on vacation. "So many followers, even after all that tragedy. Such respect. Astonishing."

She spoke too loudly. Li labored with the purpose of her statements. "We have an official saying," Li said. "Chairman Mao was sixty percent right and forty percent wrong."

"Next in line!" A guard pointed to the window of the checked bag facility, beside the entrance to the mausoleum. Another guard leaned out with a ticket in his hand. "We must check your bag," Li said. "Hats and other signs of disrespect must be removed."

Claire slipped her sunglasses into her bag and handed it to the guard. Li wasn't sure whether the bandanna would be classified as a hat. At any rate, she was pleased to see Claire remove the red cloth and put it in her pocket.

"I've been looking forward to this all day," Claire said to the guard and smiled. "The highlight of my trip."

The guard looked at her blankly.

"The foreigner's humbled to visit the leader of China's revolution," Li translated. She took the postcards out of her pocket, ready to check them. She never could be too sure in Beijing. But the man waved his hand at her, urging them to move on.

Inside the grounds, two women tended a display of artificial flowers. "You may rent bouquets to put in front of the Chairman," Li said.

"No, thank you." Claire shook her head.

The information provided to Li by her boss at the Twenty-First Century China Tour Guide Company stated that fresh bunches of famous flowers and grasses surrounded the coffin. But these were paltry items, worn out bits of plastic.

"Renting flowers!" Claire said. "What a striking example of capitalism."

Li straightened. So direct with political affairs. And yet when she'd asked Claire how much money she made annually, Claire waved her finger at Li, telling her happily that she shouldn't ask such questions.

It was anyway only right to stick to the tour.

"Chairman Mao wished to be cremated," Li said, as they moved away from the flowers. "But he was embalmed like Lenin and Ho Chi Minh before him. We did not have the technology needed to preserve the Chairman's body for public display. The experts in Vietnam gave it to us. According to Chairman Mao's doctor, the process of embalming was difficult. The Chairman's body was left in less than perfect condition."

Claire nodded. "A complicated procedure."

Several guards stood by the entrance to the first room. "It's time," Li said, barely containing her own excitement. Going through the doorway, a guard barked at the Chinese family in front of them to stay in line.

"An imitation of Abraham Lincoln," Claire whispered to Li, indicating the white marble armchair with the massive statue of Chairman Mao seated on it. "Incredible work."

Li was pleased that Claire spoke in a hushed voice, in the tones the occasion required. Behind the statue hung an immense tapestry depicting China's mountains and rivers. How homesick Li suddenly felt for the Yellow River, but she quelled the ache.

Several families ahead of them lay their flowers at the base of the statue. "We have to keep moving," Li said to Claire, who'd stopped to gaze up at the structure. Li almost touched her elbow. "Please."

The line moved gradually from one side of the room to the other. Li would have liked to pick out all the famous landmarks in the tapestry, but she was distracted by Claire's inability to stay in line. Studying the exhibit, Claire tended to stray too far in front, or a few steps to the side. A child behind Li pushed forward and Li was forced to walk very close to Claire, who lingered again. As Claire craned her neck to look back at the statue, her steps lagged so that she was walking beside Li instead of in front of her. This made Li pause in order to keep the single file rule. "One line," a guard shouted in Mandarin. "One line," Li said, relieved that Claire finally slipped in front of her.

At the entrance to the second room, the viewing hall, a guard put up his hand and the line slowed. There would be positively no talking inside the chamber.

"The crystal for the casket came from the East China Sea," Li whispered quickly. "The winning coffin was made by the 608th Factory, which was originally the 2nd Spectacles Factory where Chairman Mao's spectacles were made. The casket is mechanically raised from a freezer for viewing and lowered again at night. You will see that the body is illuminated. Lamps serve to make Chairman Mao's skin color appear closer to that of a living person instead of the gray, and they reduce the appearance of wrinkles."

"Yes," Claire said eagerly, turning to face Li. "Xenon lamps are used inside the coffin, employing fiber-optic technology to carefully light the body. Such an artful skill."

Few foreigners knew such technical details about China's history. Li felt herself flush with pride.

"No talking!" The guard peered at Li, annoyed, as he waved them through. "Single file. Keep moving."

Inside the room, a hush descended on the visitors. The Hall of Mourning was dark, except for the top-lit glass case in the middle of the room. Chairman Mao lay in his gray suit, draped with the Communist Party flag.

Ahead of Li, Claire was quiet. From her profile, she appeared unhappy. Li waited for her to blurt something out. Surely, Claire might comment on the fact that the Chairman actually looked a bit like a wax figure; that his cheeks were very red. Or that they were being hurried through and would exit so soon. But Claire remained silent.

What if she'd decided the visit to the Mausoleum was a colossal waste of time? Worse, what if Claire had concluded that she was not content in general with today's tour of the Square? Claire stepped out of the line.

"Single line!" Li hissed, tapping her once on the shoulder.

Claire pulled at her sweatshirt pockets. What was she doing? Why was the foreigner pulling at her pockets? An iciness stole over Li's face.

"What an incredibly evil man," Claire whispered. Something trailed from her hand onto the floor. "Such an evil man."

"But it's just a corpse," Li whispered fervently.

"All the wrong," Claire was murmuring. "…the disempowerment of the people." She went to the coffin, dropping things as she ran. A lighter sparked over and over as she held it against something in her other hand. Two guards moved swiftly, apprehending Claire and pinning her arms behind her. An overhead light came on, the room flooded with brightness as the casket descended through the floor. Guards barked orders to resume filing to the exit, but there was no line now, just a large group of people talking excitedly. Li stooped to find evidence of what Claire had dropped. Too late, Li noticed her postcards had fallen from her pocket, someone's shoes scuffing them. She picked up a string of red firecrackers, the type used to celebrate the opening of new businesses.

"Her accomplice," a guard shouted in Mandarin. He grabbed Li by the arm and held it behind her back.

"Please wait," Li said, but the guard muffled her words with his hand as she tried to explain. Claire was still shrieking something about democracy and helping the Chinese people. The guard dragged Li through the exit and into the Square toward a police vehicle, leaving one of her high-heels behind. The vendors stopped their haggling to watch. They stared in silence.

After it was over, when Claire was on a plane home, having been asked politely to leave and not to come back, Li sat by the window on the train. It wasn't until she was two hours south of Beijing, and while the other passengers dozed, that she pulled out the red bandanna from her bag and turned it over in her hands.

Li, too, had been asked to leave Beijing, to return home. Certainly, her town was more like the old China, not fancy or rich, with abundant opportunity, but at least it was predictable.

In the back seat of the police car, Claire, looking straight ahead, had pushed the bandanna into Li's hand. Li did not know what to do, and had tucked it quickly into her skirt. The two policemen in the front seat were anyhow more interested in Claire's gold lighter than in the two women safely in their custody.

Turning over the red square of cloth on the train now, Li knew she wouldn't manipulate it into a triangle, in order to keep her hair back. She wouldn't tie it with a reef knot at her neck, as she had as a child. But she might keep it close at hand while she was teaching English lessons at home. She would use it as she thought Claire should have used it—to wipe away the fog on her classroom windows when she wanted to really look at the world outside.

ASIA: *Iran*

When Stars Fell Like Salt Before the Revolution

Jill Widner

Sylvie stands at the window, wrapped in a blanket, the dawn in the distance, brightening the dusting of snow that has fallen overnight in the courtyard below. The dun-colored grass is frozen. The stone fountain and concrete pools, empty and scattered with leaves.

The second-floor rooms on the other side of the courtyard are larger than the room Sylvie shares with her mother. They have balconies, each with a private ceiling, a mosaic of tile in a vaulted arch that is the same turquoise blue as the dome-shaped roof of the mosque, visible through the branches of the trees. At the top of the dome, a weathervane, like an axe-head in the shape of a crescent, gleams in the sun like a coin.

And then there is no mosque. No rose hips dangling from bare branches. A girl is lifting her hand. She's smiling at Sylvie and turning it over, she touches the mound at the base of her fingers where the skin is marked with crosshatched lines like ideographs she can't read, and the girl won't tell her what they say.

When Sylvie awakens she finds a note on her mother's bed, instructing her to meet her downstairs in the Caravanserai Room where tea is served. She opens the curtains and stares through the glass. There are the pools, scattered with leaves. There is the mosque through the trees. She turns her hands over. There are the cross-hatchings like number signs etched in the skin.

Sylvie finds her mother seated on a mound of cushions facing a low table, eating dry toast and drinking hot tea with lemon in a china cup.

Sylvie tells the waiter she would like her tea the Iranian way and studies her palms while she waits. He brings a gold-rimmed vessel the size of a shot glass on a saucer scattered with transparent shingles of crystalized sugar. The waiter shakes his head no when Sylvie starts to break a piece into her glass. He motions for her to put it in her mouth. "There it will dissolve," he tells her. "This is the Irani way."

Sylvie's mother wants to shop for Kilim. They walk beneath the vaulted ceilings of the bazaar, lost in a maze of brick lanes crowded with kiosks, searching for the carpet merchants. Sometimes they find themselves at the dead end of a narrow alley, sometimes back where they started, beneath the open arches that face Shahrdari Square.

In a fabric stall, a shopkeeper unfurls a bolt of bright cloth and drapes it over the partition that divides his stall from another. Plain-colored chadors hang on coat racks and translucent headscarves, like slips made of insect wings swing from screens. At the front of another stall, a man is arranging pomegranates in tiers on a wooden cart. He splits one in half, peels the membrane back, and spills the bright red arils into the palm of Sylvie's hand.

Sylvie likes to bargain and finds that she's good at it. In a metal shop, she barters for a round box with a man whose skin is blackened with copper dust.

"That is not enough," he says, when Sylvie offers a price. "You see," he says, prying the box apart with his fingers. "This box has a lid. And here, there is an inscription."

"But the lid is too tight," Sylvie counters. "And look at your fingers," This box is very dirty."

He takes the box out of her hands and rubs it with a cloth he has pulled from his pocket. "This box can be clean."

He is very handsome, Sylvie thinks. Many Irani men are handsome. Even the old men. The goldsmith in the jewelry shop is such a man. He introduces himself as Sahar Jazin and asks Sylvie's mother if she and her daughter would like to watch him work. Sylvie's mother is reluctant, but follows Sylvie and the bearded man in the loose trousers and the long white shirt through a beaded curtain.

At the back of the room Sahar Jazin sits on a wooden stool that faces a workbench. He opens one of many drawers in a cupboard built into the wall and, with a pair of fine-tipped pincers, rummages among what sounds like bits of gravel. He drops a shard of gold the size of a fishing weight into a mortar where a small fire is smoldering.

"What shall I make for you?" Sahar Jazin asks.

Sylvie points to the turquoise ring on his little finger. Except for what looks like a moon-shaped Persian letter worn into the shaft, it is very plain. "A ring. Like yours."

"This ring is from the holy city of Mashad. It is very old. I have many rings much more beautiful than this already made. Look inside the case." He leads the way back through the curtain to the front of the shop and points to the jewelry on display, but Sylvie shakes her head no.

Sahar Jazin unlocks one of the drawers behind the counter and holds a gold loop, decked with bits of turquoise, against her nostril. "How do you like this?"

Sylvie laughs. "But I would need two. For my ears."

"Of course." He nips a fine length of gold in two with a pair of wire clippers and then, with a pair of pincers, coils one piece around the other until he has twisted it closed in a knot. He opens a different drawer and slides flat squares of macled turquoise smaller than the tip of a match onto the open end of the curved wire and motions for Sylvie to turn her head to the side. "Take the other one away."

Sylvie pulls the back of the post from her ear, and he slips the open end of the loop through the hole in the lobe of her ear.

He hands Sylvie the other ring. "You put this one on the other side."

Sylvie pushes her hair behind her ear and tries, but it won't go in. "I need a mirror. I can't see."

"No mirror. You must feel with your fingers."

She tries again. "You do it," she says at last.

When the earring is in place, Sahar Jazin asks Sylvie's mother if he may know her daughter's name. He removes a fountain pen from another of the drawers and writes something on a sheet of graph paper he tears from a small spiral notebook. He takes his time, and Sylvie watches the Persian script appear beneath his fingers, a net of filigree, the ink like water color before it dries on the paper.

When he notices how closely Sylvie is watching, Sahar Jazin writes something more. "You must keep this," he says when he is finished.

"I will."

Sahar holds the curtain aside for Sylvie's mother to pass through. The beads brush the floor and for a brief moment he is alone in the room where Sylvie is studying what he has written on the small piece of paper.

"What I have written is for you. Not for anyone else. Do you understand?"

Sylvie doesn't, but nods and follows him to the counter at the front of the shop, where her mother is opening her wallet. When they have agreed on a price, Sahar Jazin escorts them to the door. "Khoda hafez," he says, more to Sylvie than her mother. He holds the back of his hand against his chest, then turns it over and holds his palm for a moment over his heart.

At the end of the lane are the Persian carpet stalls. The bright, geometric patterns of the Kilim Sylvie's mother has been searching for are everywhere, unfurled on tables, stacked in rolls, pulled open on the dusty stone floor. But Sylvie has grown tired of bartering and tells her mother that she will meet her back at the hotel.

"It's an easy walk. Twenty minutes at most from the square. If you find a carpet you like, say you want it delivered to the hotel. You know what they say. She travels fastest who travels alone."

"What?"

"Rudyard Kipling."

She is standing on the corner, looking both ways to cross the busy Karim Khan e Zand Boulevard, when a dog with swollen teats runs in front of her, nipping at the heels of a man pedaling past on a bicycle. A girl in tall, rubber boots and a knee-length dress runs after the dog into the middle of the street. The top of her head is wrapped in a red scarf, but, beneath it, her hair hangs long down her back. The dog turns around when she calls, and, wriggling, follows her back to the sidewalk.

Sylvie squats to pet the dog and looks at the girl. Her eyes are macled like Sahar Jazin's turquoise, both rough like stone and shining, but green not blue. The girl touches the dog's head and slips her hair behind her ear. To show off her earring, Sylvie thinks, then sees that what she had thought was a silver feather is a knotted gray string.

"Eight puppies she has. You can take a white one for 20 rials. You come? I will bring you back after."

Less than thirty cents. Sylvie wants to say yes, but lowers her eyes and shakes her head no.

The girl nods. "For 20 rials I can also read your hand." She lifts Sylvie's hand and as she does Sylvie sees that her palms are painted with henna and tattooed with Persian script. She studies the palm of Sylvie's left hand briefly and smiles. "You are lucky," she says.

"What do you mean?"

"These small cross-cross lines below these fingers bring salt luck."

"Salt luck?"

"Yes, salt luck." She rubs the tips of her fingers together. "Only a little bit. A sprinkling. And only sometimes. When you do not expect to be so. And in a way that may not at first seem so."

Sylvie pulls two folded bills from her pocket and flattens them with her fingers. The paper is red and tan. On one side is a portrait of the Shah of Iran; on the other, a lion. Above its head floats a crown. Held high in its paw is a sword.

"Reza Shah Pahlavi," says the girl.

Sylvie looks at her, surprised. "I prefer the lion," she says, and hands her the two red notes.

"Two?" the girl asks.

"So you can see both sides."

Walking backward, the girl waves goodbye with both painted palms. Sylvie waves back until a break comes in the traffic. It isn't until she is running that she remembers the girl in her dream. She looks back, but the girl has disappeared with her dog in the crowd.

The street that leads to the hotel is a quiet lane. Plane trees shade the sidewalk. A wrought-iron fence borders a park. Sylvie glances through the rails as she passes. On the other side two boys are studying on a bench.

One of the boys says to the other, loudly, "You speak English to that girl."

The other boy closes his book and approaches the fence. "We wish to practice our English with you." His pencil makes a skipping sound, trailing the iron balusters as he walks her to the gate.

"Why do you want to learn English?" Sylvie asks.

"So I can speak English very well."

They walk a cinder path to the bench where the other boy waits, his chin tucked inside the high neck of his sweater. They look like brothers. The older boy pulls a few rials from his wallet and, pointing to the bicycle that is leaning against the back of the bench, says something in Farsi. The younger boy's voice rises a few notches in protest, but eventually he stands. He pushes the bike a little way down the path and looks over his shoulder before he leaps over the saddle and pedals away.

"Beshin," the older boy says to Sylvie.

"Beshin?"

"Yes, beshin. Sit." He pats the seat. "Beshin." Then adds, "Mikhahi. Do you wish?"

"Are you asking me if I want to sit down with you here?"

"Yes. And also, if you wish, to give me some English."

"Give you some English?"

"Yes."

"Ok. For a little while."

"Where have you been?" he asks.

"To the bazaar. With my mother. She wanted to look for Kilim."

"Ah, Kilim. You have been to Bazar-e Vakil. Where will you go now?"

"To the hotel." Sylvie tells him the name of the street.

"I can take you there if you wish," he says.

"But first English."

"Yes. First English."

"I think it would be easier for you to give me some Persian."

"Very well. What word would you like me to give you?"

"What is your name?"

"Hussein," the boys says.

Sylvie laughs. "No. I mean, how do you say, what is your name?"

"Esmet chie."

"Esmet chie." Sylvie enunciates the syllables carefully. She can almost taste them, metallic and ornate in her mouth.

"Esmet chie?" Hussein asks.

"Sylvie."

"Like the metal."

Sylvie smiles. "I was just thinking that Persian tastes like silver."

"Tastes?"

Sylvie points to her tongue. "How do you say, how do you say?"

He laughs. "Chetor migan."

"Chetor migan boy?" Sylvie asks.

"Pesar."

Sylvie looks through the tree to the sky. "Chetor migan sky?"

"Aseman."

"Moon."

"Mah."

"Chetor migan star?"

"Setarre."

"That sounds like English. I think you're making it up."

"No, no," he protests. "All true."

"You are funny."

"Ba-mazzehn," the boys says. "Ba-mazzehn means funny."

Sylvie smiles.

The boy touches the edge of his little finger to her face. First beside her eyelid, and then beside her mouth. "Khandidan."

"Khandidan?"

"Khandidan means to laugh. Smile and laugh. Both. And did you meet the fortune teller in Bazar-e Vakil?"

"The fortune teller?"

"Yes. In Bazar-e Vakil there is a fortune teller who keeps a small bird. You give the fortune teller so many rials and he directs the bird to pick a bit of paper from a tray on which is written a line or two from Hafiz to guide you. You know who is Hafiz?"

"The poet," Sylvie answers. "No, I didn't meet the fortune teller." She is thinking of the girl with the henna-painted palms. She is thinking of the girl in her dream. "But I have this." Sylvie reaches inside her pocket and unfolds the slip of graph paper Sahar Jazin gave to her. "The goldsmith wrote it for me." She moves her hair behind her ears. "He made these."

Hussein ignores the earrings and studies the piece of graph paper. "Did the goldsmith tell you what he has written?

"He said it was my name in Persian. Then he wrote something more."

"There is more. This is Hafiz. Shall I translate for you?"

"Please."

Hussein clears his throat. "It is difficult."

I beg you, to no one else show
These words I send in such a hidden way

Hussein interrupts his translation. “How do you say this word? Something like a secret code. It is a mathematical word. You do not know it?”

Sylvie shakes her head no.

Hussein makes an impatient noise with his mouth. “In the poem, Hafiz has given the woman he loves a secret code to understand.”

“Go on,” Sylvie tells him.

Read these words in some safe place you find.

“I don’t know how to say the rest,” he says.

“Try.”

“Only the last two lines”:

You may speak any language to me

Love speaks every language beneath the sun.

“That is Hafiz?”

“That is the great Hafiz.”

“So I did receive a fortune in Bazar-e Vakil.”

“I think so.”

“Do you think it is a good fortune?”

“A fortune is not necessarily good or bad.”

And then the younger boy is back. “Do you like ice cream?” he calls through the rails of the fence. He parks the bicycle and unwraps a sheet of newspaper from around several frozen ice cream bars.

“Ice cream?” Sylvie says. “In winter? It is so cold.”

“Yes,” he says.

“Chera?” Sylvie asks.

He laughs. “Khalikho,” he says to Sylvie and points to Hussein.

“Hassan says your Farsi is very good,” Hussein explains.

The younger boy peels the paper from his ice cream bar. “Tomorrow you come back for exam.”

“Tomorrow I must beravam Ahvaz,” Sylvie says.

Hassan smiles. “Oh. You must go home to your mother-father?”

“My mother is here in Shiraz. At the hotel.” Sylvie looks up through the trees. “Tomorrow we must go back to Ahvaz, where my father works. After that, I must go back to school in America.”

“Khoda hafez,” the younger boys says.

“Shall I walk with you to the hotel?” Hussein asks.

“I know the way. It isn’t far.”

“But it is almost dark.”

"Not dark. Twilight." Sylvie points to the first stars that have appeared in the sky. "Setarre."

"Yes, setarre. Later there will be more."

"I will look for them."

"I will also look for them," Hussein says. "I will look for you looking for them. We can meet like invisible lines in geometry."

"And I will look for you."

"Even from America?"

"Even from America."

"Goodbye then," Hussein says. "Khoda hafez."

"When school close, you come back to Shiraz," Hassan says.

"Yes."

"Goodbye," the younger boy says again. "Good everything."

It is difficult to remember exactly, but sometimes she tries. That night, unable to sleep, she took the fold of paper to the window and pulled the curtain aside to a night so clear, so black, the stars looked like salt spilled across the sky. *There it will dissolve. This is the Irani way. Salt luck. Only a sprinkling. And only sometimes. In a way that may not at first seem so. A secret code. For you, not for anyone else. Do you understand? We can meet like lines in geometry. Goodbye. Good everything.* And then, when she pressed her face to the glass—she can't be certain—it was so long ago—it might have been drifting snow, but the way she thinks of it now, the stars were falling. All of the stars of Iran. In a way they've never fallen again.

ASIA: *Israel*

COMFORT ME WITH APPLES

Rochelle Distelheim

Stay me with flagons, comfort me with apples: for I am sick of love.
—Song of Solomon 2:5

1993. Jerusalem. This is not a happy story, it does not end well, but it is my story, and I am here to tell it.

Allow me to introduce myself: Manya Zalinikov. Zalinikova, if I use the feminine form. Also, my husband, Yuri, my daughter, Galina. *Olim,* this is who we are, new Israelis. Since six months, we are here from our home in St. Petersburg, Russia for this reason: to live like Jews. This is what Yuri tells us. Learn to be Jewish, he says, after a lifetime of knowing that the less Jewish one is, the safer one is; after coming from a country where being Jewish is a birth defect.

The old Soviet Union is dead, the new Russia is a difficult place, but not as difficult as Israel. This country is like no other. It takes you in, yet you are never *in,* as a *sabra*—a native-born Jew—is in. It takes you in, and then it breaks your heart.

Israelis are proud people—chauvinists, my Hebrew language teacher called them. They want everyone who comes here from another country to love it. I have tried. I have passed dislike. I have passed distrust and confusion, without yet arriving at love.

In Russia I was a concert pianist, when I could find work; Yuri, a mathematician at The Academy, working with false identity papers one can buy for cash, papers with fancy gold stamps and a false religion: Christian. Galina was allowed to attend college, we were allowed a small *dacha* in a forest of pine trees. Here in Jerusalem I perform on the piano in a supper club, The White Nights, owned by a Russian with a murky background, meaning rich, and silent as to his history. Yuri studies how to be a Jew with a Reb, a teacher, who is brilliant, who knows he is brilliant, and considers me a creature who is beyond his powers of rescuing. Galina is at the university and, unless she marries, in danger of turning into a soldier, as happens with all Israeli young people, except—and here there is irony—the fiercely religious.

I begin at the beginning, a day on which Amit, a clever young television director, of more than average good looks and intelligence, was rehearsing his people on the set of a not-yet-opened television show, *JSingles,* that matches young Israeli women with young Israeli men, everyone hoping for marriage. You may wonder why Galina did not put herself forward for this endeavor. My daughter requires hours to select a pair of shoes, a bracelet. Imagine the time she would require to select a husband.

The host of the show, Yuri's Reb Turrowtaub, makes no secret of his ambition to be rich and famous, as well as holy. One month before, on a day of rehearsals for the show, appeared Jen, very beautiful, very Swedish, and pregnant, the father a war hero recently killed, hoping to honor her dead lover's religion by marrying a Jewish person. She met Amit, he met her, and they fell in love.

Consider this: geography, religion, sociology, psychology and, what in Russia we call *blood pull,* tell us that Jen and Amit would not meet. Having met, they should not have fallen in love. That they wished to marry, human beings being perverse, this country being complicated, was miraculous in its optimism.

To marry, to make a beginning, to say to the people you love, next year we will do such and such, and the year after we will do another such and such, in a country whose specialty is endings, is an act of courage, or, maybe a refusal to choose reality, when reality is too difficult. We Russians manufacture melancholy, we luxuriate in it. We export it. While Israelis, not yet my favorite persons, existing on a pinpoint of land surrounded by a sea of enemies, insist upon the normal: weddings, circumcisions, babies, concerts, museums, lectures, carnivals, zoos.

Let us return to the set of *JSingles,* on that day when the Reb's nerves were bitten off at the ends from long rehearsals, an absence of sleep, and from not knowing if the show would be a success. I was there with my friend, Ahuva, the Reb's wife—a woman who is very much an un-Reb type of person, or how would we be friends—

following her with flash bulbs, film, cold water, as she used her camera. The Reb, in his satin robe, looked to me like a volcano draped in slippery white, on the tip of boiling over if one detail went wrong.

Everyone knew Amit was swept up with Jen, even the Reb, who had closed his lips to speaking about it. After the lunch hour, everyone standing around drinking coffee, I heard Amit tell Oze, his twin brother, also a director, that, before the summer was past, he'd marry with her.

"Does the Reb know?"

"He will, in five minutes."

The Reb's response was, "*Marry!*" His eyes bulging, veins purpling his neck. "I heard you correctly?" He wrung the neck of his plastic water bottle. "A Jew to a *non-Jew*?" Now his cheeks were a fierce red, but Amit—Amit was smoking, and looking calm.

"Marry with Jen-from-Sweden..." Three words, pronounced as one. "...who, if I am again correct, you met not one month ago?" Everyone on the set froze, silence came down like a heavy blanket. Ahuva brought a glass of cold water and two blood pressure pills, which the Reb swallowed without taking his eyes from the younger man.

"A crack in the foundation of the Jewish people," he continued. "One small crack, then a split, a split becomes a *meetmotet.*" A cave-in. A wonderful word, I thought, writing it into my language notebook. It sounded exactly like what it meant.

"Ruth," Amit said, "think about Ruth, also a convert, also the Bible's most famous daughter-in-law and, let us not forget, a greatgrandmother."

From behind the musicians' stand, Oze whistled and applauded, calling out, "The kid grew up to be our very own King David, remember?"

The Reb asked, "Does your mother know what you are planning?"

His mother had recently died, said Amit, looking no more ruffled than did Rasputin, when accused of plotting against the Czar.

The Reb pounded onto a table. "Your mother," he hollered, "should be grateful she isn't here to see this." Ahuva reminded him of his health, and Amit said, "Go home, everybody, rehearsal is over."

The solution, reported to me by Ahuva, was sent down from the top. My fellow Russian, my employer, Dmitri Kanov, whose money, from nobody-knew-where, had bought for him the television station, was as lukewarm Jewish as I. Now he sent word that he loved controversy, audiences loved controversy. Strong, opposite points of view made good publicity, which made good television shows, which, in turn, made good business.

Amit, he said, had the freedom to love anyone. From what Kanov knew of Jen, loving her made good sense. If she loved Amit back, well, then—. Ahuva and I puzzled over the missing end of his sentence. My interpretation was that it meant whatever anyone wanted it to mean, just do not make problems for *JSingles.* It also meant the Reb inviting us to coffee on Ben Yehuda Mall to declare peace. Galina was included, because she was close to Jen's age and could possibly offer girl-to-girl friendship to sweeten the meeting.

And, so, on a blue and gold summer day, the birds slipping in and out of the budding trees, the perfect example of a day never seen in St. Petersburg, we seven persons met on Ben Yehuda Mall, that lively pedestrian walkway with book stores and restaurants and shops selling everything from ice cream to T-shirts to jewelry and musical CDs, one of my favorite happiness places in a city that is not often happy.

Jerusalem was not a city of street music: too anxious, poised always for something terrible to arrive. On most days nobody felt like music in their bones, but, on that day, on the corner, a stringy-looking young man in need of a bath played his guitar, and a young girl with dark, tangled hair and a curious, oval-shaped scar across one cheek, in orange and red and gold silk somethings, shook a tambourine and collected coins from the crowd, which she slipped inside her brassiere, or what she wore instead of a brassiere. Neither of these young people looked Israeli, but who *does* look what is called Israeli?

We watched the musician and the gypsy for a long, silent time. Strangers, we couldn't jump in with, "So, your mother isn't well," or, "I saw your son at the mall yesterday, with what looked like a beautiful girl." Finally, the Reb, in his television voice, said, "Well, well, just imagine," and we all laughed in a hollow way, like smiling at the ceiling of an elevator to avoid making foolish talking with the other passengers.

The Reb led us down the mall to a sidewalk table at the Blue Bird Café, and I watched Galina watching Jen, with her bright yellow hair, like a silk waterfall, her big, wide-awake, yet dreamy eyes, and, over it all, a look of wise innocence.

My daughter said nothing, but I knew, by the way she focused her attention on the other young woman's hair, clothes, nails, that she found much to admire. Was she the smallest slice jealous, I wondered, that this girl, not Jewish, not Israeli, not Russian, had captured this splendid young man? Difficult to say from the outside. Galina was a talented actress.

Jen that day was like a shaft of light, wearing something white and gauzy. Galina's clothes leaned in the direction of the theatrical: orange knit blouse, a short but complicated skirt, flowered in red and yellow, a silk scarf tied around her throat. She and Jen, seated opposite one another, leaned across the table to talk, Galina doing most of the talking, since her Hebrew, as bumpy as it was, was better than Jen's. Two cell phones rang in the same second, at a nearby table. "Did you know that Israel is where cell phones were invented," Galina said, "which is why our babies get their first one in the hospital nursery?"

Jen laughed and took a fiery red instrument out of her bag, passing it among us. "A present," she said, patting Amit's arm. This very small machine fit into a palm, and was meant to make and receive telephone calls, but it made other, even more magical things. On a tiny pad on the front of the phone, Jen typed in Swedish the date and position of our café, pushed a button, and the words burst onto the screen in Hebrew. Push another button, the machine wrote in English, delighting everyone.

"Do you have a phone like this?" Jen asked Yuri, as if she knew he was a mathematician, and loved new inventions.

Yuri's smile was tight, but friendly. Since the beginning of his new life in prayer, in which he thanked God every morning for not making him a woman, he was not at peace with ladies who appeared to be too technological. He shook his head. "This kind of miracle is expensive."

Jen laughed in her attractive but careless way. Amit said something about what is money for, and kissed her shoulder. Galina scrutinized Jen, sending eye signals to me, announcing approval of what she saw.

Yuri looked away, his eye tic ticking his discomfort. The Reb's responsibility as host clicked into place. He jumped to his feet, raising his coffee cup. "To the happiness of the couple," he said, a hundred million miles away from his first response to Amit's marrying an un-Jew. A general murmuring agreement floating around the table, we clicked cups with one another. Amit hugged Jen and looked at her as though, if he looked away, she might vanish. Galina took out a notebook and wrote, probably a reminder to herself to remind her current suitor, Asher, she would love to own Jen's miracle telephone.

Here now, the bitter coincidence in my story. In this city of one-half million persons, and an equal number of cafes, on that afternoon, at a table some meters beyond ours, but close enough for me to observe, sat a slender man with an ordinary face, not young, not old, wearing one of those stiff black hats that sit unnatural, high on the head, a black silk coat, the white fringe of his *tzitzis* swinging below his shirt. The *tzitzis* I did not see until he stood up but, seeing the hat, seeing the beard, I knew this was a case of *tzitzis.*

The beard: heavy, dark, not trimmed to a point and romantic-looking, like Yuri's, or even like Czar Nicholas's beard, but thick and squared and long, and side curls that bounced in a manner that was both comic and serious, and were, in a strange way, sweet-looking when he turned his head to call the waitress. All in all, an ordinary Orthodox look, in a place where this man was among his own.

And, yet, *something.* I whispered to Yuri, "Isn't that man too young to look so old?"

He frowned, and whispered back, "Manya, *please.*"

Since his change from our family's un-Jewishness, *Manya, please,* has become his principal declaration to me when I remark in public upon anyone in black clothing. Or, in private, on why the monthly visit to the *mikvah* insulted women. Or, on why refusing to eat milk products and meat products together was accepting the medieval amidst the twentieth century.

"That man is fully Israeli," he said.

I leaned past Yuri, hoping to reach Galina. Still writing, her nose in her notebook, she hadn't noticed this man. She ignored all men in black. They were beyond her ability to understand, primitives, unfriendly to women, why should she acknowledge them?

Why? Because they were there, and we were there, and every molecule occupying a single Israeli iota changed the emotional temperature of the country. Just as the beggars posted at the entrance to the central post office in St. Petersburg changed the way we entered and exited from that building, making certain to have coins to drop into their hands. Just as the *babushkas* seated in the corners of every gallery in the Hermitage Museum changed the way we'd enjoyed the art: *Do not touch, do not stand too close, do not sneeze, cough, sniff on any object other than another person.*

The man was now wearing sun glasses while reading his newspaper, shifting the paper every few moments, reading it upside down, as often as rightside up. Strange, but true, most Israelis' nerves were so jangled by everyday events, reading a paper upside down could be a result. Should I report him, like I'd report a suspicious package sitting in the post office, looking like it belonged to nobody? Report him for doing *what?* This man was not a package; he was an Orthodox.

I looked around for someone whose arm I might grab, someone where I could whisper, *Shhh, there, that man in black, does he look wrong to you?* Would an Israeli believe a Russian? Yuri fussed with his wristwatch, shaking it to assure that the time was correct, and Ahuva reminded the Reb to put only one sugar in his coffee, and Jen said, "Where, please, the bathroom?"

I said, "Me, too." Jen was the one, if my Hebrew could penetrate her Hebrew. She would understand.

When we stood up, Galina said, wait for her. In my mind even a small exodus from the table would put a cold towel on the party atmosphere, which was already teetering. I whispered that the bathroom was for one lady at a time, possibly the wrong information, but she nodded. On my side was the fact that public rest rooms in Russia were scarce, inconvenient, and dirty.

Jen slipped her arm through mine, as easily as she would with an old friend, smiling her sweet, radiant smile that so loudly announced her happiness. "Come, come, Missus Zalinikov..." She laughed. "I said it correctly?" I felt a warm wave of affection for this brave young woman, thousands of miles from her family, now eager to move on into a new version of her life, as though she, like Israel, refused to be beaten down. She struck me as having a wisdom I had not yet discovered. Maybe I never would. Maybe she'd be willing to tutor me, to infect me with her optimism.

We walked together to the restaurant building, not ten meters from our table, passing the man in black, who had a look of happy expectation on his face, or what I could see of his face, all that beard to hide in. Jen went inside, but I stopped at the entrance to look back at him. He stood up. I thought, *good, he's leaving.* But no. He didn't walk away.

I continued in the doorway, just inside the restaurant, holding the door open to see what he'd do next. He called out to the waitress, "Please, a glass of water." In this same moment, a small bird with a shimmering blue head flew onto the tip of the umbrella shading his table. The waitress, a slender young girl with pale, silky curls all over her head, a starched white apron over her blue jeans and T-shirt, and a springy walk that announced good health, brought the water. To look at her was to know that somewhere, even if they lived in a far-away time zone, was a family that telephoned her often, just to inquire about her happiness, and to say, "Good night, we love you."

I continued holding the door open. The bird was pecking at the yellow umbrella as though someone had planted it with bird seed. The man drank the water, dropping the glass, or throwing it, a crash that caught everyone's attention, except the bird's. Then he said, very loud, to no one, to everyone, in Hebrew more poorly accented even than mine, "Goodbye. I will not see you again," before thrusting one hand inside his jacket, and throwing himself forward.

The sky shook, the earth rocked, birds flying over must also have rocked. Bright light shone everywhere, so much brightness, it lifted up the man in black, exploding him into bits and pieces of bone and flesh that splattered onto the tables and chairs, until there was no man left, only a body without a head or arms. All around him, or what was left of him, where people one second before were eating and laughing and telephoning and kissing, there was empty air above, bloody pools and body parts below.

Glasses, dishes, pitchers flew off the shelves at the waiter's station behind me, windows cracked, some blew away, along with the door, knocking me to the ground. A man hollered, "Everybody, be calm, sit." He didn't mean me. I had to go out. Yuri was out, Galina was out, but he pulled at me and screamed there would be more explosions, come back, stay inside. I went.

A man shouted, "*Pigua, pigua! Terrorist*!" Then an eerie silence, the earth holding its breath, followed by three shrieks of a siren, as sudden as a gunshot. Two shrieks were an everyday sound, announcing an everyday ambulance coming through, carrying someone with an everyday heart attack, a baby impatient to be born. Three blasts meant terror attack. Three blasts meant: once again.

A woman was crying; a sound beyond anything human, beyond

pain, beyond grief, as if sorrow had been given its own voice. She wouldn't stop and wouldn't stop, until I called out, "No more, *please!*" and realized, as I kicked something soft, a hand with four fingers, that the voice was me. Then bodies to step over, some without faces. My right eye felt stabbed. I touched it. My hand came away with blood.

Ahuva and Amit were slumped over our table, not moving; the Reb was underneath, murmuring something I didn't understand. Yuri, lying on his back, stared at the sky, his jacket and shirt shredded, blood running from an opening in his throat, splashing onto the bird lying next to him, now without its shimmering blue head. Galina, one minute lying flat down, the next, sitting up, looked at me with a face heavy with blood, her stunned eyes registering that she had never seen me before.

Down on my hands and knees, I begged Yuri, "Breathe in, out, in. Breathe." *Don't die before I tell you how much you are loved.* He struggled to take in air, I thumped on his chest, which did nothing except give me something to do. I wiped Galina's face with her silk scarf, tying the ruined fabric around her head so that only her eyes showed up. The wild bird trapped inside my chest beat its wings, trying to get out. In minutes, less than minutes, ambulances screamed onto the mall, as though all morning they had waited around the corner, knowing, with that sorrowful Israeli knowing, that, sooner or later, something terrible would happen. Why go home, why bother to take the ambulances into the garage? They will be needed again.

All around me, cell phones rang and rang and no one answered. News played on the radio and the television day and night in this country, a country smaller than Belarus or Ukraine. Everyone listened. Everyone expected tragedy, and all the phones worked. A bomb gets exploded, and everyone called everyone they loved.

The everyones I loved, besides Yuri and Galina, were my friend, Nadia, who was that day in Eilat, and my American-turned-into-an-Israeli friend, Yael, in her office. Should I call? *We're fine, my eye bleeds and Yuri's throat is slit, Galina's face is in pieces, but we're able to move, there are no big pieces of shrapnel or nails in important parts of our bodies. If there are, they're lying quiet.* My cell phone was in my purse, and my purse blew out of my hand when I fell.

Now came the police and the fire people, and the experts in explosives to search for other bombs. Then the *Zaka* workers, who began at once the work of cleaning up. Israelis are efficient people.

Have you seen these *Zaka* men executing their dance without music? Men in yellow and black vests, skull caps, white gloves, carrying plastic bags, peeling scraps of flesh and bone from under the tables, the chairs, scraping from the few whole windows that remained, scooping from the bloody river running down the street, wading into the ankle-high sea of broken glass that surrounded everywhere, to pick, pick.

"Remnants," I heard these men say, "collect every remnant." Every pinpoint scrap of human being must be buried, with the body or without. Did you know intestines are yellow? Have you ever seen an arm or leg lying on the ground, attached to only air? And this: DNA.

The DNA of a hand, even an ear, a finger, can connect a body part to a body, to a life that was, up to the moment of the explosion, busy at the business of living.

Men wearing masks to keep out the stench of burned flesh, a smell strangely like the smell of rotting food, carried out the people on stretchers. Bleeding bodies and ringing pockets. I saw a young girl in an apron smeared with blood, and blue jeans, a head of curls, passing too quickly for me to ask: Alive? Farther off, the ambulances waited. A man in a white coat made wild gestures with his arm, calling to the rescuing people, "Don't give me the dead ones, bring out the injured." A pair of wet brown boots stopped next to me. I looked up, into the face of a young girl medic person. "Are they alive?" she said. "We're taking out the living ones first."

The funeral was the following day, Jewish law requiring burial within twenty-four hours. Just as well. So many Jews being killed every day, this way the burial teams can keep up, the roads into and out of the cemeteries don't get clogged. Even in hell, details are important.

Amit's family owned an area in the small garden cemetery on the western edge of the city. Jen and I went. The ceremony was short and terrible, in Hebrew, Jen not a part of it, nothing. His mother, also red-haired, was not, as Amit had told the Reb, dead but, after burying her child, wished she could be. Jen wanted to say something to this woman, she didn't know what, some word of recognition, of alliance. They had, after all, both loved the same young man. Oze, looking like he couldn't remember where he was, or why, tried to help, but his mother looked at no one and said nothing, her face frozen into deep furrows of grief.

The Reb and Ahuva were minor miracles: serious scrapings, a broken wrist, a twisted neck, damaged ribs, singed hairs. My eye was bandaged—a good thing, because this way my tears spilled from only one side. I ran outside too fast, the doctor told me, didn't I know any better? "Doctor," I said, "please understand. This was my first suicide bombing. I'll do better the next time."

Two weeks later, Yuri and Galina were still in the hospital, his throat stapled together, living on blood from people we never met, light ones and dark ones, rich ones and not-so-rich, most of them speaking languages I didn't understand. So much blood, so many people, we'll never be able to thank everyone.

I played the what-if game in my mind, with Galina. What if we'd sat down at another café? What if we'd sat at another table, farther back, farther out? What if I'd said yes when she asked to go with me to the women's room? What if we'd never come to Israel?

Her room was down the hall from Yuri's. She had, in the first ten days, many times surgeries. To save her face, the surgeon said, also to pick out the nails from the bomb, and the flying metal and glass from everywhere. She'll have a scar, he said, running the nail of his pointing finger from the corner of his eye to his mouth. I asked, how deep, how wide, how bad? He shrugged. "It isn't fatal, so how could it be bad?"

Only a face. I imagined him thinking this, especially on a day when he perhaps sewed a finger back onto a hand, or stitched a kidney, a stomach, back into somebody's body. I did not say this to anyone but myself: one person's *only* is another person's *everything.*

Those first days, my bed was the floor of Yuri's room; the beep-beeps of his monitors, the squeak of the nurses' shoes moving down the hall, these were my lullabies. Lying alone, I thought terrible thoughts about not being able to go on, about why were we here—*why?* Israel was dying, I sobbed one night to Yuri, who blinked. He heard me. I wanted to go home, my real home. I'd never felt so alone, so sinned against, so angry.

Nadia came with a bottle of red wine. "To help you feel more human," she said, "especially when taken with music, possibly a nice view of the ocean."

"Where nearby is an ocean?" I said. "Do you see an ocean?"

She sniffed at the air: soap, disinfectant, floor wax. "The smells in here could kill you."

Yael came, with her uplifting outlook that usually rescued me—but not that day. She brought a pink flowering plant for Yuri, a book of Israeli poetry for Galina, plus a bag filled with the newest fashion and movie person magazines, "for her less intellectual moments."

"How are you holding up?" she asked me, in the hallway, away from Yuri's hearing.

"I'm not."

"These are terrible challenges."

Challenges? A psychology word, a word for people who don't know what it feels like to be blown up. "Challenge means something difficult to do, with the promise of a reward at the end. My reward is a husband living on borrowed blood and a daughter with a ruined face."

"Both alive, both recovering."

"I want to lie down on the floor and howl, I want to..."

"But there *is* a reward." She pulled me to her, an un-Yael thing to do. "Now you're one of us, more *sabra* than *olim.*"

"You invite me into your exclusive club of survivors of terrorist attacks?"

"You invited yourself, you went through the initiation."

"So, I uninvite myself. I was never one to join clubs."

Jen came to say goodbye, looking that day like a woman who had forgotten about details like lipstick, or making up her eyes. Even her hair, pulled back with a rubber twister, looked without life. "I could have saved him," she said. I didn't agree, but I didn't argue. She was going home to Stockholm, to reflect on how everyone she loved ended up dying.

"Not your baby," I said.

The doctors called Yuri's wounds superficial. Not true. Nothing about being blown up is superficial. I asked my husband if he knew what the Reb was saying under that table when the bomb went off. I stayed with minutiae, clinging to the ordinary. The *shema*, he said, the prayer for the dying carried by Jews into the gas chambers in the camps.

"Where did you learn these things? You have only just now become a Jew."

He smiled, a pale, melancholy kind of smile that left his eyes unsmiling—his birth gift from being born a Russian. I squeezed his hand to say what I couldn't say: All the talking we went through about his God not being my God, unimportant.

Now, the question that plagued me, still plagues me. What decides on a daily basis who is to go on living, who is to die? Luck decides. Good luck says: Live. Bad luck says: Die. As harsh and final and unfair as that. Don't tell me about the Book of Life. I like my answer better. If I could choose between being born with the gene for luck, or the gene for wealth, or power, or talent, or even intelligence, I would choose luck. I would choose the *mazel* gene.

My second question was this: The Jews have been chosen, the scholars say. We have an obligation to carry out God's commandments, to demonstrate that we choose Him, they say, to demonstrate that we honor our covenant with Him.

Chosen? *For this?*

If any of you out there speak with Him on a regular basis, please, the next time I want you to say, "Hey, Mr. Big Shot, I have a message from my friend, Manya Zalinikova. Take a minute from your important God work, look down, you'll see her, a dark-haired woman in her over-the-middle forties, usually wearing something red, now with an eye bandage."

Tell Him I appreciate His good intentions. He meant well, but ask Him to leave us alone to live our lives in whatever decent way is still possible, one day into the next, no special connections or special memberships with special groups up there where He lives. Ask Him for me to unchoose us, please.

A Husband and Wife Are One Satan

Jeff Fearnside

Neither of them could remember exactly when their arguments began bringing more business to their cafe. A certain amount of public obnoxiousness could be expected in Kazakhstan, especially when vodka was involved, but normally the deeply personal affairs of a husband and wife were kept secret, behind the locked doors of crumbling Soviet-era apartments or closed gates of tiny village homes.

That doesn't mean people were above prying into their neighbors' lives, especially in the villages. Raim and Railya made it easy for them.

It started out playfully.

"Mare," Raim would say, smacking his wife on her great round behind, which shivered like a horse's flank under her cotton skirt. "Stallion," she would return, grabbing him by his fleshy hips and then pushing him away, laughing.

The sparse few customers who came at first, mostly their friends and relatives, enjoyed this little theater. Then one day Raim returned drunk from a trip to the bazaar to buy onions, and Railya soundly scolded him for "coming in on his eyebrows" in front of the entire cafe.

"You're really under her heel!" roared the big foundry boss, Kolya, and everybody laughed. Raim, normally good-natured and too drunk to fight back anyway, grinned sheepishly.

"But it's a very pretty heel," he said, trying to wink but blinking both eyes instead.

Once the taboo was broken, they began arguing as freely in their cafe as they did at home. Being ethnic Tatars, descendents from the Mongols who had ravaged the region some eight hundred years before, they already enjoyed a certain reputation for wildness. At some point, they realized that business had become brisk. Just how much was due to their tasty homestyle cooking and how much to the entertainment was uncertain, but Railya shrewdly observed that there were certain phrases that always pleased her diners, who even insisted that the thunderous pop music, normally a cafe's main attraction, be turned down in order to hear what the combatants were saying.

It was a summer Friday night, and the regulars were all there: married, bear-like Kolya and his doll-like girlfriend, Larisa; Murat, a quiet little Kazakh man, and Tikhan, the equally quiet Russian youth who always sat with him; Dilya and Olya, excitable and extravagant teenage friends; and Alikhan, a widower everyone assumed was alcoholic because he strangely sat by himself and never spoke except to order.

Raim bustled between his roles of greeting customers, grilling large skewers of meat, and dishing out portions from a massive cauldron of *plov*, long-boiled rice, carrots, and onions topped with mutton.

"*Assalamu-Alaikum*," he greeted Murat as he did all his fellow Muslims: "Peace be with you."

"*Wa Alaikum-Assalam*," Murat returned. They gripped hands lightly but warmly, their free hands holding each other's forearms to show respect.

Since Kolya was Christian, Raim greeted him in Russian and shook his hand in the vigorous Western style. In such a way Raim visited each table to ensure that his customers were happy. They all settled into their seats while Railya topped off everyone's glasses with their drinks of choice.

Then the show began.

"Your portions are too big," Railya complained, emphasizing each word by pointing a spoon nearly as large as a ladle at her husband. As a schoolgirl in Soviet times, she had often starred in the many holiday pageants the authorities staged, and she relished reliving the emotions of those days.

"People come here because they're hungry," Raim said. "I feed them."

"They'll have to feed us soon if you keep giving away everything we own."

"It might do you good to relax and open up a little, you dried-up old galosh."

"I gave you the best years of my life! If I'm dried-up, it's because you sucked me dry."

"Stop your talking, snake."

"Bloodsucker!"

"Stubborn ewe!"

"Deaf farter!" Her eyes twinkled, for she often used this epithet affectionately with him. "You're lucky I married you—you from a family of cattle thieves. I'm a head taller than you!"

Kolya began laughing so hard tears streamed down his ruddy cheeks. "That's exactly what my wife says!" he exclaimed between sobs before downing a shot of vodka. His girlfriend patted him consolingly on the arm. He placed his enormous free hand upon hers, and half her slender forearm disappeared.

They came for different reasons: Kolya to escape his wife, Larisa to be with Kolya, Dilya and Olya to find men, Murat and Tikhan to lose boredom, Alikhan to be alone in a crowd. Or so they thought. But had some sensitive soul come in, some spiritual master or poet, this soul would have felt them connected by a common energy, an energy unseen to them but to the spiritual master or poet as tangible as the blue-white glow simultaneously broadcasting the same flickering patterns from identical square boxes out window after window onto street after street night after night.

"We're already nineteen," Dilya lamented one night to her friend. "Do you think we'll ever get married?"

Both had broad, plain faces heavily made up, short, tight skirts pulled over wide hips, and large breasts only faintly harnessed in halter-tops. They could have been sisters except that Dilya was ethnic Kazakh, with a dark complexion and long, black hair, Olya ethnic Russian, with a fair complexion and long, blond hair.

"What about Timur?" Olya asked.

"He doesn't love me. He only thinks I'm pretty. I let him buy me presents."

"If he steals you, will you marry him?"

"Of course. I'm a good girl! I wouldn't disgrace my family. But," Dilya sighed, "he really is a bonehead."

"You would learn to love him."

"Yes, that's true. As God wishes. Mama was stolen by Papa, and they didn't love each other at first."

Dilya began looking around the room and quickly focused her attention on one table.

"What do you think of him?" she asked.

Olya glanced to where her friend seemed to be looking, then to the left, to the right, and back to her friend.

"Who?"

"Tikhan!"

Olya shrugged and then turned her attention to another table. "Kolya, though," she sighed. "Now there's a man!"

"What about Larisa?"

"Who cares about her, tiny little princess. I'd show Kolya what a real Russian woman is like."

"Olya, what are you saying?"

"After we're married, of course." She took a sip of beer. "I'm a good girl."

At the other table, as if he could sense that he was being overlooked again, Murat shifted self-consciously in his chair. Nobody could remember what he had done during Soviet times, and nobody exactly knew what he did today. Almost apologetically short, with elegant hands and glasses that made his eyes look like an owl's, he gave off the air of an academic in how he always ordered his food in perfect, precise Russian, the way he arranged his napkin neatly on his lap. In truth, he was a businessman involved in some shady dealings, as most even modestly successful businessmen in the country were, backing up his lack of physical stature with money.

Tikhan also appeared to be an academic and in fact had studied so well at the university that he hadn't needed to bribe his teachers for his good grades. Everyone assumed he now spent his days and nights in lofty intellectual pursuits, perhaps preparing for a master's program, but he actually spent much of his free time watching television. His favorite show was *The Big Wash*, which featured regular people talking about such themes as "I lived in America," "I want to be a star," and "I will never forget my wedding." Other guests listening in an adjacent room would then join, and arguments often ensued. He also liked *The Burden of Money*, where people competed for a fat cash award by telling a serious-faced "jury" their most sorrowful personal tales. Tikhan's main connection to Murat was that they both enjoyed drinking pot after pot of strong green tea with sugar.

At that moment, Tikhan caught the girls looking in his direction again, and they both immediately looked away and bent their heads together in conspiratorial giggles. At length they collapsed back in their chairs, two glorious fallen angels, spiritual emptiness radiating from them like halos.

A favorite crowd-pleaser at the cafe was any variation on the "I told you so" theme, usually with Raim ignoring the advice of his wife to his unacknowledged detriment.

"Look at this," Railya said, pointing to the empty cauldron with her ever-handy spoon. "Not only are your portions too big, I told you we didn't have enough rice."

"It was enough," he said meekly.

"Enough? Then why are our customers wanting for plov in the middle of lunch?"

"How should I know? Perhaps you ate some while I was at the bazaar."

"Do I look like I can eat that much?"

"When a man has a good woman, he wants a lot of her."

"Hornless devil!"

"At least you didn't give me horns," he asserted, quickly distancing himself from the notion that she was cheating on him. Even Murat laughed merrily at this, and Kolya pounded the table with his great paw.

"Never," Railya responded with a frankness that seemed too frank in their little theater. "You may be an old tree stump, but I would never do that to you."

Raim was somewhat taken aback. "Is that a compliment or the truth?"

"It's the truth. You're an old tree stump."

Everyone laughed again, and Raim slipped comfortably back into the improvisation.

"A sore on your tongue!" he cried.

"You see?" she said. "You know that I'm right, so you have nothing but empty words."

"Stop your nonsense."

"Words, words, words."

"Take yourself by the mind, woman."

"Oh, this is better than *Windows*," Larisa squealed happily. She loved the outrageous allegations people confronted one another with on this show. She especially loved the story—one she secretly considered trying out herself someday, though, of course, she would never tell Kolya—of the boyfriend who claimed to have caught his girlfriend making love to her sports bike. "Don't you think so?"

Kolya nodded, vigorously stroking his long, bushy sideburns. Raim was staring steadily at his wife.

"Why are you looking at me like a goat at new gates?" she finally asked.

"A goat am I? Why are you so stubborn, like a ewe?"

"Goat!"

"Ewe!"

"Yes, yes!" Kolya cried. "This is life!"

Summer's desert heat gave way to autumn's coolness flowing down from the mountains, not like a flash flood but like the watery molecules that slowly saturate the air, then become dew on morning grass, then rain. The process is imperceptible day by day. In the same way, something changed in how Raim and Railya behaved.

One morning he came back from his trip to the bazaar without returning her greeting.

"Oh, did we sleep together?" she asked sarcastically.

"Hm?"

"A 'hello' for your wife would be nice."

"Hello, Dyuimovochka," he grunted distractedly. She understood this reference to the one-inch tall fairytale girl, suggesting that she wasn't looking well—understood it as perfectly as the smell coming from his lips.

"Again you came in on your eyebrows!" she cried.

"Not in either eye," he snorted back, though he took care not to move too close to her.

"Let me take a look."

"I told you, there's nothing to see!" He busied himself with washing his hands in the corner washbasin, and when he turned back around, she was in the exact same position as before, hands on hips, reproach in her eyes.

"Why are you looking at me like Lenin at the bourgeoisie?" he spluttered. As they traded insults this time, their eyes remained hard.

"Deaf farter!"
"Old galosh!"
"Wood-goblin!"
"Witch!"

Eventually Alikhan caught Railya's attention and silently pointed to his empty shot glass.

A month later, everything appeared normal—Larisa picking her teeth while Kolya stroked her hair, Murat and Tikhan drowning themselves in tea and sugar, Dilya and Olya alternately whispering and giggling giddily over beers, Alikhan a sleepy-eyed statue over his vodka. But Railya sensed that something was different. When Raim returned from the bazaar this time, she instinctively pressed toward him to catch a whiff of the vodka she was certain was evaporating on his lips. She caught a whiff of something else instead. She recoiled as if he had smacked her forehead with a teakettle.

"Who is she?" she shouted.

"Who's who?" Raim returned, backing away.

"She, she, she! The whore whose perfume is all over your neck!"

"Perfume? That's not perfume. It's gasoline. I spilled some on myself when I was helping Baltibek fix his car."

"You spilled some on your neck? Why do you lie to me? Why do you protect that filthy bitch?"

He only stared at her, and with a sudden feeling of great fear, she softened.

"Raim," she pleaded, "please tell me it was just an accident, a little kiss, a one-time thing. Please tell me it was nothing."

Something about her fear and complete vulnerability annoyed and then angered him, bringing long-buried feelings to the surface, where they simmered, then boiled—an irrational stew of feelings that he could no longer contain.

"You drove me to this!" he shouted. "You want to know, yes? All of the details? Okay. It's Gulshat, Baltibek's wife. We've been sleeping together for a month. There. Ever since we opened this cafe, you've grown colder and colder, and with your constant nagging, what else could I do? Maybe to you it was all a joke, but I'm a man, I have my pride. You—"

He cut himself short. His confession itself didn't startle the patrons of the cafe. A certain amount of infidelity was expected of men, even seen in the village as manly, and Gulshat had been the subject of certain rumors for some time. What startled them was that Raim had managed to keep it a secret until now.

Railya, however, was more than startled. She felt as if she had been cut with a knife—a real physical pain, searingly hot around the edges of the cut.

Her customers now experienced something they had almost forgotten about, silence, and this silence settled deeply inside their souls as their busy minds stopped churning for a moment and they realized, startlingly, they were in a cafe with real bodies and feet connected to the floor. They moved uncomfortably in their seats, and to see Railya standing before them silent and cut made them more uncomfortable, and at that point they would have done anything to make the merry machinery they were accustomed to begin madly whirling again.

Raim felt the same way, and he instinctively put that machinery into motion.

"You drove me to this!" he repeated. "What was I supposed to do? What could I have done?"

Railya remained unmoving and silent.

"It was this, all this," he stuttered, spreading his hands before him, unsure of what to do or say next, his eyes sweeping the room from the lone tap of the single beer they sold to the cauldron of plov steaming over the fire. For a moment, he seemed mesmerized by the gleaming metal, the licking flames.

"I did it for our business!" he suddenly screeched. "Don't you understand? I did it for us!"

"You always gave away too much," she finally whispered.

For the first time anyone could remember, Alikhan said something other than to order food or drink.

"*Pravda... pravda,*" he said, nodding emphatically: "Truth... truth."

In these times, Railya could have divorced him. However, for a traditional Tatar woman living in a village, the known world stopping at its boundary, not so much its physical boundary but the much stronger one of society and its mores, where would she have gone? And what could she have done? No one in her family had ever been divorced, and more importantly, they relied on her to help support them. For Raim and Railya, the cafe was their sole means of income, and one they managed themselves; they couldn't close it or take time from work. So they moved into a nether world ruled by neither matter nor spirit. They continued to come day after day, more like memories of themselves than anything else, going through the motions of opening the shop, preparing the food, and serving their dwindling number of customers.

Autumn's fluid coolness gave way to winter's freezing snows, which blew down from the mountains and regularly, imperceptibly at first, added to what remained from before. In the same way, Raim brought bouquets of red roses whose petals over time withered and fell, softly, to the floor, gathering in drifts that neither Railya nor anyone else bothered to sweep up. After a while the cafe was filled with the frail, crushed scent of roses underfoot.

Raim hadn't touched a drop of alcohol since his confession and had even, in an entirely novel development for him, visited the mosque on a few occasions. He understood what he had done and felt sorry for it, but he also understood, with a knowledge that only could have come from some spontaneous and miraculous form of grace and certainly not from his own limited consciousness, that words were not needed—moreover, that spoken now they would permanently ruin everything between them. He continued to bring flowers and wait.

Then one day, which just happened to be a day when the regulars had all assembled for the first time since the confession, or perhaps exactly because of that, Raim decided to speak.

"Railya," he said softly, though it sounded like an explosion. "Dear."

She didn't turn to look at him, but she stopped preparing tea for Murat and Tikhan, her body tense, as if ready for flight.

Raim thought quickly but carefully. This new feeling in him was too fresh to trust to his own voice. As a Soviet schoolboy, he had been forced to memorize countless poems, many of which, all these years later, he could still remember. He searched his mind for his favorite poet, Pushkin, and for a verse that would appropriately reflect his feelings. He found one well known to everyone in the room:

I loved you: yet love may be
In my soul faded not completely.

But let it not disturb you again;
I do not wish to sadden you with anything.
I loved you silently, hopelessly,
Tormented now by timidity, now by jealousy;
I loved you so sincerely, so tenderly,
May God grant you such love from another.

He spoke slowly, simply. When he was done, he stood like a child at the head of the classroom, not knowing if he should say more or sit down.

"Perhaps..." he began and then stopped, for the thought was far too fragile and important to give words to.

Railya blinked, slowly, twice. Then, as if for the first time, she noticed all those petals on the floor. Mechanically she moved toward the broom, and when passing her husband, though she still didn't look at him, she spoke:

"Not yet," she said quietly. "But we will see."

Kolya's eyes began burning redly, and Larisa patted his arm.

"Two boots make a pair," she said.

Kolya hoisted a shot of vodka to his thick, moist lips and said to her, the whole room, and no one in particular, "A husband and wife are one Satan."

THE ART OF LIVING

Teresa Hudson

For Tanya

Lara Glazunova carefully descended the old staircase as she did every morning, trying not to trip on its badly chipped tiles. Their apartment building had once been beautifully decorated in art-deco style, but that was a long time ago. A few pieces of colored ceramics laid in a decorative pattern on the landings and a wrought-iron banister were all that remained from that part of its life. It hadn't aged well, but at least it had survived. That was more than could be said of many relics in St. Petersburg.

Sometimes Lara felt like a relic herself. There were days when she felt almost as ancient as the art in the museum, as if she had been alive for centuries. Sometimes she swore she saw her own eyes reflected in the paintings. What would an artist call a portrait of her now? "Woman With Cancer"? "Russian Woman"? Perhaps "Lara, Middle-Aged Museum Guide."

Lara had worked as a guide in the Hermitage for many years. Both she and her husband Vladimir were trained as archeologists, but after studying ancient Orthodox churches Lara had decided to become an art historian specializing in iconography instead. She began working at the museum after finishing her dissertation, and now gave tours about everything from icons to armor. She enjoyed her work very much, but these days just walking from one end of the museum to the other took a lot out of her.

She had made it to the bottom of the staircase and was just about to walk outside when Vladimir called down to her. "Lara! You're going to pick Julian up from school today, yes?"

"Of course, Vova," she said. "I told you I would." Vladimir was very preoccupied with his current project, studying the site where Gazprom wanted to build its new headquarters. He was very anxious about his work, and that made him anxious about everything else, too.

"Because I definitely cannot do it, and you know how he gets if we're late."

"I will be there, dearest. I promise. Don't worry."

"All right. See you later."

"*Poka.* I kiss you." Sometimes Lara didn't know who was more difficult to care for, Julian or Vova. One was an archeologist, the other was a student at Special School for Children with Psychiatric Needs, Number 16.

She walked outside and began to make her way toward the bus stop. Their street, Bolshaya Monetnaya, was in one of the oldest neighborhoods in St. Petersburg, on the opposite side of the river from the Hermitage. On workdays the number forty-nine bus carried Lara across the Neva and deposited her five blocks from the museum. If the weather wasn't too bad and she could walk fairly fast she could be at work by ten. Today it was windy and cold, but at least it wasn't snowing.

The wind was coming straight from the north, so she hugged the sides of the buildings along her way. Some were in better shape than others, with bright new facades and shiny, soundproof glass. They'd been renovated by rich oligarchs who wanted a prestigious-sounding address in Petersburg and thought that "Big Money" street sounded like a good place to live. Lara took comfort in knowing that the buildings had survived revolutions, wars, and famine. They would survive the oligarchs too. Like human beings they had changed over time, but in spite of everything they still stood. Vladimir's archeological team had recently unearthed an ancient cemetery under the Gazprom site. He had dated it to a time before the Swedes lived here, before the great Peter or Catherine's reigns, before oil was discovered in the Arctic circle and Bentleys cruised through their neighborhood. There were more skeletons in this city than people suspected. Perhaps they were what kept it standing.

The bus was on time. She rode the rickety old thing across Troitsky Bridge, and got out near the Marble Palace. It occurred to her for the hundredth time that if she worked for the Russian Museum instead of the Hermitage she could work right here. She wouldn't have to leave her apartment as early and could get home faster too. But it was too late to change jobs now, and besides, who knew how much longer she would be able to work at all?

As she started down Millionaya Street she could just see a short figure in a bright purple coat about half a block ahead. Only her friend Katya had a coat like that. "Katya!" she called. "Katusha! Wait!"

Katya stopped and turned. "Is that you, Lara? Come along then!" She stamped her feet on the pavement to keep them warm, and pulled her red woolen cap down over her forehead. "Hurry!"

"This wind is about to blow me over," Lara said breathlessly as she caught up to her. "Horrible, isn't it?"

"Yes," Katya said, pulling up her collar. "Like living on the taiga. Come on, let's go."

They began walking toward Palace Square. Lara was soon out of breath, but masked it by holding her scarf up to her mouth.

"How's Julian?" Katya said. "Have the tantrums gotten any better?"

"Yes. I put his medicine in juice every morning, so he doesn't even know it's there."

"How resourceful of you."

"He's much less violent now. He's even rather thoughtful at times. When I was giving him a bath the other night, he said 'Mamachka, why are there holes in the wall?' He didn't remember that he'd made them himself. I said, 'Darling boy, your papa was very silly. He put his hand on the wall, and it went right through!' You know what he said?"

"I can't imagine."

"He said, 'My papa is as strong as a pharaoh!' I don't know where he gets such ideas."

"From the books you've read to him, of course. You've been a saint. He never would have made it this far without you. He'd have been institutionalized long ago."

"Oh, don't say that," Lara said. She couldn't bear to think of what might become of Julian, or Vladimir, without her. "The people at the school are very good with him too."

"And how are you? Any stronger?"

"Much better. The doctors say the tumor is shrinking."

"It's wonderful what they can do with chemotherapy now."

"Yes."

The two women walked in silence the rest of the way to Palace Square. Neither of them wanted to talk about illnesses long. An innate superstition made them turn away from such subjects.

In a few minutes they were on Palace Square. As strong as the wind had been on Millionaya, it whipped across the huge space around them like a gale. They met it head-on, skirting the museum's walls as they made their way to its entrance.

"This wind is simply ghastly," Lara said, her eyes watering.

"Just think what it must be like for them." Katya gestured toward a few construction workers on scaffolding. They were repairing the Chariot of Victory sculpture over the arch leading into the square. "Poor guys. And all because of some hooligans and their fireworks."

Lara couldn't see the men very well, but she was glad to know they were there. Perhaps civic pride shouldn't take precedence over people's health, but the Chariot sculpture was important. It was a symbol of resilience in the face of enormous odds, commemorating Russia's victory over Napoleon. It was there to give people hope when all seemed lost.

"Ivan Borisich!" Katya called to a man up ahead. "Hold up!"

A middle-aged man in a worn overcoat turned toward her. He wore thick glasses and looked slightly disheveled, as if he had just gotten out of bed.

"How are you on this blustery day?" Katya asked as she approached him.

"Frozen solid. If I didn't have so much alcohol in my blood I'd have turned into a statue on my way across Palace Bridge," Ivan said.

"We would have saved you," Katya said. "We would have chipped pieces off of you and put you in our tea to thaw."

"No need. You see, excessive alcohol consumption has many benefits." Ivan fell in step beside them. "How are you, Lara?"

"Fine, thank you, Ivan Borisich."

"And your eyes? Still bothering you?"

"Much better, thanks."

Lara saw Ivan and Katya exchange a look, which she ignored. "I'm very glad," Ivan said. Everyone knew that her vision problems were not a good sign, but they also knew it was important to be upbeat. There was nothing worse than a glum friend.

"Why does the wind always seem stronger here, coming off the square?" Lara asked, changing the subject. "Just look at those branches." The handful of trees that stood at the center of the museum's courtyard bent and swayed as if caught in a miniature squall.

"Something about the way the building's positioned between the river and square," Ivan said. "The arches act like tunnels, condensing the air."

"You're such a scientist," Katya said. "Is there anything you don't know?"

Ivan considered her question. "Yes. Does art imitate life or life imitate art? I've never been able to figure that out."

"Art imitates life," Katya said. "That's why people love it so much. It allows them to see things they wouldn't otherwise."

"Those people must be true art lovers," Lara said, pointing to a queue where at least a hundred people stood waiting. "Some of them don't even have decent coats. We should give them blankets."

"Good idea," Ivan said. "Why don't you take down the Gobelin tapestries and use those for a start?"

"You think there'd be enough?" Lara said, enjoying the joke.

"Definitely," Ivan said. "Plenty of tapestries to go around."

"We could always use the chasubles from the chapel too. About time somebody got some use out of them," Katya said.

"Once an atheist, always an atheist," Ivan said.

"Naturally," Katya said.

Lara didn't say anything. Her study of icons had given her a different perspective on religion than that of her colleagues. Artists brought the icons into being through prayer. Lara wondered if the icons, in turn, brought the artists alive too.

The three walked through the heavy doors of the staff entrance. A security guard named Maxim nodded at them from his perch on a stool behind a small horseshoe-shaped desk. He was a small man with sharp, pointed features who suffered from a slight deformity of the spine. It kept his shoulders raised to his ears in a perpetual shrug. "Good morning, Maxim," Katya said as they hurried past.

"Good morning," Maxim said. His gaze never left the door. He was the museum's first line of defense and took his job very seriously. He was unarmed, but kept his finger on the button of a phone that would alert other guards, ones who kept revolvers on their hips.

"What's your first excursion today?" Katya asked Lara as they hurried down the long entry hall. It was always chilly there even in the summer. The vaulted ceilings were twenty feet high, and the floor was made of marble. "General or special?"

"A general tour for a school group from Astrakhan."

"Oof. Let's go have a smoke and prepare ourselves," Katya said.

"I went to Astrakhan once. We ate caviar every day," Ivan said.

"The good old days, huh?" Katya said.

"Yes, eating the eggs of fish that nibbled on dead revolutionaries made me the pacifist I am today."

"Ivan, you make me laugh," Lara said.

"Then my work here is done. Speaking of work, I must leave you now and make my way to my mausoleum." Ivan worked in the Department of the Scientific Examination of Works of Art, located near the Egyptian mummies and sarcophagi. "I wish you both a productive day," he bowed.

"The same to you," Lara and Katya replied, almost in unison.

The two women walked a little further and opened a door that led to a small spiral staircase. They climbed up one flight and entered a low room called the *entresol*, the break and waiting room for museum guides. It consisted of a coffin-like antechamber adjoining another long, narrow room where the senior guides kept their desks. Younger staff members made do around a common table in the antechamber.

The walls of the entresol were dingy and yellow from decades of tobacco smoke. Its furniture consisted of a wooden conference table, a few chairs, and a bookcase full of out-of-date magazines. Two overflowing ashtrays sat on the table, together with some stained mugs, a few pieces of scrap paper, a rotary dial phone and a broken pencil. An elderly woman sat behind the table, looking through a month-old magazine. Her gray hair was in a bun, and her hand trembled slightly as she flipped through the pages.

"Good morning, Maria Grigorevna," Katya said.

"Good morning, Katya," Maria said. "Hello, Lara."

"Hello, Maria Grigorevna. How are you this morning?"

"Not too well. My arthritis is acting up."

"Oh dear. I'm so sorry," Lara said.

Maria Grigorevna had worked in the Hermitage for over fifty years. She had taught both Katya and Lara when they first came to work. She was officially retired, but still came to the museum almost every day. Her husband was dead, and her children lived elsewhere. Without her work, she was lost.

Lara followed Katya into the adjoining room where they both took off their coats and hung them in a rickety wardrobe. "She should have stayed at home on a day like this, for God's sake," Katya whispered.

"You know she won't do that. As long as she has breath in her body she will come to work."

"Can we get you a cup of tea, Maria Grigorevna?" Katya called.

"No, thank you," Maria replied. "I had some at home."

"Just as well, there's no water left," Katya said, picking up an electric kettle and shaking it. "Why don't people ever refill this?" She set the kettle back down, and she and Lara returned to the break room.

"What are you doing here today, Maria Grigorevna?" Lara asked.

"Reviewing a paper I wrote for a conference some years ago about my *cassoni*." Maria's specialty was Venetian wedding trunks of the Renaissance. She was widely respected and had traveled abroad many times to present papers on the subject. "Deputy Director Vilinbakhov wants to see something about them."

"That's wonderful. You're an inspiration to us all. Katya, may I have a cigarette?" Lara asked.

"Of course." Katya handed her one, then lit her own.

"I'm hoping he'll improve the lighting on them," Maria said. "People can't appreciate workmanship if they can't see it properly."

"I agree. Those rooms are very poorly lit. Perhaps paintings take priority, but still..." Katya raised her eyebrows. "I think they hardly to know where to begin. So many things need improvement."

Lara didn't say anything. Every room had seemed somewhat darker than usual to her for a while.

"I should get to work," the old lady said. She pushed back her chair and shuffled toward the door. "I wish you success with your tours today, girls."

"Thank you, Maria Grigorevna," Katya said. She leaned across the table toward Lara. "If I still insist on coming to work when I'm that old, do me a favor. Tell me it's time to go to home and make jam," she said.

Lara smiled. "Katusha, I can't see you making jam under any circumstances."

"You're right. Maybe pickles. They suit my character better."

Lara stubbed out her cigarette. "I need to go find my group. When's your first tour?"

"Noon. But I have to interview a new girl this morning. If she does well, she can take Liuba's place." Liuba was a young colleague who had recently emigrated to France and was now working at the Louvre.

"I hope it goes well. I know it was a blow to you when she left. You put so much work into training Liuba."

"Well, what can you do?" Katya said, extinguishing her cigarette. "We teach them well, but I don't blame them for leaving, do you?"

"No. But it is difficult to see them go, isn't it? Don't you miss her?"

Katya shrugged. "I try not to be resentful."

"Of course," Lara said, standing. "That does no good."

"Listen, call me if you want me to take your second tour. If it's too much for you, I mean."

"Thank you, my dear. I'm sure I'll be fine." Lara said, smiling and waving her hand. Then she went downstairs in search of her group.

She spotted them easily. They were waiting for her, fifteen high school students and two teachers, at the foot of the Grand Staircase. They were wearing light overcoats, always an indicator of southerners unused to the "Northern Palmyra."

"Good morning," Lara said, approaching them. "My name is Lara Glazunova. I'll be your guide today."

"Good morning!" One of the teachers came forward with her hand outstretched. She was an attractive, dark-haired young woman with a southern accent. "My name is Victoria Yeleseevna. This is my colleague, Ludmila Stepanovna." A slightly older, heavier woman came forward. She smiled, revealing several gold teeth.

"Pleased to meet you," Lara said. "Tell me, is there anything in particular you wish to see, or would you like the standard general tour? We have approximately two hours."

The teachers looked at each other. "I know Ludmila Stepanovna recently finished teaching a section on mythology," Victoria said. "Perhaps she'd like for the students to see some paintings featuring myths?"

"That would be marvelous," Ludmila said. "But of course, you are the expert. This is our first time here, so anything will be quite acceptable."

Lara smiled. There were works of art based on myths in almost every room. "Well, we will certainly include the Gallery of Ancient Painting for you," she said.

"That's wonderful," Ludmila said. "We're so excited. We've been looking forward to this for months, haven't we, guys? It's hard to believe we're actually here." The students murmured their assent.

Lara felt again how fortunate she was to work where she did, and how much she would miss the museum if she couldn't. She understood why Maria Grigorevna continued coming to work every day. Life outside was so difficult. There wasn't nearly enough beauty in it. "I'll try to make your visit memorable. Let's begin on the staircase and work our way up, shall we?"

Lara led them to a landing where they could get the full effect of the ornate Baroque decorations, pointing out the gilded plaster, Carrara marble, and painting of Mount Olympus on the ceiling. "Notice the mythological figures!" she said. "This is the Grand Staircase, also called the Jordan Staircase. The Romanovs used it to go out to the Neva..." She had given the general tour so many times she could recite it in her sleep. But the group was enthralled. They had never seen such opulence.

She led them through the Peter the Great and Armorial Halls, the Gallery of 1812, the Malachite Room, St. George Hall, Large Chapel and White Hall. She swept quickly through the French Collection and Pavilion Hall, as well as the Rembrandt and Dutch rooms. Every room reminded her of something or someone in her past. Every piece of art was an old friend waiting to greet her. Lara, in turn, gave the school group as much energy as she could muster. But as she continued she could feel her strength waning, and began to wonder if perhaps she should ask Katya to take her second tour after all.

They made their way to the New Hermitage and the Gallery of Ancient Painting. "Here you can see an illustrated history of painting over a period of a thousand years," Lara said. She was very tired, and looked for a chair or bench to lean on. "Many of these paintings allude to myths, as well. There are also sculptures here by Antonio Canova." If only she could sit down for a minute, she would be all right. "Canova was an amazing artist. He had an uncanny way of bringing marble to life."

A female student pointed to a sculpture of a woman nearby. "Excuse me, miss. Is that one of his too?"

"Yes, that's the 'Repentant Magdalene.' Canova sculpted monuments for many tombs, including one for Pope Clement the Thirteenth. The 'Genius of Death' over there," she pointed to a marble bust a few feet away, "is a detail from that."

"Why was he so obsessed with death?" the student asked. "Was he depressed?"

Lara looked at her. She was so young. She had so much time. How could she possibly understand? "That's a good question," she said. "Art is about lots of things. Sometimes it's about love, sometimes it's about sadness. Sometimes birth, sometimes death. Sometimes it's about all of that."

She could see from the student's expression that she didn't understand. "You all know about the Blockade of Leningrad, yes?" Many in the group nodded. "During the Blockade, guides here at the Hermitage continued to give tours of the galleries. Did you know that?" They shook their heads. "It's true," Lara continued. "Even as their friends and families were dying, they kept coming to work. Sometimes they lived in the museum's basement when the bombing was really bad. The art was sent away for safekeeping, but that didn't matter. All that remained in the museum were empty frames, but that still didn't keep them away. Sometimes they even gave tours as if the art was still there in front of them. And people came and asked questions, just like you're doing today. So, you see, sometimes art is everything there is. Sometimes it's more important than anything else."

"Excuse me," a young man said. "How could they ask questions about the art if it wasn't there? That just doesn't make sense."

Lara considered his question. She looked down at the figure of Mary Magdalene and saw her own eyes staring back at her from the marble. "It wasn't the presence of the paintings that mattered," she said. "It was enough that they had ever existed at all." She wondered if the cancer had begun to affect her brain. She wondered how many more tours she would be able to give before her eyes were as blank and empty as the Magdalene's. Then someone coughed, and she collected herself. "Let's go into the next room," she said, "and see the Caravaggio."

AU LIEU DES FLEURS

Matthew Pitt

"Everything's fine in the world so long as I keep my head down."—Mouna Aguigui

Latin Quarter, Paris—May 11, 1999

My, was there a pall that day. Birds and bees were about but barely active. Their paths were aimless, their motions half-hearted, as were those of the red squirrels foraging for new nest material. The morning was clear enough, light-scorched, but that was a thin illusion. The sun rose sluggishly as if dragged from the horizon. Young children were in the park, but most were dozing or picking their noses. The playground was bare of their little hands and acrobatics—the jungle gyms were vacant and lonely skeletons of birds picked clean. Not enough wind to fly kites. Not enough energy in mommy or daddy to heft their children and bound around making flying sounds. Passing pleasantries between strangers lacked even seeds of sincerity, and the editorials in *Le Monde* were full of forced treacle. The student artisans seated on wooden stools on Boul St. Mich must have kept sketching—but what was there to inspire them? Probably all they drew that day were portraits of their own scuffed, untied shoes.

I was a simple failure then. My income was generous, my suits, solid, the trip to sleep from the moment I first shut my eyes, brief and uneventful. But let me say this clear, my head was going under, my mouth filling with salty foam, I was drowning. It can't be said that I embraced my routine, not quite; it's far more truthful to say that my routine was feasting on me, consuming me confidently. And my hand played the biggest part, as it was what each morning wrapped the fat, striated neckties around my throat.

That May Monday began just like any other. I woke. Ate grapefruit and hummed idle notes in the toilet. Toiled through a cheap cigarette and with a flimsy comb whipped my hair into a style disrespectfully imitative of a cockatoo. I arrived by car at work, where I balanced the books for the largest housekey duplicator in France. Sat at a cardboard brown desk at a windowless office on the 7th floor and pretended, pretended, pretended to devote myself. Prayed for the hours to pass. Unastonishingly, they did. Finally, lunch. I knew it was time because I watched my supervisor approach the elevator. I saw her tug at the elevator door's iron knob, which was hollow at the center like an open inarticulate mouth. Heard the door shut, saw the light disappear down the shaft, heard her strike a match as she exited the building. These acts amounted to my permission to leave.

I walked alone to the bistro where I had been dining without alteration for fourteen years. Two men who had finished their meals stood in front, smoking. An acquaintance of theirs bummed a drag. "What's the advance report?" he asked the two men. "Menu up to snuff?" The diners looked glumly at one another. One stood at rigid attention and covered his eyes with his necktie, while the second held his hands in a pantomime of a sniper in a firing squad.

It was indeed a disaster. The proprietor's wife was finishing two angry phone conversations at once, slamming down both receivers simultaneously. Whole shipments had not arrived at the bistro that day, and those that had were spoiled—forcing the proprietor to serve the only food that had kept from the night before: fish soup.

I draped my serviette over my lap. Without realizing I'd ordered, a bowl of the stuff was set before me. It smelled of clams and sewers. I recoiled at the odor. I wasn't alone in my distaste: Others turned from their bowls, trying not to inhale. Those patrons beside me who had already finished their soup settled up quickly to escape the scent—their francs, normally a frisky currency, lay limp on the countertop. My own gray spoon was turned away from the bowl as though insulted. And there was fish soup as far as the eye could see. Fish soup broken only by water glasses and occasional elbows. I watched a nurse seated next to me scoop up a snortful. She winced; her eyebrows had a terrible collision. Still, she ate.

Still we all ate. I grunted down sip after sour sip. When the proprietor's wife wheeled around to ask if I was happy with everything, ashes from her cigarette tumbled into my bowl. I was grateful, frankly, for an excuse not to eat another bite. Back on the street, I walked with my hat off. Took as always the long way back to work, through the crooked streets that led past Priscille's parents' home...seven months had passed since that terrible day, the day of Priscille's wreck...I took stock of my stumbling life...I would kiss the rough walls of her parents' home when I knew no one was watching...my lips would brush against the stone...return to my desk late, avoiding promotion...the week, then the weekend...luxuriate with the ducks on Saturday instead of finishing Proust... stroke the felt that lined the wooden box I kept my fountain pen in, not writing down a single word...I didn't mean to galvanize my life so divisively between the tended and the intended, but such a division did strike me as correct. What I did was not what I wanted to do, but only the pale suggestions of what I wanted more...

Cackles coming from the bottom of the street broke my train of thought. Two circus roustabouts were fighting in front of a three-speed bicycle, which leaned against the façade of a building foreign to me, fighting over the use of colored markers. From where I stood their cackling sounded muted, just a series of bitchy whispers. Yet I knew what it was—what it must sound like—where they stood: unbridled laughter, bellies of it. I inched forward, yet the sound seemed to have come no closer to me. I had no business approaching those clowns—my mind was already back on the 7th floor, entangled in cobwebs, ears filled with the dripping tick of our office clock.

Yet I rattled off, semi-mad, down the street. Only to see the roustabouts hitch up their pants, drop their markers and whistle away, as though they'd been committing some vandal's act that I had uncovered. Pulling up short of the bike, I examined their handiwork. They had scrawled messages on posterboard, which was glued to both sides of the bicycle's banana seat. The side of the sign aired to the street read: "Grab What You Can—JUST 5 Francs! Macho Meat-Filled Pastries, Raspberries, Rice, Pickle Relish Choucroute...We Don't Mind, Rob Us Blind! Inquire Within." I had to go inside. I was still so hungry, I couldn't bear to pass up the tempting offer.

Ignoring the consequences that my tardiness to work might bring, I opened the door, hung my blazer on a hook and continued in, past the lounge and guestbook.

Inside I waited fruitlessly. There were no busboys, no maitre d'. I wondered if I'd missed the meal. I peered out the window to read the backside of the billboard on the bike: "Always Serving."

Well then?

I strolled down the corridors to make myself more conspicuous to the waitstaff, and to steal glances at what the other diners were having. A group of three caught my eye. The first two I knew from newspapers: prominent spokespersons from *les Verts* and *Parti communiste*. For years I'd admired their ability to inspire and incite, to lead strangers to action by virtue of voice alone. In my more inspired moments I had concocted fantasies of quitting work and dashing to their side.

The woman from Green Party spoke, martini sip not quite settled down her throat: "Only death can engineer so pointless a silence." But it was the group's third member, a tall, enviably tanned fellow with a foamy salt-and-pepper beard and eminent nose, whose words stunned me. The tall fellow turned to the woman, smiling, as though he'd considered her statement the moment before she'd made it, and was about to bring everyone up to speed on its merit. He was dressed with cosmopolitan flair, in a purple flowing pullover shirt, a tailored navy blue jacket, with a brightly-beaded brooch in the shape of Africa on his chest (broadcasting that the condition of the suffering greatly dictated the shape of his days). "That is true," he said, consonants whistling past his teeth. "And yet only Mouna I think would have had the wherewithal to *violate* such silence."

Mouna?

Then this was not a restaurant's dining room at all—but in fact a funeral parlor, in which services for that old Frenchman Mouna Aguigui were being held. You'll forgive what must seem on my part blunt stupidity. But before I had eavesdropped on that brief conversation, I'd peered into what I'd guessed to be the banquet hall. Sure enough there was a rolling cart positioned at the center, lid peeled back. Though my view was obscured, I guessed the cart was the centerpiece to a buffet. Assortments of people had passed by the cart, looking inside—and while they weren't holding any knives or forks, I'd imagined they were simply sizing up their pickings, and would return soon with plate and saucer.

No. As I took a second glance, I realized my mistake. It was a coffin they were looking inside. I had thought that the people clustered around it were sniffing. And they were. Not as diners examining the bouquets of varied entrees—but as mourners overcome by the gears of grief. This was not a cart stocked with house specialties, but a miniature hearse, held steady by four gigantic bicycle wheels just like those I'd seen outside.

I approached.

I had heard a little of this dead clown, Mouna: He was a sloganeer, a snitch—and as such too dangerous a topic to introduce around the water cooler, too mercurial for journalists to consider an ally, too marginal for Mitterand or Chirac to have to engage in debate. And just extreme and eager enough to be an easy victim of historians, who play a game of reducing the passionate to footnotes.

I suppose we've come to the story part of things: my lover's sudden death. Priscille's death. When such a tragedy befalls the living, we wear our epitaphs publicly. Mine read: I am disconsolate but my smile tries to tell you differently. My own emotions? Couldn't catch them with a glove. I had spent the entirety of the night she died lying in my bathtub, water cresting at my chin cleft, refusing to accept any memories of her, as though they were unwelcome immigrants. I remembered how shamefully I'd acted...after I'd heard the news I had not come calling to her parents' house. I never paid my respects. And although I was given the day off from work, I had failed to even show for the funeral. I had disowned her family's anguish. Had excommunicated them ...refusing to take their calls, refusing to revisit photo albums with them, to touch my face by way of conjuring her. A crime of abandonment that shamed me now no less than in the seven months since I'd perpetrated it.

My eyes blinked open, and their gaze returned to the scene at hand. At the coffin's head and foot were sets of chrome handlebars, given a recent polish by the look of it. Garish ribbons sprouted from the handles; there was a horn, little bells—how had I missed seeing these? I felt at that moment as though I were covered with sheets of glass—windows that all needed opening at once! I tried to dismiss this feeling, and concentrate instead on the deceased. Indeed his corpse was captivating, exquisite even. A short body for such a long coffin. Under his feet, as though to boost him, were stacks of newspapers, the headlines of which bore his own name. I marveled at the many dazzling artifacts embroidered into his person. Little posies threaded through the hinges of his eyeglasses; other flowers ran in and out like tinsel in his scraggly beard. A Guatemalan worry doll…a strain of rosary beads…and a noisemaker peek-a-boo'd from his shirt pockets. An outbreak of metal buttons, like cheery measles, were pinned to his cap and corduroys, their messages tilted at angles impossible to read without craning my head: "Full Retirement at 15!" "My Heroes are the Happy," and "Concerned Scholars for Bathing."

Not all his messages were festooned with such absurd mirth. There was a billboard tied to his chest pleading for a landmine ban. And all over his clumsy potato-sack pants were bumper stickers, one decrying the use of child soldiers, another reading, *"Hurlez à la lune, pas avec les loups."* I continued reading Aguigui's body, pausing only to wipe his still smudged spectacles with my handkerchief.

As I studied him I was possessed by a belief: that the bumper stickers covering his pants were serving as makeshift patches. I had to know if I was right, and if so, what the patches were concealing. I had to know. I bent down and yanked off one of the stickers. Instantaneously a fragment of cloth erupted from the hole I'd torn in Mouna's pants. The cloth rose a few inches above his body, then fluttered in suspension, refusing to sink from its highest point. I snared it. It continued like a butterfly to beat in my hand, its lacy edges tickling my palm like eyelashes, flapping gently against my fingers. I held it to my chest until its beating subsided.

Mouna's own handkerchief. Of course there was an inscription stitched into its fabric—*"Au Lieu des Fleurs Faites Quelque Chose"*—In Place of Flowers Do Something.

Then…odd. I felt I should leave, felt…rewarded…as one might after having driven many miles from home simply to secure the sight of sunset from an unusual spot. But my brow was moist, my eyelids heavy. I was no longer myself. I pursed my mouth and let the loops out from my belt, finding myself at once stricken with loose lips and a tight stomach. What was wrong with me? Could it be that rancid fish soup? Hunger? Or was it Aguigui's handkerchief—had I acquired some contagion from it?

I knew I was near Luxembourg Gardens, so I headed there, hoping the new scenery would improve my condition. As I turned from the coffin, I felt others' eyes. I was not so alone. Many of the mourners stood near me, impassively staring at the handkerchief I'd taken from Mouna's trousers…and then when I walked out the front door, several of them followed me. I took a glance backwards: Their eyes were sunspots, the kind of intense gaze rooted in either fascination or indictment. Taking no chances, I picked up speed. My quick pace prompted sharper pulses in my gut. My pursuers remained just steps behind. I ran toward the arc that fronted the park; from there I darted into a throng of pantomimes and street performers, hoping these people would provide me with camouflage. But no matter where I moved, or what sharp turns I took, the mourners shadowed me. In fact, they were gaining ground, as though they knew my destination better than I. I sprinted for the park's toilets, further undoing my belt, further tightening my mouth. The sensation wasn't nausea…in fact it was a sensation to the contrary. It reminded me of other forms of suppression. How, for example, I'd had to resist sobbing until closing time on the day Priscille was killed in the wreck. I'd been told at four…my company's profit numbers for the quarter were due, and I was obliged to stay and finish, aligning decimal points and countersigning my own figures, before rushing to the morgue. But the feeling was contrary even to this. It was lighter, a sensation like you or I might have shared if we'd exchanged dirty jokes in grammar school—an intense suppression of laughter, practically crapping ourselves trying not to burst with giggles in front of teacher, as though we were carbonated canisters that had been violently rattled and shook…

By now I had reached the park bathroom. But just as I gripped the door, I was seized by the waist. I made no move to escape. The mourners had chased me down. The reason was clear. They were menacing me for the disrespect I'd shown in accosting Aguigui's coffin, violating his body, stealing the handkerchief that was rightfully his. Dropping my shoulders and lifting my palms I turned to accept my punishment, like a dog who cannot help but confess to a mess his owner has just uncovered.

I turned to face my attackers, but there was only one. I recognized her from the funeral parlor. She'd been kneeling by the flower arrangements lining Mouna's observation room like river tributaries. A mature woman, fifty anyway, old enough not to chase men into bathrooms unless driven by expectation. Her lips jutted outward, and her plum eyes pointed down…as though she were playing a child's game…trying to see what she could of her own face without aid of a mirror. With her face frozen in this fearsome pose, she spoke: "This park is not, you could say, my favorite. For starters there's that odiously precious fountain. Plus, its visitors keep house casually. And those hard green chairs! They really take a toll on a person's rear..."

She drew closer, eyes squinted nearly shut. I somehow knew that she hadn't read the brief will and testament written on Mouna's kerchief—it was possible she'd seen me read it though, and wanted to know what the hanky had said. Well, that information was simply enough imparted; I could recite the text back to her, it was only a phrase. Or I could just hand the cloth over to her outright and be finished here. I could resign myself to a docile position, curling up maybe like a hardened sponge on the park lawn. It was the lazy middle of May, after all, the start of spring; I had a right to resist thought, to waste my liberty where and how I chose; a right to bend my ear to the sounds of roots gobbling groundwater, of squirrels constructing nests, the sound of nature asserting itself—which seemed somehow always more soothing than my own efforts at assertion.

"Excuse me," the woman cut in, "I couldn't help but overhear your thoughts."

"Thank god for that!" I cried. "I couldn't help but think them." The woman giggled and I hiccuped. Now the tightness in my stomach attacked me in waves. "I want to apologize for my behavior, Madame, I do, but at this moment I find myself frantically sorting through the slop of my brain, trying to, you know, dig up a piece of etiquette to present to you, but I'm damn fresh out."

She lifted, for the first time, her head. Her neck was gooselike, both grand and gangly. "You are above reproach, monsieur...for one, I'm expertly qualified to receive huge amounts of uncouth behavior at one sitting...and for two, this whole time that you've been speaking you've been speaking into my deaf ear."

"Marvelous soulmate!" I responded. "What you say fills me with gladness. With other attempted confidantes, no matter how much I want to tell them what feels true at the time, I find myself constantly covering my words with little Band-Aids. I have never proven an able forum for my own confessions. I allow nothing to vent through me. I am a plugged bottle when straight talk is in the air."

"But you'll repent now? With me?"

"Oh sweetie, indeedie, indeed! Do you realize that right now I'm missing work for you? Well," I amended, gleefully, "I'm not *missing* it at all, really, I'm just not there. But hang work! Tell me about yourself and what yourself is about. Show me to your name—speak just the sound of it, marvelous soulmate, and instantly it will become my mantra!" She did just this—she was Dawn—and her words were flurries of snow melting on my tongue. Our improvisations filled me with lightness. It felt like I'd learned a new magic trick, one whose secret I would lose again the moment I stopped practicing. The moment we quit speaking, I would squander this found lightness forever...and yet... with my stomach railing again, I had to leave Dawn behind. "But not without a parting shot," I said, guessing that she still had access to my thoughts. "I must momentarily take leave, but upon my return, we'll have a discussion, our topics ranging from Chilean refugees to the death penalty to fish soup!" Then I ducked into the bathroom. I vomited, caught my breath, let the blood splash and wade through my veins—a sensation like watching my little niece play in my office, putting paper clips up her nose, making believe the stapler was a second phone; creating a playpen, in other words, out of space I had long regarded as colorless.

As soon as I was able, I walked back out, only to find that Dawn was gone. Another woman had replaced her. This new visitor was attractive and stunningly poised; her long hair was clearly a prized asset, it gleamed in the little light left of day. She had full lips and unassuming eyes. Searching for Dawn as if for housekeys, I scanned the garden. The harsh gleam of sunset kept me from seeing far. And this new woman kept bobbing in front of me. She was as insistent as she was young.

"I saw her leave, monsieur. She was in a serious hurry!"

"The woman? The one here a moment ago?" I wanted badly to chase Dawn. But it was no use; she was not in sight. Besides I didn't dare stray too far from the bathroom until my stomach settled. Damn. In disgust I tore a piece off my thumbnail. What a fuck I was! Dawn had only humored me until she felt courageous enough to escape on foot. Escape from me did seem the wise choice. Fun as it was, what had my ramble amounted to? Gibberish, a few leftist heartstring-tuggers spouted her way, and then? Fish soup? Why did I say I wanted to talk about fish soup, for God's sake? I felt like the bread bags and cigarette butts lying near trashcans, longing to be left alone.

But this new visitor wouldn't be denied. Like the first, she courted my attention with idle chitchat. Hers did not concern the conditions of the park, but instead, the new art installation she'd just come from at Centre Pompidou. Though this woman—a generation junior to Dawn, clearly of a different class, almost clearly not Parisian—outwardly seemed to share little with my experience, we warmed to one another, moving rapidly between topics. Some of what we said was inappropriate, even scandalous, fodder for public streets. More than one passing reference to anarchy, of poking holes of civil disobedience into the police state; the street riots of '68, which she was not born for and I not interested in until that moment. We were freeing ourselves from language's heavy boot—and from consternation, the tax levied upon we who question our leaders (which is supposed to be like doubting the atmosphere).

However, the tremors in my gut soon overwhelmed me, miserably mirroring the sensations I'd felt in Dawn's presence. Again I entreated this new sister, please wait for me, won't be gone along, keep near: "And upon my return," I began, and this time I suggested we debate the horrors of the nuclear meltdown in Ukraine, the repatriation efforts in East Timor—and then, to my agony again, "fish soup." I rushed into the bathroom, and again when I returned, I returned to a replacement. The evening drew its pattern. Strangers took the place of strangers whose company I'd just begun to enjoy; we caught some robust oral and intellectual wave; I turned queasy, made a plea for what we might discuss at greater length once I had purged; and my suggestions invariably dovetailed into fish soup, always my last, inapt words to these brief kin. Words that couldn't be further from the ones I'd wished to leave them with: Not the delivery boy rolling up evening editions like sleeves to throw at professors' doorsteps…not the schoolgirl who dashed her head slightly askance as she summated her arguments…And certainly not Paul, my last visitor, a haunted man who'd just spent a year on business in Beijing. There, he'd witnessed several scorching human rights abuses. And he longed now to have a stage to prowl, to broadcast his testimony to the rafters of this world. I didn't even get a chance to tell him I would like to come along. "Sorry" was all I could muster before rushing to the toilet. "It's been like this all evening…" "From bad soup, you say?" he asked, but I had already slipped inside, and he'd already begun to turn away.

Finally it ended: moon up, park emptied, I hitched my trousers to the loop they were accustomed, sighed, and exited the restroom. It must have been past midnight. Petty crooks walked with territorial cockiness along the cobbled paths, not with the stealth they submit to in early evening, and the indigents slept soundly on their stone sofas. It was the beginning of the dead hours, the formless ones, the only hours that seem to belong to anyone who wants them. I walked home. The stars were still as dogs awaiting table scraps.

I spent the next few nights retracing my steps in the garden. Hoping to get sick again. Waiting for at least one of my cronies to reappear. Trying to decipher what it was that happened that night. If anything of significance in fact really had. As my despondency grew, the walks shortened. I read and reread the handkerchief. What had overwhelmed me when I first read it, what had I hoped to accomplish? I'd been a fool, soapboxing about abuses and tyrannies I knew little of, simply because a vague statement on a corpse's old snot rag supplied the fuel. It was as though a rocket had returned to Earth smelling of crocuses and grandfathers, and from that our scientists claimed alien life to have been proven beyond a doubt.

After several weeks I gave up my search, feeling foolish and overwhelmed.

Overwhelmed. I returned to that word, and knew it to be true. Since I'd first moved from the South of France to Paris, fourteen years ago, it had been true. You can do that, move your whole life to a city with abandon. Then you open your apartment windows, and the sensation that the city has already annulled you overwhelms. This is a city's supreme weapon, indifference, indifference bordering on the unreal, as though the Parisians had given me up for dead and were not officially recognizing my gait or odor or smile. It was an art form, a competition: Who could care least? Who could turn the deafest ear? You pretended not to see the person walking toward you or that you'd disrupted their path; pretended not to notice haggard women smelling of linseed shouting, "*Je suis drôlement emmerdé*!" (Christ—a few years of city life and you laughed open-mouthed at such women!); pretended not even to notice pigeons clustering round your brioche—the sound from their green throats the groan of plaintive stomachs. And you did not, under any circumstances, notice the pleas of panhandlers and passersby. You learned to subtract those pleas from the range of your senses. Even pleas coming from your former lover's parents...whose house you finally reach out to, on July 12th, with a plea of your own, slipping a letter into their mailbox that reads, "I beg you—let me speak with you about her. Let us remember her together. Let me be to you now what I should've been then." The next morning, ungainly as it is, my plea is answered. Priscille's parents messenger a response over to my office. It reads: "We know you've meant well, know you've been meaning to meet us. It does surprise us that you have the time to see us now, given your sheer activity in recent days. But we are overjoyed that the silence between us is broken, and will call you the day after tomorrow, after the holiday." Though their middle sentence was cryptic, the rest was clear and comforting. My only wish was that we could speak at that moment, but I respected their wish to wait until after the holiday. I would simply have to busy myself until then, like a boy who can't sleep through Christmas Eve but must wait out the sunrise.

Bastille Day had no business being the day the stuck stylus jumped its groove. But there is all that diverting noise, and blue white red confetti whirling, so that I cannot help but look out the window at least briefly when I hear fighter jets snap the sonic boom as they fly showoff routines above. So yes, I venture out, if only for the cheap thrill of feeling, for a moment, in the company of an electric crowd. No sooner have my eyes adjusted to the light than I am approached by an old woman, who, clasping my hand and pointing to the swelling parade, angrily remarks, "Look at them!" Where she points, two gleaming Algerian girls unfurl a banner. I ask the woman where I've seen them before. Seems in late spring they interned with the Parliament kitchen staff. While in this capacity, they made a point of carving chips in the ceremonial soup bowl of our nation's leader. So that when Chirac dined with President Clinton in June, he found himself wiping off drips of ptarmigan bisque that drooled into his lap. The old woman huffs to punctuate her contempt, then huffs again when she gets a good look at my face.

Bravo to those girls! What a gorgeous trick! Yet that wasn't where I remembered them from. It seemed I actually knew them. But—no—it's an illusion, I say to myself, your mind is hopscotching from too much wine. Get some food and fill your stomach.

...From there I walk by the fish market, with no intent of stopping. Yet the display window captures me—moisture drips from the imbricate scales of grouper and trout, salmon levitates, sea bass too, all tied to an almost invisible wire, floating like a morbid trapeze act. And there's a face on the television set I swear I know. So I step in. Oh, it's no one. Just some actress doing community work while cameras roll around her. No...excuse me...come again—it *is* an actress, but not one I know from movies. She has a ladle in her hand; she is spooning out bean soup in Macedonia to a refugee family. She looks up only once from her work. Yet that lone look is enough to prove what I'm hoping for. That hair of hers? Unmistakable. Unbelievable! It's the young woman I spoke to that night in Luxembourg Gardens, just after Dawn, and just before Paul...

...Paul I see on the TV that night: an invited panelist for a political roundtable in the UK. An ambassador from China has just bestowed some trinket on the British Prime Minister, a token of affection for opening up trade relations. Now, Paul stands up and, walking over to the ambassador, says, "Let me respond with a gift in kind. For your record of human rights violations against dissidents, I present you this bowl of scorpion soup. A delicacy in your country. Enjoy! Just mind the tip of the tail. It's lethal, and I suppose in my excitement I overlooked its removal...I pray your removal isn't similarly overlooked." In *my* excitement, I nearly run into my TV set, rushing to turn the volume up on my friend's performance. On *our* performance—for Paul is doing his routine the very same way the two of us laughingly rehearsed it that night in May. He has perfected a delicious quality of showmanship. As he prowls the stage, I feel pride spiraling into my marrow.

...Next, just after the commercial break, comes Dawn. She heads a group of legal advocates who are advising death-row inmates to file frivolous lawsuits to protest poor treatment. Their first case? A suit by a prisoner complaining his chicken consommé was served "a tad on the chilly side." When the TV reporter asks about the inspiration for her creative outburst, Dawn arcs her shoulders in a humble shrug. "It happened on that spring night near Luxembourg Gardens. You know the one I'm talking about—I'd tell the story but you've all heard it by now." Yes. I know the one she's talking about too. But now I have to hear it told again: "This little spinning top of a fellow, only thing that could match his words in terms of tumbling speed was his sour tummy, starts to speak. Gives his take on everything dark under the sun. I listen, then give back. He turns pale. Fish soup, apology, he gimpily runs to unravel his guts in the toilet, and then I—just like everyone else from that night has testified—found myself quivering with purpose, unable to stand still or stand for stillness another minute longer."

After that, I found them everywhere, all my fleeing companions. Couldn't help but find them, even when I was not looking. I recalled my talks with them that mad night in the garden, what had enraged and haunted them, and so I knew where to spot them. Even those that I hadn't met myself—say those Korean students spearheading a hunger strike, sipping soup as a symbolic last meal and chanting, "*We are happy, we are very happy,*"—I knew. Each one I knew. And as I read on and witnessed and marveled at their grand breaches of order, I felt like a twin to them all.

EUROPE: *Germany*

IN THE GERMAN GARDEN

Jay Kauffmann

The moment his plane touched down, Henry wondered if what he was doing made any sense. Would his son even want to see him again, let alone make an effort to reconcile? It was dawn in Berlin, a Saturday—or was it Sunday?—in August, the sky low and gray, with just a hint of light on the horizon. Henry ran a hand through his hair, which felt greasy after the long trip, and considered his lap where a tray of Chicken Kiev had overturned. He slipped on his sport coat and buttoned it shut, though the stain was still visible.

The prospect of facing his ex-wife and her husband made him physically ill. Henry may have left Germany, but it was Martina who had left him. As he strolled down the bright, echoing hallway to passport control, he remembered, twenty years before, the first time he had arrived in Berlin. He was twenty-five, cocky, his uniform intentionally small to show off his physique. He had come with no illusions; then again, he didn't expect to be a flunky, either (administrative assistant, they called it) to that pompous tight-ass, Colonel Chamberlain. He could still smell the man's sweet pipe tobacco.

He entered Schoenefeld's vast hall, set down his bag, and waited—he hoped—for his son to appear out of the crowd. He wondered if a hug was appropriate after so many years. Michael was seven the last time Henry saw him, thin and pale, prone to bouts of giggling, with white-blond hair. Every morning they would bike to the bakery for *brötchen*, then race home, neck and neck till the finish, at which point Henry would touch his brakes and let him win.

He had always meant to be a better father. How many times had he invited the boy to Washington? Ten, twelve? But Martina always managed to come up with some excuse. There was summer school, *Fussball* camp, chicken pox.... In more recent years, it was simply: "He doesn't want to." Of course, Henry had meant to return, but somehow something had always come up. That was even how he explained it, lame as it sounded: "Sorry, pal, but something's come up." And though Henry wrote and called, it was sporadic. As he climbed the ranks—finally reaching (like Chamberlain, no less) full colonel—his military career took precedence. It's not that he stopped caring—there was always that longing, that throb of guilt—it's more that he was just so busy Michael invariably fell to the bottom of his list. And now he was seventeen—*Seventeen!*

Henry spotted a blond teenager moving in his general direction, wearing trainers and baggy sweats—*Michael?*—but, no, the youth stopped short of Henry and embraced an old woman—probably his grandmother. He hoped Michael would like his gift—the latest iPod, so new, in fact, the salesman had assured him, that no one in Europe would have one.

"Henry?"

Henry turned to face his ex-wife. Smiling, blond hair pulled taut against her skull, she hugged him with surprising warmth. She felt slimmer in his arms than he remembered. "Martina, I didn't expect...."

"Oh, you look so disappointed." She smiled. "Michael couldn't make it. But don't worry," she said, mimicking his glum expression, "you'll see him later."

She drove at an alarming speed, weaving through traffic with no apparent concern for lights or signs or other drivers, working the Mercedes's stick-shift like a cock, it seemed to him, which she wanted to dislodge.

"I've made a reservation at the Omni. I think it's on *Kurfürstendamm*."

"Nonsense," she said, eyes ahead. "You stay with us."

They drove along the *Grunewald*, sunlight streaming through the dense woods. They had met at a summer party near here, he remembered, in one of those old mansions once owned by Nazis. She couldn't believe he was in the army, she had said, he seemed too sensitive. She was in nursing school, crushingly voluptuous, full of

Marxist ideas, spoke English like a Brit. How she loved turning everything he held true on its head.... There were stories about these woods, he recalled, about wild boars that mauled dogs, carried children away, even killed a jogger. She had teased him about it once while they were strolling through the dark forest, causing him to jump half out of his skin whenever a twig snapped.

"So, how is Michael?"

She rolled her eyes, exhaling. "Unbelievable. A whirlwind most of the time. Frankly, I can't keep up."

They stopped in front of a large, modern house made of steel and glass, surrounded by tall pines, designed by Franz, no doubt—her architect husband, the man she had left him for. Suddenly, there he was in the doorway, Franz, waving, pot-bellied and balding, still in his bathrobe—not in the least slick, nothing, really, like what Henry had imagined.

"Henry, *hallo*, please, please, come in." The man actually hugged Henry, took his bag out of his hand. "Hungry? *Ja, natürlich*. I prepared *frühstück*."

Henry felt guilty for all the times he had thought badly of the man.

After washing up and changing, Henry joined them around a large wooden table covered with dark bread and cheeses, müesli and yogurt, pots of tea and coffee.

"Well, well, here we are," said Franz.

"I hope this isn't too awkward—my being here and all."

Franz pursed his lips and frowned. "Why? Why should it be? Absolutely not...."

"*Guten Appetit*," said Martina, reaching across the table to stroke the back of Franz's hand.

They began to eat. Henry had forgotten how good a slice of bread could be. Outside, a half-dozen sparrows fluttered excitedly around the birdfeeder. It came to him then, out of nowhere, her reason for leaving him: "Please understand, Henry, I need to find my German self again." More at ease than he remembered, she seemed to have found it.

"How is Kirby?" she asked between sips of tea.

"Um, fine," said Henry, stunned that his present wife, her very existence, had momentarily slipped his mind. "She's taken up running."

"Oh, Americans are so sporty. I just can't with these...." She cupped her breasts in her hands.

Franz chuckled.

Henry looked at his wristwatch—*embarrassed, threatened, turned on?*—then, adding six, realized it was 11 a.m. "So, where exactly is Michael?"

"Sleeping," said Martina. "You didn't know? Welcome to the world of a teenager."

Henry stood over Michael as he lay in bed, uncovered, face-down, wearing nothing but briefs. My son, he thought, stunned by the boy's size (close to six feet, he figured), his lean musculature. His hair was short, almost a military cut, light brown like Henry's. He sat down on the edge of the bed and placed his hand on Michael's tan shoulder. "Hey, pal," he whispered, "time to wake up. Your old man's here."

Michael groaned, stretched, rolled onto his back. His blue eyes stared without expression. Then, gradually, as they began to focus and recognize him, Henry watched his son's eyes imperceptibly harden.

Well, he knew it wasn't going to be easy.

Michael sat up and yawned. *"Morgen."*

Henry wanted to wrap his arms around the boy, smell him, *eat him up with a spoon*, as if he were still a toddler. But he held himself back, envisioning how his son would cringe. "Man, I missed you. You have no idea...."

"*Ach*... slow down." He shook his head in frustration. "My English is rusty."

"Right, sure, I'll let you wake up first." As Henry stood to leave, he passed his hand through Michael's hair, which felt bristly, like the end of a broom. Abstractedly, Michael reached up and brushed his hand away.

They sat together in silence, beneath the canopy of pines, forming a triangle—Michael, Henry and Martina. Now and then, a warm breeze passed over them, triggering a shower of needles. As Henry crossed and uncrossed his legs, the wicker chair squealed beneath him.

"Such a lovely day!" said Martina. "Why don't you two go for a walk and catch up... or how about a bike ride? Yes, that's an idea. Henry, you can borrow Franz's bike."

"Where *is* Papa?" asked Michael.

Henry felt it like a blow.

"Michael," said Martina.

"It's all right," said Henry.

Michael leaned back and extended his legs, crossing them at the ankles. He wore a white T-shirt and jeans, freshly pressed. His bare feet looked enormous, a size twelve at least. He reminded Henry of an officer on leave, arrogant, carefree, a bit blasé.

"Oh, I almost forgot... I have something for you." Henry leaned forward, reached into the plastic bag at his feet, and withdrew a small white box with Mac emblazoned across the side. "Catch," he said, tossing the gift. Michael grabbed it out of the air and for an instant—as a look of wonderment passed over his face—Henry caught sight of the boy he once knew. He laughed, more for the release of it than anything else. "The salesman called it *cutting edge.*"

Michael tore open the box, looked it over. "I already have one," he said, setting the iPod back in its box. "But thanks."

"But this is the newest version."

"Looks the same," said Michael.

"Well, it isn't."

Martina, to his right, reached over and patted his thigh. "How thoughtful, Henry."

Henry felt like a fool—infuriated, whether more with his son or the salesman he couldn't say. "Never mind," he said. "Give me the damn thing. I'll get you something else."

The boy handled his chopsticks deftly, dipping his maki in wasabi, then harvesting shaved ginger before tossing it into his mouth. His wristwatch looked expensive, absurdly so, far more than anything Henry could ever afford. He made a mental note to undo Martina's indulgences—starting immediately.

"How would you like to come live with me in Washington—just for a while, see how you like it? You could go to Georgetown. A hell of a school. I'm sure we could get you in...."

A slight smile, more a smirk, crept over Michael's face. "Mother will never agree."

"I don't see why not."

"Besides, I don't want to."

"Ah, well, that's a different story...."

They sat at a small table against the window. Dark and cramped, the restaurant reminded Henry of a compartment on a train. Outside, young night-clubbers strode past.

"Your mother says you're interested in politics. Is that right?"

"Hmm." He seemed bored, watching people go by.

"You're going to have to give me more than that."

He took a sip of tea. "Bush should be assassinated."

Henry laughed. "Why don't you say what you really think?"

Michael stared, soberly. "Forget bin Laden, your president—*your boss*—is the real terrorist."

"He's your president, too."

The boy's mouth fell open in a cartoon-like expression of horror, cheeks flaring red. "I refuse to be American."

Henry drew away, stunned by his son's rage, which he then understood to be directed at him. At the next table, two women held hands, smoking clove cigarettes. The smell left Henry feeling nauseous. He also felt jetlagged, as if swimming against a fierce current.

Rain began to pelt the sidewalk as hip, faintly punkish kids rushed past, boots slapping the pavement.

Michael considered his watch. "I have to go," he said, then stood and slipped on his leather jacket. "Tell mother I'll be home late."

"How late?"

"*Tschüss,*" said Michael, ignoring him, and walked out.

A moment later, Henry left some money on the table and—surprised by his own impulsiveness—set off after his son.

Once on the street, he looked left and right, then spotted Michael, hunched against the rain, hands in his pockets, striding away. Henry followed from a distance. The boy wound his way through Kreuzberg, heading God knows where. The narrow cobblestone streets glistened like a river. Taxis rumbled past, the smell of diesel in the air. Henry felt ridiculous, vaguely criminal. After all, since when did stalking become acceptable parenting?

Michael stopped in front of a Kebab shop and embraced—kissed on the mouth—a short mustachioed man in his twenties, Turkish looking. Henry ducked into a doorway. It smelled of piss. He shivered, felt wet to the bone. The German word for fag—*Schwul*—popped into his head, though he remained surprisingly detached.

When he looked out again, he saw that they had crossed the street and joined a small crowd, bathed in bright bluish light, pressed in front of a nightclub beneath an awning that read: *The Blue Angel*. His son kissed and embraced more friends—girls as well as boys. Perhaps he wasn't gay, after all, thought Henry, reassured. Someone handed Michael a cigarette, no, a joint, from which he took a long drag then passed on. Every few seconds the club's door opened, releasing a deep throbbing beat that Henry felt in his abdomen.

A woman, clearly a prostitute, dressed in fishnet stockings and a leather bustier, walked past, then, noticing him, said, "*Hast du Lust zu ficken?*"

From the coarse timbre of the voice, Henry realized at once it was a guy, or rather a transsexual, for his breasts looked large and real-ish. "No… *Nein*."

"Ah, you're American… I used to live in L.A."

Henry nodded, peering around the corner at Michael, who was still waiting to be let in, bobbing to the rhythm.

"Who are you watching?" The transsexual slipped in beside Henry, smelling of old woman's perfume, her shoulder-length hair plastered to her head and dripping.

Henry inched away.

"Oh, come on…" said the transsexual, craning her neck, "which one?"

Henry felt trapped, eager to flee yet unwilling to expose himself to Michael. "The tall boy in jeans and leather jacket."

"Mmm, *Schön!* And why are we spying on him?"

Henry faced the transsexual, whose nose was flat and twisted like a boxer's, and whose mascara ran down her cheeks in black rivulets. "For Christ's sake, go away."

"Ah, you're in deep—I can see it. And you wonder how you can make him love you again. Isn't that right?"

Henry realized at once it was true. When he looked back to where his son had been, he was no longer there.

Crystalline light shone through the woods, the sort of light that appears after a storm has swept the air clean. Henry followed Michael as they rode their bikes into the *Grunewald*, passing massive estates once owned by the Third Reich's elite, their gardens ravaged, some transformed into open pits.

"Boars," said Michael, nodding toward the damage.

They pedaled along one of the lakes, where dozens of people sunbathed naked in a field. One old couple, with pendulous body parts and great rolls of flesh, strolled hand-in-hand without the least self-consciousness.

They continued deeper into the woods, crossing an occasional jogger. The web of trails ran for miles in every direction. Within minutes, there was no one.

They slalomed through mud, bucked over roots, sluiced through puddles. Michael stood out of the saddle and hammered up a small rise. Henry strained to keep up, sweat dripping off his brow. "Hey, pal, ease up a little."

Michael stopped. Henry pulled alongside, panting. It was late afternoon, nearly dusk, the air warm and still. Shards of light filtered through the trees. The rich black earth smelled of decay.

"Jesus, you're going to give me a coronary."

Michael smirked. He did that a lot, Henry noted.

"Listen, Michael…" *This was as good a time as any,* he thought. "I want you to come live with me and Kirby. Give the States a try."

Michael snickered, passed a hand across his face—the German gesture for someone who's crazy. "*Du bist total verrückt.*"

"Your mother and I agree: things have gotten out of hand… Anyway, it's already been decided."

Michael stepped off his bike, letting it fall. "You can't make me."

"Michael, listen to me… I'm your father: I love you. But it's time you shaped up." He wiped the sweat from his eyes.

Michael balled his hands into fists. "*Du Arschloch,*" he growled. "*Ich hasse dich.*"

Before Henry could say another word, the boy straddled his bike and stomped on the pedals. As Michael bolted away, Henry watched him grow smaller and smaller till he disappeared.

For a long time he stood there, expecting his son to return at any moment. Then it began to turn dark. The forest seemed to expand and contract as if taking a breath. Wherever Henry turned, it looked the same. He set out with only a vague sense of which way he had come, the bike at his side, now and then stung in the face by a branch. Soon the blackness enveloped him.

He laughed out loud at the absurdity of his situation, then, hearing the faint echo, felt a chill come over him and shuddered. He reminded himself that he was in Berlin, not the Congo, which offered small consolation. Beneath the dense canopy of trees, he could make out his hand gripping the bike's chrome handlebar but little else. It was pointless to continue. He began to look for higher ground—one of the lessons he remembered from boot camp—a place to wait out the night.

He felt his way to a clearing atop a small hill, laid down the bike, and sat on the damp ground. For an instant, he pictured Michael, as in a snapshot, back home in Washington, smiling across the kitchen table.

The wind picked up. The treetops swayed, limbs creaking. A gamey smell drifted past.

Then he heard the boars—an unmistakable sound—rooting and snorting in the underbrush. It sounded like a half-dozen or more. A branch cracked and fell to the ground. He stood and searched for a rock or stick, then settled on the bike, wielding it back and forth several times. They drew nearer, squealing feverishly, as if having seized upon his scent. He had never been on a battlefield before—a career desk jockey—but imagined this was what it was like. His every fiber felt coiled and electric. He considered his options, trying to stay calm, lucid. He abandoned fleeing at once, envisioning how they would drag him down from behind. No, better to hold his ground. As they scrabbled up the hillside, he crouched behind the frame, holding it as a shield, and waited.

They surged over him like a current, knocking him down. Something metallic—a pedal?—dug into his thigh. One slobbered over his ear and neck, its soft, rubbery snout exploring, almost tenderly, before gouging his scalp with its tusk. They moved clumsily over and around him as big as cows. He lay on his side, curled up, keeping the bike on top of him. As they gnawed on the tires, he heard the high-pitched release of air. He lashed out with the frame, cursing them. They grunted angrily, stepping back, then reconvened, tearing at his clothes, dragging off a shoe.

Then, as abruptly as it began, it ended.

Henry pushed the bike aside and listened as their snorting, stump-legged shuffle faded in the distance. In increments, he let himself relax, then surveyed for injuries. Though bloodied and sore, he was essentially unharmed. He sat up, nearly vomited, then lay back again.

Long before dawn, Henry set out, limping with one shoe, pushing the bike on shredded tires, the woods veiled in blue fog. Eventually, he reached a road along a wide body of water and squatted at the water's edge. He washed his hands and face, looking up now and then to watch the sun bleed over the shoreline. A boat passed, its sail ablaze with blood-orange light.

Having made it through the long purgatorial night, Henry felt rejuvenated. He didn't want to go back. He could imagine the scenario: the police car sitting out front, Franz and Martina looking concerned and apologetic, and Michael looking sheepish and guilty and resentful for having to feel guilt. He rose and headed south along the byway, though he hardly cared about the direction. He was resigned now to whatever might come—from his son or otherwise.

A pack of cyclists streaked past, followed by a line of cars. Then a beat-up Trabant pulled alongside, its windows down, George Michael blaring.

"Hi there, stranger," said the driver. "Need a lift?" It took Henry a moment before he recognized the transsexual. "Honey, we won't bite." The car was full: *four transsexuals in a Trabant*—which sounded like the start of joke. She looked him up and down. "Looks like you've had quite a night."

They stuffed the bike in back, the trunk propped open, then made room for him in the backseat. He wedged between the two transsexuals, their breasts pressing up against him, the car smelling like a cross between a perfumery and a locker room. The one to his left was three inches taller than Henry and built like a wrestler, while the one to his right looked almost pretty, vaguely like Natalie Wood, only a butch version.

"Where to?" said the driver.

"Well, I don't know...," said Henry. "I am a bit hungry."

"I know just the place—best bakery in Berlin... Of course, I really shouldn't. A girl's got to watch her figure, you know. But for you, just this once...."

"*Quatsch*, don't listen to her," said Natalie Wood. "She'd fuck you for a *Strudel.*"

They followed the water till they reached an intersection and cut through a wealthy residential area. As the car rumbled over cobblestone streets, they passed a joint around between them, a mixture of tobacco and hash. Henry took a hit, something he hadn't done in twenty years. *What the hell*, he thought, smiling to himself, *I deserve a little R & R.* Then, by chance, they passed in front of the house.

There, standing in the garden with the policeman, were Franz, Martina and Michael. As the car shot past, Michael looked up. Thrilled despite everything to see his son, Henry reached across the mounds of silicone to wave. Though he couldn't say in that brief moment if Michael recognized him or not, he did, however tentatively, raise a hand.

EUROPE: *Hungary*

THE RING

Marc Nieson

But Anna, we are a family here.

—Hah! Gypsies with a big tent, I tell him.

This afternoon, our last performance here. I am happy. Sunday, only one show. Miklos does up the zipper of my costume, the weight of his hands on my shoulders. In the mirror I see him but he will not look at me. I have offended him with talk of gypsies. Look at him sulking off to the far end of the trailer, folding our bed into the wall. This has been a good town for us. Good audiences. Good weather. But tomorrow we leave, tomorrow the road. I am sad. Once upon a time I was happy to do the road, but now I like more the towns when they are good. Like this one. I could live in a town like this, I think. But tomorrow we will be moving west. Always west it seems.

—And the axle, I ask him.

—They said Sunday, Anna. Is it still not Sunday?

Always the optimist, my Miklos. After so many years. Even when he knows like me there will be no one to fix a trailer on a Sunday. That the man will come tomorrow, late, and then we will have to drive through the night. That these people he calls family care only that we do our act, the next night, the next town. He knows these things but he will not think these things, he will not think ahead. For Miklos, today is today and tomorrow is tomorrow. And yesterday? Hah, he probably doesn't even remember the last time we broke down. Two days sleeping in Zorzi's trailer. I would rather sleep with the horses.

—I would rather sleep with the horses, I tell him.

—Anna, he says.

I waste my breath. We talk only in circles. Look at him now, on the floor doing the exercises. His eyes closed, his lips counting. He does not think about his legs moving up and down, up, down. He is not even here in the trailer anymore. Gone. Someplace else in his head, someplace like music, like sleep. Up and down, back and forth. His pointed toes, his fingertips, his beautiful chest.

No, I will not look anymore. I will do the makeup. Do *my* ritual. Open the lids to all the jars, then rub color into my cheeks. My cheeks, ach, look at them. Look at the corners of my eyes cracking, and my hair like straw for the horses. How does he do it, my Miklos? There on the floor with his young arms pumping and his skin like an angel's. Maybe this is his secret, maybe this is where he goes, into a prayer. Maybe he is counting words.

—Look. In the mirror, Miklos. I get old.

—No, you are beautiful as ever, Anna.

Again he is behind me, palms on my shoulders softer now. The magic palms of the greatest poleman of any circus in Europe. And I say this not because he is my husband, but because I have seen the others. They are good, some younger and even stronger now, but there is none like my Miklos. None whose hands become part of his partner the way Miklos's hands become me.

I let those fingers melt into my shoulders, almost let my feelings go, but then the trailer door swings open to Irena. Ah, the daughter returns. Her cheeks are pink from the wind and when she takes off her coat I see she is wearing yesterday's clothes. The sweat of Miklos's palms grows cold on my shoulders. I watch his eyes follow her across the trailer. Watch how he watches. I even heard him say once how he could not tell us apart from behind. This, he thinks a compliment. It is true she has my body, but of fifteen years ago. I watch him. He is not watching, he is remembering.

—You are late, I say to her.

I wait for Miklos to say something, but he says nothing. I can hear her behind the screen, the rustle of her costume. She thinks I know nothing, but she is wrong. Once upon a time I was a girl her age, only a little older when I met my Miklos. I know all about her empty stares and waiting at windows. Her scribblings on paper in the night. I know all about this boy of hers.

Look at her fixing her tights now and coming to sit down beside me at the mirror. Staring straight ahead and dipping her fingers into *my* jars. And now Miklos coming to do up the zipper for her, too. Patting her on top of the head. His eyes get small, thinking to maybe give her another new trick for our act. Maybe even the great arch with only one arm. I look at this seed who has stolen my body. This little thief who looks in the mirror far too long. More than even I do. And at what? She has maybe five minutes of things to check in the mirror.

—If your father will say nothing, then I must. This is the last time, I say. I will not have you love this lowly Punjab.

In the mirror, her jaw falls. Her eyes make me into a witch, then search for their father. And finally, finally he sees me in the mirror.

—Go and check the rigging, he says to her.

Finally, the father speaks. Bravo, Miklos, bravo. Irena stands in the open doorway, slipping on her clogs. The wind pushes hair across her face.

—You cannot have my love, she says. It is my love to have or not to have.

The door slams, the walls shake. Miklos is back on the floor, counting. My superstitious Miklos. I am sad. I am sorry, but he always makes me be the witch by saying nothing. By knowing nothing. But I do not want her to be sorry. I do not want this more than anything.

—Miklos. In the mirror, look.

—Oh Anna, stop. Do you know any woman who looks like you and has your years?

But he doesn't step behind to touch my shoulder. He steps outside, his breath trailing. Fine. You go off too, Miklos. I can sit here alone with the mirror, my true enemy. Taped to its corner is a photograph of me as a little girl. I remember the photograph and the day inside the photograph. Standing there in my favorite white dress with the blue edges. And our dog beside me in the grass. And that big old house behind me, with its many rooms and solid roof. Springtime it was, with all our trees wearing flowers.

But now it is November, and the wind presses against the trailer.

How nice, a full parking lot for our last show. Some days I like full shows, sometimes no. I never know how I am going to feel. Sometimes I can enter the big tent and see only our tired faces and the slow circling of animals. The dust in the tail of the spotlight, the accordion swallowing its own pity. Then other times it's more the hot beating of the drum and the hungry breath of the audience I feel. The Punjabi all in a line waiting with the tiger cage, the squealing of children. Sometimes, if I close my eyes just enough, the tinsel in our costumes become little circles of gold.

Behind the tent, the machines have stopped pumping in heat. Damn managers, cheap as squirrels. Thankfully they have changed the order this season. Put the big cats after us so at least it is still warm when we perform. I hear the music for the jugglers' finale, and catch the two of them taking their deep bows, the last smoke of their fire batons still rising. They skip through the curtains past me, his face all wet with sweat, her chest. I like how the audience can see their love, so close. With Miklos and me it is different. We are too high up and the people see only that we are spinning. They cannot see what happens inside our circle. But I am happy. This, ours and only ours.

The lights go down, then up on the fat ballerina. And there's Irena, watching from the shadows. Since she was a little girl, this her favorite act. Look, she still laughs and laughs. After so many years. I move over toward her, fix the cape across her shoulder, but she pulls away. Miklos comes up behind us and we are three in a row, ready.

Ah, the music starts. Clowns tumble out with their suitcase, struggling to get past the exiting ballerina. The crowd roars. Now the Punjabi follow with our pole and rigging. I hear their hammers setting the base, the ping of cables. More laughter for our clowns. Then I feel Miklos's hand slide down to touch my bottom.

—To the spit of gypsies, he says.

—To the spit, I reply.

I cross myself and reach down to Irena's bottom.

—To the spit, she says.

The Punjabi rush by, and I glare at each one, searching for her boy. But then the music. The curtains. A push on my shoulder, and we run. Irena and I circle the ring while Miklos checks the pole and climbs to position. He needs time to attach his feet so I cross before the last of the clowns, who slowly unfolds a pink dove for me in his palms. I blow him a kiss as the clap of Miklos's hands calls from above. Irena climbs, then me. The rope. The straps. The vise of Miklos's grip. The spotlight, a little late—that fool drunk again—but it doesn't matter, I am moving on air. Breathing deep, but flying. And happy. Yes, today I think I am happy after all.

We do the first pass, Miklos and I. The second. I arch the length of my body for the third, then curl back in for the strap and pole. The clap of hands and I see Irena's body stretch out from his arms. She is much better this year, stronger. Perhaps Miklos is right. Perhaps she is ready for the one arm. I watch him carefully move her below me. Watch his body spin round and round. My breath returns and the hum of the audience rises to meet the music. The cooing of pigeons. Ah, Miklos motions me to get ready.

I am moving. I think of my turns, each one so as not to get drunk. I feel the force that spins us round. That with one hand draws the beauty of our circle and with the other pulls at my feet to die. But at the center of our circle glow the saints of Miklos's hands, the grip of his eyes now telling me to give him my leg and become the bird for the people. We are spinning. Faster. I see the red in his neck spread into his cheeks. He is lying, I am growing fat.

—Fat, fat, I say. Everything's falling.

—No, you move like the breeze. What falls, falls into place. Now the veil, the veil, he says.

I set the brace in my neck and tilt back my head. There is the color of the tent's sky. I am moving. Big and round. I point my knee, my toes. I take out the pink veil and hold it by the corners behind me. We are a cloud. A great pink cloud over the ring. They are watching. They are all watching now. I feel their eyes. The circles of their eyes. I wait till I have the circles of their mouths too and then, I let the pink cloud drop down upon them. Now they are pink too. The whole audience, pink. But above me is Miklos. Red Miklos.

—Fat. Old and fat, I tell him.

—It is me who is red. You are beautiful, he says. Now spin, damn you, take the bit and spin.

There is only the metal between our mouths. Miklos sets the speed. We go round once, twice. And now I spin. I spin. I spin. I feel my body move without me. I feel Miklos's mouth flow into mine. I am spinning. Weightless. I think of nothing. I am nothing. No longer Anna. Nor Miklos. I am we. I am color. I am not getting old. I am beauty. I am happy. Happy. Happy.

It is dark now. Outside, the lines of cars with their red taillights have all disappeared. Heading back to homes, no doubt. Me, I move through our row of trailers, their dim lamps burning within. Each one, that is, but ours. Our broken trailer. I slip off my clogs and set them outside the door. Irena's aren't there. Nor Miklos's. Most probably he is over by the gypsy camp, bringing them leftover bread and oranges from the food tent. He brings them these gifts because they are hungry. Because he remembers. Because he knows I will kill him if he gives them money. Because he thinks the circus life is a rich man's life. He doesn't notice each town puts us near the train station, too.

Inside, I sit before the mirror and take up some cream to wash the makeup from my cheeks. Through the window I see one of the acrobats inside his trailer taking off his shirt. Outside, his brother unwinds the hose for a shower. I am tired. Sometimes I am so tired.

Then in comes Miklos. He passes behind me with coils of rope in his hands. Settles onto a bench and cuts at their edges with a knife. I don't want to talk, and yet I must.

—And where is your daughter, I say.

—Anna, he came all the way back with his own gas money.

Ach, still he does not see. The boy is a Punjab, maybe not a dirt Punjab who runs behind the elephant with a shovel. Maybe clever enough to be promoted to the road and the posters, but still a Punjab. Touching our Irena with glue on his hands. But my Miklos cannot see this. Cannot see anything but good in others. Nothing. Even if I said the words. Even if I said Miklos, I do not want this same life for her. Even then he would not understand.

—You live in the air, Miklos, I say.

He says nothing. What can he say? What other life can he imagine? Through the window I see each muscle in the acrobat's back tighten under cold water.

—Anna, I try to be a good father. I am sorry, I will try even more.

Ah Miklos, look at him with his eyes to the floor. Turning the little circle of our wedding round and round his finger. The little circle I hold so tight up on the pole. It is true, he does try. Maybe it is me who is wrong. Maybe it is because I was born into a house that I think this way. Maybe. He is behind me now, brushing against my shoulder.

—What if I told you I let her go so we too can share the moon, alone.

—Hah, I say.

But then his hand moves round to brush my cheek. Outside, Sunday's last train is pulling away from the station.

—And the axle, I say.

—Anna, he says, with a voice beginning to rain.

Sometimes his voice is like this. When the show is all over and my legs like stones and night falling outside the window and nothing, nothing at all I can do about any of it, his rain voice.

I feel his weight from behind, then his palm cup my breast. He touches me soft, softer than he used to. And I know this is how it will be, our love growing softer and softer until it is like old fruit ready to throw out. I can talk about this now, but it is raining. It is raining and I curl my shoulders into the rain.

Miklos walks to the far end of the trailer and folds out our bed from the wall. I put the cover back onto my jar of cream, but the mirror shows a new rip in the collar of my costume. And my skin so dry. I do not care, I tell myself. Let my cheeks turn to wood and my hair to straw. Let Irena love this Punjab and Miklos make him into a poleman to give her the life of the road and the ring. Let everything fall into place. Let her be happy, like me.

—I do not care, I tell my enemy the mirror.

—Huh, says Miklos.

Ah Miklos, who will never understand. Who makes me beautiful for all the people. Who makes me fly, and makes it rain. Deep inside I know he would leave all this if I really wanted him to. He would go to my family's village and make a job and a home. And I know he would hate the job and the home but still love me. Miklos, my Miklos.

—Why do you listen to me. I am such a witch, I tell him.

—No, he says. You are beautiful and I love you.

EUROPE: *Italy*

THE WIDOW'S TALE

Joseph Cavano

If ever you have been to the small farming village of Malpaso, you well may have heard the story of the widow and her daughter. The great Caesar himself led his legions through the countryside here, and if you are lucky you still may stumble upon the ruins of an ancient aqueduct that once brought water to its inhabitants. Today, its days of glory long since having passed, it is a village waiting to die. Most of its young men are gone now, killed in the war or drawn to the prosperous North, or to a distant America with its streets lined with gold.

Daytimes are too hot for the old ones to venture outside, so you are unlikely to see anyone until evening when the ghosts of the village make their way to the square. Evenings there are a welcome relief from the oppressive heat and the monotony of days that pass so uneventfully it is nearly impossible to tell them apart.

And so, they come. All that remains of a once proud people. Arms interlocked—men with men—women with women—they slowly make their way into the square and its promise of a glass of cool mineral water or, if the monthly checks have arrived, a bottle of one of the bittersweet sodas that seem to mirror the villagers' very existence.

Once inside, you can see the old Opera House. It is a sad reminder of better days. Not a note has been sung there for twenty years. Its only visitors now are the bats that cling at night to its silent walls.

She comes on Sundays. It is only then that she can rouse herself to make her way to the church of San Angelo where she was baptized and married, and where seven years ago, Father Antonelli prayed over her daughter's body and commended her soul to the eternal care of our Lord.

She arrives at dusk so she can select a spot out of view of any worshiper who has been drawn there to pray for forgiveness or offer thanks for an answered prayer. Not until the echo of any last footstep has disappeared, will she make her way toward the altar and kneel before the rows of candles, take a single coin from her pocket and drop it into a metal box. Then, lighting a single candle, she will begin to pray.

Outside, the old ones will have filled the square. It remains the sole bright spot in a life that has become a single shade of gray.

For a few golden hours the villagers come together, friend and foe alike, drawn to one another by a cruel and immutable fate. They talk about the weather. The need for rain. Of children and grandchildren who left a lifetime ago. Pictures are exchanged. Another child has been born in America. The gift of happiness wrapped in so much pain.

It is never long before everyone gathers near the giant persimmons to hear the music. I have been playing my mandolin there for as long as I can remember. I play the same simple songs but nobody complains. I think they remind the people of better times.

Those who come have little money, but it doesn't matter. They are my friends. I would offer to play for free, but I do not wish to offend their pride. I enjoy seeing the smiles as one of them tosses a coin. I am poor, too. The most trifling amount helps keep the wolf from my door.

I love the children best. Between songs I make funny faces and pretend to chase them. I know most of their mothers well. Several of them have shared my bed.

Still, it is not the cool drinks, or the music, or the comfort of old friendships that draw so many to the square. It is the widow and the story she will tell when at last she leaves the church and joins them. It is then that all conversations will end—births and marriages—voyages to America—all postponed—put off for another time.

The barman will signal for me to stop playing and everyone will look to his neighbor, until a brave one will rise and ask the question that all have been waiting to hear: "Senora, what news do you bring about your sainted daughter?"

The widow's husband, Francesco, had yet to turn twenty when his father died and left him a parcel of land. Though little more than a hectare of the poorest soil, the acquisition gained the young man admission into the most exclusive of southern Italian clubs, a society so secretive it never met formally or sought new members—a fraternity of "possidente"—land owners—whose one order of business never varied. *Take more!*

Over the next several years, the young Padrone labored from dawn to dusk, spending every waking hour working the land—nursing it—making it pay.

Too tired to sleep, he would lie in bed nights dreaming of the day his small parcel of grape and olive would stretch beyond what any eye could see. By the time he turned thirty-five, he was well on his way.

Confident his future was secured, he decided to take a wife. Do not imagine, however, his thoughts were those of other young men who stirred at night dreaming of a woman's warm, supple body molded to their own. Indeed, if the Padrone thought of it at all, it was not of heat, but of a body of cold facts and how they could be manipulated to make marriage profitable. What soft, feminine hand pointed the surest route to riches, he wondered. Which young lady's heart was as hard as his own?

Adopting the same cautious approach he used when purchasing a cow or negotiating the price of seeds, he labored night after night until he found the answer for which he had been searching.

Caterina was hardly a beauty. Tall and willowy and appearing older than her twenty years, she looked like an interloper from a foreign land. Still, the Padrone had never been one to be blinded by superficialities, especially when there were more important factors to consider. Like Caterina being the only child of Giovanni Ferruci, whose property was the only tract of land between Francesco's and the government forest which lay beside it. Controlling it would give the Padrone sole access to all the land that surrounded the village, assuring him of an endless supply of labor and a captive market with no choice but to pay his price.

His mind made up, Francesco acted quickly. After a single, short meeting with Signor Ferruci and a furtive glance at his bride-to-be, Francesco Amorano married Caterina Ferruci in the Church of San Angelo, before family and friends, and in the presence of God. It was the first of a series of events that would forever change the village of Malpaso.

It wasn't long before it became obvious that the Padrone's choice had been a wise one, although the marriage was hardly passionate.

Nearly fifteen years separated the two. Caterina soon came to view Francesco as a wise, older brother from whom there was much to learn. On those few occasions when the Padrone was not too tired, he would wake his dutiful wife late in the evening and make love to her as dispassionately as if he were setting out another row of tomatoes. For her part, the widow seemed relieved by her husband's lack of enthusiasm and performed her wifely duties in a most perfunctory manner.

Still, the marriage prospered and their fortune grew. As the years passed, the Padrone grew to respect this unique woman whose single-minded pursuit of money seemed to surpass even his own. More and more, he began to love her.

One day, he stood leaning against a small hazelnut tree and watched with unconcealed admiration an exchange she had with Roberto, one of his most valued workers.

"Signora. I must speak with you."

The widow eyed him cautiously. She had learned from Francesco such requests usually cost money.

"Signora," he said politely, trying to recall the speech he had rehearsed on the way over, "you know I have been with the Padrone since long before he took you as his bride."

"And?"

"Well," he said, removing his straw hat and juggling it from hand to hand, "I believe there has never been a complaint about my work or a question about my loyalty."

"And?"

His confidence waning, Roberto rushed to finish. "I need more money. When first I came to work for the Padrone, I had only a wife to consider. Now there are three other mouths to fill."

"You should have thought of that before you unbuttoned your pants and burdened your wife."

"Signora, you do not understand."

"I understand perfectly. You are a good worker. If you were not you would have been let go long ago. You are paid to be a good worker. It is expected."

The widow started walking away but turned after a few steps. "If the money is not enough, find someone who will pay more."

"Oh no, Signora," Roberto said, slamming his hat onto his head and clicking his heels. "I could never leave you and the Padrone. It is unthinkable. It is only money, after all."

Francesco was right. Give a worker an apple and he soon will want pie. "Get back to work," she said.

Francesco couldn't help but smile. Caterina had learned the lesson well.

The seasons passed quickly and profitably for the Padrone and his wife. One after the other, they unfolded as inexorably as they had since that first skin clad farmer thrust a sharpened stick into the wet primordial soil and looked hopefully to the sky.

One year, however, a winter arrived that was not the usual short interlude of cool days and wet rainy nights, but a time of light and noisy laughter. Another seed had been planted.

It was a time of joy and much anticipation for the entire village. Even the most jealous heart had been softened by the prospect of the Padrone and his wife having a child after so many years. Everyone was praying for a boy. The Padrone himself had begun to make frequent visits to church. He long had dreamed of having a son, who one day would spread the name Amarano throughout Italy.

Sometimes, however, he would sit alone at night considering the things he had done. He had spent a lifetime taking advantage of the villagers. He had inflated prices mercilessly and squeezed the last lira from every transaction even when he had no need to do so. More and more, he wondered about retribution. Was there ever an evil that went unpunished? Would God let a sinner pass?

One night late in Caterina's pregnancy, Francesco heard a scream. He rushed upstairs to the bedroom and found Caterina, her face ashen and her body doubled in pain. Though she was not due for weeks, Caterina assured him her time had come. She begged him to go for the midwife, who lived a short distance away. By the time Signora Sabbatini arrived, the screams had become more frequent. She ushered Francesco out the door and instructed him to bring hot water and towels.

The night moved with inexorable slowness as Francesco busied himself with thoughts of the new son he would name Giuseppe, in honor of his own father whose death had given him the plot of land that had started it all. "As much as my father has given to me," he whispered, "I shall give you one hundred times over."

Early the next morning, his ruminations interrupted by the distinctive cry of a newborn, Francesco rushed into the room and looked toward Caterina. An infant rested upon her chest. Nervously, he searched for the one adornment treasured by him above all others— the one small adornment that would indelibly stamp the name Amorano across the life of the country long after he himself had passed. Finding no such treasure, he turned to Signora Sabbatini who raised the child in triumph. "Congratulations, Padrone. God has given you a beautiful, baby girl."

So bitter was the Padrone's disappointment that he refused to give his daughter the name of his mother as was the custom, leaving the chore to Caterina, who named the child Angelina. For more than a year, he refused even to look at her, convinced she had been sent by God as punishment for his sins.

Although she tried, Caterina could not convince him the little girl was a gift from God Himself. "God helps those who help themselves," she reminded him. "After all, whatever you may have done, you have done for your family. Surely, God could never blame you for that."

One autumn evening not quite five years after Angelina's birth, Francesco was late coming home. It was not unusual for him to be thirty minutes late, but when two hours passed and he had not returned, Caterina left the house and began calling to anybody who might still be around. Fortunately, a few of the workers had decided to spend the night in the orchards, hoping to get an early start harvesting the grapes, which were abundant that year and offered a rare opportunity to make extra money. Roberto was there, and slow-witted Vincenzo, and a few temporary workers who had been hired to help with the harvest. As soon as they heard the Padrone had not come home, they set out across the fields, carrying two small lanterns to illuminate the way.

Caterina returned to the house and sat by the window looking out into the darkness. There were all manner of terrible things that could have happened. After an evening rain, you could make out the tracks of wild pigs that roamed the nearby woods. A young boy had been injured less than a week ago. There were robbers, too. A rich man like Francesco, who was known to distrust banks and supposedly carried large sums of money, would be a prime target.

She had been at the window nearly an hour when she heard a noise.

She rushed to the door and glanced outside. Two small lanterns swung back and forth, providing a kaleidoscopic view of trees and men struggling under a heavy burden. She ran toward the light and saw Francesco lying on a hastily constructed stretcher. He was alive but in obvious pain. His hands were pressed against his chest and his face was gray and soaked with perspiration,

"I think it is his heart, Signora," Roberto said.

The heart had always been an Amorano problem. Francesco's father had not turned fifty when his heart stopped and made of Francesco a young Padrone. The grandfather, too, died of a heart attack at an early age. How strange, Caterina thought. The Amoranos who controlled everything else had never been able to control their hearts.

A taciturn man, Dr. Fontana, nodded and went about the business of examining his patient. Caterina looked on anxiously and tried to infer something about Francesco's condition from the occasional grunt or the arching of the doctor's brow.

When the doctor finished, he placed his instruments in a worn black satchel and headed to the door. "The first twenty-four hours will tell the story, Signora. I'll return tomorrow. Pray to our Lord."

That night Caterina couldn't sleep. After checking on Angelina several times, she made herself a cup of coffee and tried to take her mind off what had happened by reading a popular Italian movie magazine. Francesco would buy one occasionally and, knowing Caterina disapproved, he'd hide it. She'd always find it. Sometimes she'd wait for Francesco to return from the orchards and meet him at the door.

"How many times must I tell you? I do not want this filth inside my house. What if Angelina should find it? The way those women dress. They may as well wear nothing."

"I put it where she cannot reach. What is the harm? I read the stories. They take my mind off the farm."

"You're a fine one to talk of such a thing. Follow me for a day. See what I do. You wouldn't stay up so late at nights."

The poor man. He always worked so hard. Please, God. I'm afraid I'm going to lose him.

Dr. Fontana arrived early the next morning. The news was good. Francesco's condition had stabilized.

"The worst is over, Signora. He'll have to take it easy for a while, but I think he's going to be all right. See that he gets plenty of rest. I'll check in on him again later tonight."

As soon as she saw Dr. Fontana out the door, Caterina rushed into the bedroom. Francesco had fallen back to sleep.

"You've given me quite a scare, old man," she whispered. "Don't ever do that again." Then she placed her head next to his on the pillow. By the time she woke it was late afternoon.

There was a one-legged man in the village who told anyone who would listen how fortunate he had been to have lost his leg in the war, because he had been forced to move slowly.

Confined to his bed Francesco came to learn the same lesson. For the first time since he was a boy, he found the time to look around. What he saw amazed him. Viewed through the prism of a small bedroom window, the world seemed changed. Objects no longer rushed by, vague and colorless, but seemed to hang suspended, frozen in time and achingly beautiful. The workers too, no longer looked so alike, so interchangeable, but as unique as snowflakes on a northern winter's day.

Most of all, he noticed Angelina. No longer the cause of his wounded pride, she became his daughter, so small and so perfect, that merely to see her brought joy to his heart.

From that moment on, she became the center of his life. He was determined to make up the five years he had missed.

There was nothing he would not do for her. No childish request was too outlandish. No amount of money too much. He invented special days in order to lavish her with more gifts. "Today," he would say, as he sat her upon his lap, "is exactly three years since you lost your first baby tooth," or, "Four years ago this very minute, you took your first step. We must celebrate that wondrous achievement."

As she grew older, the gifts became increasingly lavish. Hats and dresses from Milan or Rome. Shoes from Paris. There was nothing she could not have.

Caterina, however, began to worry. She had begun to notice a change in her daughter's behavior. Perhaps Francesco had made a mistake in giving her so much so soon. After all, life might not always be so easy.

"You worry too much, Caterina," he told her one night as they dressed for bed. "She is a child. Let her enjoy her youth. Why not make her life easy where ours has been hard? Who knows what the future may bring."

For the next few months, Caterina followed her husband's advice, but Angelina's conduct did not improve. Instead, she became more willful and disobedient. More and more it became only Francesco to whom she ran.

One afternoon, Francesco was getting ready to go to work after a leisurely lunch, when Caterina motioned for him to sit.

"What is it, Caterina? I am late already."

"This will not take long. It is about your daughter's behavior."

"What is it now, Caterina? We have talked about this before."

"And now we shall talk again. The fields will still be there when we are finished."

"What is it this time?"

"This morning, Angelina asked if she could have a few friends visit. Since it is Saturday, I told her she could." Caterina pushed her chair back and walked over to the stove. "I think I will have coffee. Will you join me?"

"Tell me what happened."

"When her friends arrived everyone went out to the veranda. There was her best friend Sophia, the mayor's son, Pietro, and that banker's boy Vittorio."

"Please, Caterina. What is the point of all this?"

"Things had been fine for an hour, when I heard a loud noise and Angelina screaming."

"Go on."

"I ran outside. The table had been knocked over and the floor was littered with playing cards and money."

"I'll tell her not to play cards for money when I return from work. Now I must go."

Caterina grabbed him by the arm. "It's not the money that concerns me, though there was far more than a few lire on the floor."

"I am a simple man, Caterina. Speak plainly."

"She had lost a lot of money when she discovered one of the boys had been cheating. She'd turned over the table and was using the vilest language. I tried to calm her, but she wouldn't listen. I'm telling you, Francesco, I'm concerned about her. She's become willful and very disrespectful."

"She is just like her mother. You know what they say about the women of Calabria. They would rather eat their babies than lose money." Francesco rose from his chair and grinned. "And," he added, as he stopped at the door, "the women of Calabria love their babies very much."

Over the next several years, Francesco enjoyed the life of a Padrone as never before. He arose late in the morning and retired early. One sunny afternoon he rushed into the kitchen and surprised Caterina who was browning garlic in a pan of olive oil. "I have died and gone to Paradise," he said, "for surely there is no place on earth with such a heavenly smell."

Caterina turned off the burner and poured the hot oil into the sauce pot.

"Well," he said, "I have finally done it."

"What have you done now, Francesco?"

"I have quit. As of this moment I am no longer employed."

"What?"

"My working days are over. I am a free man!"

"Sit," she said, pointing to the kitchen table. "Now what is this nonsense?"

"I have spent a lifetime in the fields. I'm tired, Caterina. I'm tired of the early mornings and the late nights. Of sun and wind and rain. Of workers who do not show up. Of those who do, but accomplish little."

Caterina stared in disbelief. "And who shall run the farm? The birds? The bees?"

Francesco rose from the table and bent to kiss her. "I have in my mind somebody who will do all that needs to be done."

"And who is this Savior?"

Franceso couldn't help but laugh. "Genaro, of course!"

"Genaro," she yelled. "Has the sun made you crazy? He's a gigolo who plays at life. He cares only for his poems and his music and his whores. He lacks ambition!"

Francesco grabbed her and began swinging her around the room.

"Exactly. That is why he will want no more than we choose to give him and he will leave the rest alone."

Caterina pushed him away." You are a foolish old man. Why would such a man want such a job?"

"It suits his nature. Besides, all the important work has already been done. All he needs to do is to keep the men happy and look at the clouds."

Caterina smiled. Even after so many years, Francesco's wisdom still surprised her.

It turned out exactly as Francesco had planned.

The farm prospered. There was more laughter now. More singing in the orchard. And, it was not only the birds that sang every morning in praise of another sunrise, but the men, who had found in Genaro a most congenial overseer, and Genaro himself, who had finally discovered, among the rows of grape and olive, a most appreciative audience.

One early morning, soon after his sixty-fifth birthday, Francesco's heart stopped. Caterina put on her black dress and prepared to meet the crowds that came to pay their respects.

As was the custom, the wake was held at the house. For seven days Caterina did her best to politely greet the mourners. Most came out of curiosity rather than any deep affection for their Padrone. When the last mourner had gone, she shut the front door, and she and Angelina moved separately to the casket for one final kiss.

The mass and the procession to the cemetery went smoothly. When the last mourner had gone, Angelina hurried away.

Caterina stood at the grave for a while and stared at the stone monuments as if envious of those whose struggles had come to an end. With her husband gone and a young daughter to care for, however, she tossed one final flower and moved slowly toward home.

I enjoyed being on the farm. I had always enjoyed being around people, and Francesco, God rest his soul, and the widow had formulated a well-thought out plan for its smooth operation. In truth, there was little for me to do. Angelina, however, had become a problem.

Her misbehavior began innocently enough. Small lies. Minor indiscretions. A curfew narrowly missed. Another fit of temper.

Over time, however, the lies and indiscretions grew more serious, and the cause of them became clear.

There was a boy. His name was Vittorio. He was the son of the local banker and his good looks and easy charm had earned him a reputation among the girls of the village that made mothers take their daughters aside and fathers threaten murder.

The more Caterina warned her daughter about him, the more attractive he became. It wasn't long before Angelina saw in him the perfect companion for her entry into the exciting new world that beckoned.

I have often wondered what the villagers would have thought if Caterina had told the whole story, neither adding nor subtracting from what really happened that fatal night. What would they have thought if she had begun her story at the beginning and not at the end? How would they have felt about her if she had told them how it all started that long ago night when she first called to me?

"Genaro. Vieni qui. It's hot outside. Come have a cold drink."

The workers had left for the day, and having nowhere in particular to go I accepted.

"Grazie, Signora. Old Sol is still hot."

"Come inside."

I went inside and watched as she took two large glasses from a cabinet, put in a bit of ice, and filled both glasses to the top with a fine wine. For a lady with a well deserved reputation for frugality, it was a very generous portion.

"Here," she said, passing a glass to me. "I would like to propose a toast. To our very successful collaboration. Long may it last."

I touched my glass to hers and waited to see what might follow.

"I must be honest, Genaro. When Francesco first told me he had you in mind to become overseer, I had my doubts."

"As well you should have, Signora."

"I saw nothing in your past to suggest you could handle such a job. As usual, the Padrone was right."

"I am happy you think so, Signora. The Padrone was a very great man."

She took a sip of wine and held it on her tongue as if trying to extract every last flavor. "Yes, in many ways, he was very special."

I have spent too many years in the company of women not to have learned how careful they are in choosing their words. I began to wonder in what way the Padrone had disappointed her. I was pretty sure I knew.

The time passed pleasantly and a lovely quiet had settled over the house, when she reached for my empty glass and our hands touched. She looked pretty sitting there in the shadows, her large, brown eyes set off by the faint glow of the kitchen light.

"Genaro, may I offer you another?"

Having never seen a profit in moderation of any kind, I readily agreed.

"Do not be angry with me. There is a question I want to ask you."

"Signora, there are no words you could utter so harsh as to make me angry with you. Ask anything you wish and I shall answer as honestly as I can."

"Are those stories about you and women true?"

"Which stories, Signora? I am afraid there are quite a few."

"I see," she said, pretending to be angry with me. "Are there are so many that I need to choose? Very well. What about the story they tell about a day in August when three women had your child? Can that possibly be true?"

I couldn't help but laugh. I was finding it easy being alone with her. "Fractionally true, I suppose."

"Fractionally true? What a strange way to put it. What do you mean?"

"Just that," I said. "The third woman did not have my child until a week later!"

I had never seen the widow laugh so heartily, but she did then and many times thereafter. Maybe it was the wine or the cover of darkness. Or maybe it was merely the comfort we felt in speaking with another who had nowhere to go and too much time to get there.

Over the next few weeks, her invitations became more frequent.

Most were similar to the first. A few generous glasses of wine and conversations heading nowhere in particular and arriving there at no particular time.

One night, however, when we had been sitting at the table chatting amiably about this or that triviality, Caterina suddenly turned serious.

"Genaro, I know you are an intelligent man. Francesco, rest his soul, often spoke to me about how much he enjoyed his discussions with you. Everybody admires your family. Two brothers who are attorneys and your father a well-respected professor at the university in Naples. How is it that you…? I don't know quite how to say this…"

"Let me finish your thought, Signora. How is it that I am such a failure?"

"No, that is too harsh. I only..."

"Please. It is a fair question. The answer is simple. I am a failure because I was born too late."

"What do you mean?"

"I am a man born at the wrong time. I should have been born five hundred years ago, when people realized art and music and literature are the important things—that it is precisely those things that define us—separate us from the beasts in the field."

I remember stopping to take a drink and trying to calm myself. It was not that I was angry at the widow, but the question she asked had brought me to a place I had tried to leave behind. "Today it is different. Now we worship the trivial. We are devoted to the counting of beans and acquiring things that make us poorer."

"I agree that is the way things are. Still, why punish yourself for something not your fault? Why settle for less than you could have by refusing to apply yourself to the world you have been given?"

"Because that is the way I am!" It was a while before I calmed myself enough to apologize. "There is an unfortunate paradox today. In order to have the so-called finer things of this life, you must give up the leisure prerequisite to enjoying them. I have always chosen to cultivate leisure and forget the rest."

The widow was quiet for a while. I sensed she was thinking about what I had said, trying to balance the rumors about me with what she had just heard.

"It is strange how different our lives have been. While you have spent a lifetime cultivating leisure, I have spent mine avoiding it."

"It seems, Signora, we are indeed a couple of strange people."

"Yes, Genaro," she said, choosing each word carefully, "we are a strange couple indeed."

I have always wondered what it is about certain moments that convince us they are more important than all others. Yet sitting there with her that night, I knew such a moment had arrived, and I would be a fool to let it pass.

I reached across the table and took her hand, and when she did not resist, I rose from the table and stood beside her and waited for her to join me. When she did, I gently placed my arm around her waist and led her to the bedroom.

From that moment on the days dragged until I could see her again.

She was not a beautiful woman, but there was something about her that drew me helplessly to her. Our times behind those doors were the stuff of dreams. There was a wildness to her too—a sensuality—that made me regret I had wasted a lifetime going from bed to bed when all I wanted was waiting so near. It was as if each of us had found in the other a part of ourselves too long missing—a part we vowed never to lose again.

One day, Caterina surprised me in the fields. We always had been discreet in meeting, so it was unusual for her to seek me out in the presence of others. Farm business had always been transacted early in the morning before the workers arrived or late in the afternoon after they left.

"Follow me."

As soon as we entered the house, she closed the door and kissed me.

"Something has happened that worries me a great deal."

"Yes?"

"You must promise you will never repeat what I am about to tell you."

"Of course, Caterina."

"You have heard the stories about the great sums of money supposedly hidden in this house?"

"I have never believed them. I was in town the day your husband came to make a very large deposit in the bank. I remember him telling me he had finally given in to modern ways."

"That is exactly what he wanted people to believe—that all of his money was in the bank, and that anybody contemplating robbing us would do well to consider how little he might find for all his trouble."

"Is it not true then?"

"No." Caterina moved to the cabinet, retrieved a bottle of Lacrimi Cristi, and filled two glasses. "He did, as you say, make a large deposit. Enough to ensure that by the end of the day everybody would have heard about it. The sum, though large, represented but a small portion of the money we had accumulated over a lifetime of living well below our means."

I can't say I was completely surprised. The Padrone always struck me as a man who left no stone unturned. "So the rumors are true then. There is a large sum hidden in this house."

"Yes. But no longer is it merely hidden in paper bags or boxes spread haphazardly behind doors or under beds."

She took another sip of wine and held it, rolling it slowly around her mouth before swallowing. "As our wealth grew, so did our fear. We realized we had to come up with a better plan to protect what we had worked so hard for. Since I had only recently become pregnant, we decided to take advantage of the perfect timing. We knew there is a big difference between a man hammering away for no apparent reason and a man working late into the night preparing a room for his new child."

"Of course."

"We worked away dividing our time between fashioning a room for the baby and erecting a false wall behind which we hid our money. Francesco worked with great fervor and such craftsmanship, so that even today an expert would find it difficult to discern what is real and what is not."

"I would expect no less from the Padrone."

She rose from the table, took our two empty glasses and refilled them. When she returned, she placed them on the table and moved close to me.

"I am very worried about Angelina and that banker's son, Vittorio."

"He is a bad one."

"He has too much influence on her. She is young and I am afraid it has gotten to the point where she would do anything to please him."

"What has that to do with the money?"

"This morning, I heard a noise coming from her bedroom. When I went inside I saw Angelina. She seemed nervous. She was standing at the very spot where we had constructed the false front. This is the third time I have caught her standing there tapping on the wall. I am afraid she may have discovered something."

"You are right to be concerned."

"I am afraid she will tell Vittorio what she suspects, and he will not rest until he discovers the truth. I have worked too hard to lose everything."

"What will you do then?"

"I don't know. You are a man. Men know about such things."

I paused for a while and thought how strange life is. How it can drag for interminable stretches without the slightest variation, and then without warning how it can jump out at you and force you to think about things formerly unthinkable.

"Vittorio is a problem. At first, I thought I would offer him money to go away and leave Angelina alone. Then I remembered what Francesco told me many years ago. 'Give a man an apple and one day he will return for pie.'"

"Vittorio is not your problem. Angelina is."

"What are you talking about? She is a young girl, hopelessly in love. How is she the problem?"

"Angelina is a woman now. A woman needs to be loved. It is just the way women are. If it is not Vittorio, it will be somebody else."

"Perhaps. Still, not every young man is a scoundrel."

"Forgive me, Caterina. I must speak freely."

"Go on."

"Angelina is not the daughter you think she is. I cannot tell you how often she has come to me since her father's death and told me how unhappy she was. How lonely she felt. How with him gone, there was nothing to keep her here on the farm. She blames you, Caterina. Not for who you are, but for who you are not. You are not Francesco. That is something she cannot forgive."

I knew what I had said hit hard. When I tried putting my arms around her, she pulled away. She was a strong woman who never hid from the truth. I could see why the Padrone had chosen her.

"There have been times," she said softly, "when I have sensed it. Always, though, I tried to pass it off. I tried to imagine it as a time mothers and daughters must go through. I looked to a day when things would change and we could become friends again. All the while, though, I suspect I knew. "

It was hard for me to sit and watch. It is always hard when the one you love is in pain.

"By the time I became a mother, something in me had died. The part of me that should have been soft had turned hard. When I dreamt at night, it was never of her, but of land—getting it and keeping it and always wanting more. No wonder she hates me."

"Do not blame yourself, Caterina. It was the Padrone who made her what she is. I am sorry. She is a selfish young lady accustomed to having what she wants. If she has discovered what you think, she will be a problem with or without an accomplice."

It was surprising to see how rapidly Caterina could leave sadness behind. How quickly she could recognize the need for action. I had never loved her more.

"Then we must act at once, Genaro. Perhaps I could send her away to a convent school."

"And how long would she remain? The solution would be at best temporary. There needs to be another way."

I hesitated for a moment because I knew I needed to make sure there was no mistaking what I was about to say. "Soon we must decide exactly how much we are willing to do to make our problem disappear."

"What are you saying? Disappear? She's my daughter! My only child!"

"A daughter can be a beautiful thing. But this is a harsh country, Caterina. We must do whatever is necessary in order to survive."

A lifetime of experience has taught me two things about women. First, they are capable of a subtlety far beyond any man. Second, once a woman has decided upon a course of action there is nothing that can stop her. That is why it did not surprise me the next day when Caterina again called out to me.

We had no sooner entered the house and taken our seats at the table, when she grabbed my hand. "Last night I had the most terrible dream."

"Yes?"

"It was about Angelina. We were having a terrible argument about Vittorio. She called me the vilest names. She told me she would never forgive me and wished I was dead. I tried to calm her, but it was no use. She slammed the door and left before I could stop her."

I did not move. I was interested in what might come next.

"Of course, I ran after her but it was too late."

"A dream can be a frightening thing. Still, I believe each contains an important truth."

Her eyes that night were those I'd seen so many nights before as we lay in bed when she would call to me to come and love her.

"It was terrible, Genaro. The way she looked at me. Her face was so sad. I never could be brave enough to look upon that face again. How I wished you were there."

I moved close and held her tightly. I knew what I had to do as surely as if she had written out the instructions on a piece of parchment. "It is settled then. You will never need to see such a face again."

She grabbed me by the arm before I could open the door to leave. The sadness had passed. Her voice was clear and resolute.

"Everyone knows you are not a religious man, Genaro. Nobody will think it odd when you do not come to church Sunday, or join the procession to the mountain chapel that will follow." She wrapped her arms around me and kissed me and would not let go. "Angelina told me she will leave for the chapel at two. Perhaps you could look in on her."

"I shall," I said.

Caterina has told the story about what she saw that long ago Sunday many times. How, when she returned from the mountain chapel and looked into Angelina's room she saw her daughter lying in a pool of blood, her throat cut ear to ear.

Vittorio was, of course, the prime suspect. When he could offer no credible alibi for his whereabouts that night, it was widely assumed he would soon be arrested. By the third day, however, he must have realized that incurring the wrath of an important official was preferable to spending the rest of his life in prison. He admitted he had spent the evening pleasuring the mayor's pretty young wife while the mayor was in Rome on business. The mayor's pretty young wife tearfully concurred.

One by one, each of the other suspects was carefully questioned and released. By week's end, the police were desperate. Even I was called in, but the lack of any physical evidence and the brutal nature of the crime ruled me out. Everyone agreed that although a village curiosity, I was harmless and had neither the heart nor the ambition to commit such a crime.

After exactly one month, with no suspects left to examine, the police gave up the search and placed the blame on a stranger several villagers had reported seeing in the area at the time of the murder. In one bold step, they had absolved themselves of any hint of incompetence and assuaged the fears of the villagers who were free once again to resume their humdrum existence.

I suppose if what happened were only a story and not real life, there would be a need for poetic justice. I can envision a scene where Caterina and I, our passion destroyed in a paroxysm of guilt, become progressively more distant, until finally, unable to bear the pain, one or the other of us confesses to the crime and justice is done.

That is not at all what happened. By the end of the year, Caterina had put away her black dress forever and we started to see each other openly. Even those who expressed outrage at the shamefulness of it all had to admit that life was both hard and brief, and a woman without a man was a sad thing, indeed. This was Italy, after all.

That first year was unlike anything either of us had experienced. We drank glasses of chilled white wine under the noontime shade of the giant walnut tree or sat on the veranda at dusk, and picked at a plate of cheese and olives, while watching as the sun made its nightly journey toward the horizon. We were happier than we ever thought possible.

Nighttimes, we would move inside and head to the bedroom. I have heard criminals often experience a rush of sexual excitation after the commission of a crime. While I cannot speak for others, I know neither of us could have enough of the other. Most nights we spent hours in each other's arms.

As the years passed, the earth turned more slowly and the days stretched beautifully before us. I had given over my position as overseer to an energetic and bright young man whose enthusiasm for the job far exceeded my own.

Caterina and I soon fell into a life of easy routine. Mornings, we'd rise early and after a light breakfast of bread and jam and strong, black coffee, I would move to the veranda and work on the manuscript which is now nearly completed and will soon rest in a safety deposit box. Our lawyer, Salvatore Fiscella, has strict orders not to open it until Caterina and I have passed from this earth.

She now spends her mornings reading. Recently, she has developed a taste for Dante and is reading the *Commedia* for a second time.

Although we could afford to pay a cook, Caterina still prefers to prepare meals for us. If you are not Italian, I cannot convey how lovely it is to sit in the kitchen while the aroma of a midday meal fills the air.

After dining, we sit and talk until one of us begins to nod signaling it is time for our afternoon nap. It is wonderfully quiet that time of day. The work in the orchards and fields has stopped for a while, and the men have gone home to share a meal with their families. It is as if the rest of the world has died and we are all who remain.

Dusk has always been our favorite time. It was dusk when Caterina first called out to me, "Genaro. Vieni qui. It is still hot outside." And it was dusk that cloaked us from the rest of the world. Evenings now, we sit outside and watch in wonder as another day passes by.

Our land continues to stretch far beyond where our ancient legs can take us, but there is plenty to see right where we sit. Row after row of trellises, bent under the weight of grapes of green and purple dot the hillsides. Hectares of olive trees, their leaves a most wonderful silver, stand as sentinels watching over our land.

I read somewhere the olive tree can live a thousand years or more. That somehow it has found a way to sink its roots deep into the inhospitable soil in search of the water that sustains it. I like to think Caterina and I are like that. We have sunk our roots deep into the harsh soil of Calabria and found that which sustains our lives.

Everything we want is here. Caterina has stopped going to the square so often. It seems as if she has lost the need. During those infrequent times when we feel the land constrict, we need only open a book, or view one of the many paintings that hang upon our walls, or listen to the sounds of music that always fill the house. Soon we are transported to other lands that only seem so far away.

I know someday everyone will have learned what really happened that long ago night when Caterina came down from the mountain and saw her daughter's body obscenely sprawled across her bed. I doubt there will be many who will find it in their hearts to forgive us. I feel sorry for Caterina. People will be harder on her. A mother should have protected her child's life, not been an instrument in ending it.

As for myself, I have no illusions. I have taken another's life and that is the gravest sin of all.

Still, I think of others who have died. Of artists who have spent their days in search of that which is most beautiful—that which is most true. How many of these noblest among us have perished by their own hand when they could no longer endure a life of not-so-benign neglect? How many more have died the death of a thousand blows parceled out one cruel punishment at a time?

Perhaps I have deluded myself. Misrepresented that the blow I struck that night was a blow struck for them. That finally, one of us fought back and claimed what should have been ours from the start—a lifetime free from want and filled with time enough to shape and celebrate the world around us. Maybe it was nothing but lust and greed from the very start. Two deadly sins, masked by the thinnest of veneers.

If there is a God I am afraid he will not go easy on me. After all, I have spent my life refusing His promise of eternal life in favor of a life of pleasure here and now.

Still, there is within me a sense that a God who knows all things knows this about me:

That I have loved His world as few others. That I have stood, as if transfixed, before the singular beauty of every plant or animal or rock he has placed upon it, and I have cherished every man and woman and child I have met along the way. And, even if I have misjudged my place—been guilty of the sin of Pride—sought to create a world of my own, as every artist does—then I have done so only in imitation of Him who they say created us all.

Oceania: *New Zealand*

Jean

Holly Painter

I've only ever known my Aunt Jean as a hundred-kilo sourdough plop. She wears coral- and mustard-colored polyester pantsuits with these necklaces her daughters made in primary school out of marbles and drapery fabric. Except her daughters are teenagers and mortified to be seen with her. So when she drops them at the mall to meet their friends, if they see her later, hanging around the calendar stand, browsing through page-a-day tablets of Yorkies or terriers, they steer their friends into Jay-Jay's until Mum takes the hint and moves along.

Oh I know, poor lady. But you wouldn't have too much sympathy if you actually met her. She's a righteous old bitch. Like, when I dyed my fringe blue, she kept trying to get me to pray with her to Jesus to free me from my sinful pentagon lifestyle. I told her I just liked the blue, but Aunt Jean could not handle it. And she hates that we're not Christian. Well, I guess she kind of loves it, too. She's still trying to save Mum a full decade on from my parents' divorce. Since she moved to Dunners, she's forever popping round on Sunday afternoons with Anzac biscuits she nicked from coffee hour. She'll recount the fire-and-brimstone sermon she just heard, and when she really gets going, the sweat trickles down behind her earlobes and her double chins start to slip against each other until the foundation rubs off on her polyester collar.

I know I sound like a bitch. But you wouldn't believe the shit that comes out of Aunt Jean's mouth: Women are morally obligated to give their husbands sex anytime they want it. Sexual assault survivors shouldn't be allowed the morning-after pill. Asian immigrants should be deported to China, regardless of whether they're even Chinese. And active faggotry, her word not mine, should be punishable by death so as to prevent the smiting of a nuclear apocalypse. We're talking full-on Destiny Church whackjob.

But my dad told me that, before she got cleaned up with AA and NA and all those other religious recruitment schemes, my aunt used to be a badass. She left school at sixteen. This was the early eighties. She had a boyfriend called Ralph, who was a little older, and the two of them rode Ralph's Harley up to Auckland and got involved with one of the motorcycle clubs up there. The photos are amazing. Auntie Jean is totally emaciated, with dark, sunken eyes, pouty lips, and blond-rooted black hair that's so mangy it's starting to dread itself. In one picture, she's wearing a white beater with 'You cunt' scrawled across it in Vivid and tight leather pants with holsters on each hip for her flasks. Ralph looked almost identical to her, except he was slightly taller and had a fluffy blondish goatee he used to blacken with grease. It left smudges on Jean's chin when they kissed. Or so says my dad anyway.

Even before they left Christchurch, they were always amped up on any number of things, twitchy and mouthy and spoiling for a fight. The weekend before they left town, it was just after New Years, they got together with a bunch of their mates, and the whole thing ended in a bottle fight. Jean wound up with a gash on her lower jaw and Ralph lost a bit of his left ear and his knuckles were completely raw, one of them shaved down to the bone. But they were all mates, and the next day, none of them could remember exactly what happened, so they let it go.

In Auckland, they crashed with Ralph's cousin, Brett, and joined up with his small-time biker gang, the Kingpins. Brett wasn't the leader or anything. He'd started off as just a weedy, croaky dishwasher boy at the Kingsland pub where the crew held court during the day. But he had some mechanical chops, and the gang's boss got a lot of pleasure out of sitting back, draining a beer and watching the pimply little fellow grovel for the chance to work on his bike. By the time Ralph and Jean got up there, Brett was the club mechanic, working out of a shop down the road from the bar. Instead of bleached red scrubber's hands, he had permanent grease stains in his nails and knuckles and a neatly gridded chess board tattooed on both arms and across his back. Eventually, he got a complete set of black chessmen inked onto the swells of his biceps and shoulders. Minus the king. That went over his heart.

Brett set Jean up as a dishwasher at the pub, but she got fired after a week for watering down the spirits behind the bar. She was only sixteen, remember. Meanwhile, Ralph made inquiries among the Kingpins and found himself a supplier, so he was usually off playing middleman between the dealer and his West Auckland clients. At night, he brought home a sweaty wad of crumpled bills, and pills and pot to share with Jean and Brett. Some nights, they'd all troop out to the bar or ride around with the crew, but most of the time Brett would go without them, and Ralph and Jean would strip down to their bony asses in the heat, turn on the cold tap in the shower, and go at it until the frenzy passed and the pills made them lose interest. Then, in the morning, Ralph would be gone and Jean would wake up to a day of nothing to do.

So she started going around to Brett's shop every afternoon, emptying one flask on the way and offering the other to Brett when she arrived. He'd take his breaks with her, tugging off his singlet, sponging the sweat from his dark, curl-crusted forehead, and holding the dull coolness of the flask to his chest before tipping it back and glugging down the vodka straight. Then he'd snag her wrist and yank her down to kneel with him so he could point his thin, steady fingers at glossy circles of water in the fuel tank or a crack so small he hadn't seen it until the sun hit the fracture directly and the reflection split into two slices.

Jean was captivated by this new world of tiny pieces and hulking men with delicate loving hands that operated on puzzles she could barely see. Her dad, my granddad, was an insurance agent and her mum kept house. When the car or the Hoover crapped out, they got out the phone book. They didn't reach in themselves and jiggle the parts around. She'd been raised to think of mechanics as low-lifes and gods, too ignorant to land white-collar jobs, and yet the only ones trustworthy enough to unscrew a panel and replace a simple wire. Even though she'd been despising her parents and their way of life for years, she still retained a sense of awe that any mere mortal could casually bring to life something as whole and god-given as a motorcycle. When Jean started hanging about the whole afternoon, Brett made her his apprentice.

Ralph was good with his hands, too. He did most of his own maintenance on the Harley, but he'd never thought Jean would be very interested. In his own way, he considered himself the romantic type. He didn't want anything about his relationship with Jean to be mundane. Of course, when he got on the wrong side of drunk, he'd piss on Brett's stereo. Then the two of them would scramble to mop it up and spray the room with Ralph's two dollar cologne before Brett got home. But when he was soberer, Ralph dreamt of a perpetual state of Hollywood love, full of fireworks and violins, or whatever's the heavy metal cliché version of that. His grand idea of romance didn't include motorcycle repair.

But Ralph was pleased that Jean had found something to do with herself. He was making plenty of money dealing to Westie kids, so it didn't matter that Jean wasn't working. She just needed to stay entertained so she wouldn't get lonely and homesick for Christchurch.

So they carried on just like that for over a year. After a few months of watching and fetching things, Jean began to work on the bikes herself, doing little things Brett taught her. Eventually, the shop hired her to assist with repairs, and she finally had her own money in her pocket. That same year, Ralph proposed to her.

He did it at a construction site. I know it sounds trashy, but actually, it was perfect. He'd found the site weeks before while on a delivery out near Waitakere. The entire section was surrounded by a solid wooden wall three meters high, and a drawing on the outside showed an architect's dream that never got built. The space inside was a field, re-grown with knee-high grass since the builders had given it up. The day he proposed, Ralph picked up Jean after work in a borrowed ute with a ladder in the back and drove out Waitakere way, stopping for takeaways in New Lynn. When they reached the site, Ralph followed Jean up the ladder and they landed in the field a few meters from the candlelight dinner he'd already set up that afternoon, minus the actual food. He'd scrounged up two folding chairs, a card table with a white linen bed sheet thrown over it, a pair of purple advent candles stuck to the bottoms of shot glasses by their own melted wax, a fistful of tulips in a blue op shop vase, plates and cutlery from Brett's flat, two wine glasses, and a bottle from Waiheke Island.

Ideally, Jean would've liked to wash up before all of this, to exchange her grimy garage clothes for her best pressed 'You cunt' clothes. But fortunately, the romantic tableau already included a meter-high mound of dirt left beside one of the section walls and a newspaper parcel soaked through with dripping fat from the fish and chips inside. After they'd polished off the fish and an enormous pile of soggy chips, Ralph knelt beside her, the tips of the long grass clawing at his chin. He wiggled a ring out of his skinny jeans pocket and just held it in the air with the pawn shop jewel extended toward Jean. She blinked at him like she didn't understand, and maybe she didn't. So he took her left hand and rested the cheap circle on the end of her ring finger like a question until she twitched back to life and thrust her finger through the ring. He promised her a better one when they had more money, but she shrugged. She couldn't wear jewelry at work anyway, so it didn't matter. And that was it. Probably not the squealy, syrupy moment Ralph was hoping for, but the next one more than compensated, as Jean toppled him into the grass and they consummated their engagement. That was the high point, I guess. After that, everything went pear-shaped.

First there was the bar brawl. The Kingpins rarely got into it with any of the other clubs, but they often scrapped with each other, escalating petty, mundane domestic disputes into full-on leather-armored knife-fights. But Ralph and Jean weren't expecting any trouble when they announced their engagement at the pub. They were full-fledged Kingpins by then, and their news was met with cheering and back-slapping and quite a lot of drinking. But after several rounds shouted by the crew, the boss blearily hammered the table and called for something harder. He hooked Ralph by his belt loop and sat him on his lap.

"What have you—" I'm going to do him in my grizzled alky voice: "What have you got on you, m'boy?"

As it happened, Ralph was carrying quite an assortment of pills and a lot of pot. He'd stopped off to see his supplier before arriving at the pub, so he had not just his own stock, but also the weekend supply of drugs to be moved out west. But that supply was off limits to him and anybody else who wasn't paying. So Ralph offered up his own stash, carefully drawing it from an inner pocket of his old messenger bag without revealing the larger treasure that he stored under the false canvas bottom of the same bag.

But the boss wasn't satisfied. He snatched the bag and shook it beside his ear to hear the giveaway rattle of a hundred pills in collision. At this point, Ralph still might've smoothed things over. He could've apologized and given the boss everything he had. But he knew he couldn't cover the value of the drugs, and Ralph was more afraid of his supplier than he was of the Kingpin boss. Only very slightly, but enough so that he hesitated, failed to react to the immediate danger before considering the next one that might come along if he got through this.

When he did open his mouth to speak, a lackey's backhand sent him sprawling to the floor. He tried to stand, with one hand already fumbling for the switchblade in his back pocket, but the boss's knee cracked him square in the jaw. Another man hoisted Ralph by the collar of his jacket and walloped him in the stomach while the boss's right hook set off a nosebleed that saturated Ralph's singlet and drizzled down into his undies. In the next moment, Jean launched herself into the fray, hauling a man off Ralph by a fistful of his hair. The man reared back and hurled Jean against the bar, her mouth wide and raging as it slammed into the sticky countertop. She spat blood and splinters and teeth and left two burrowed in the soft wood.

She slid to the floor and when she woke, there was Brett, cradling her head in his lap, with a deep red rag pressed to her mouth. Ralph slumped against the bar, his face crusted with dried blood while his nose continued to gurgle fresh streams of it. The others were gone, and so were Ralph's bag and his Harley.

Brett treated them at home. They didn't want the attention that a trip to urgent care would bring, and besides, they didn't have the money now. Ralph's nose was broken and his eyes nearly swollen shut, but he had no broken ribs and his cuts weren't deep enough to need sutures. When his bruises finally faded, he was almost good as new. Jean was a different story. She'd taken only the one smack into the bar, but it had been enough to snap five of her top teeth, leaving another one wiggly and loose.

So Brett took her to see Caldwell in South Auckland. Caldwell wasn't a dentist exactly. He was a man who pulled teeth and made dentures on the cheap. He'd studied some dentistry and he'd studied some engineering, and though he didn't have a license, Caldwell provided a useful service for those who couldn't afford the real deal.

When Caldwell examined Jean's mouth, it was still slick with puckered canyons of raw gum, sheltered by her massive top lip. He found that two of the teeth had been pulled free, roots and all, but the other three had only broken at the gumline. One more was dangling by half its roots. Caldwell told her he could make her a bridge, but he'd have to pull the loose tooth, dig out the remaining roots, and sand down a couple of her good teeth to make room. He could do it with or without ether, but the drugs were the expensive part, since he too had a supplier, and it was not your average dental equipment company. Jean was silent, but Ralph saw the quaking of her overgrown lips that he knew prefigured tears.

She'd said almost nothing since the fight. Ralph rightly suspected Jean was furious with him, but he was afraid to ask. He'd begged her to come with him to Christchurch. He was set to leave right after the appointment. Brett would ride him south to Hamilton, beyond the territory of either the Kingpins or the drug lords. From there, Ralph would hitchhike down to Christchurch until everything blew over and he'd scrounged up enough money to pay off his dealer in Auckland. He wanted Jean to come. He wanted them to be together and he wanted to know that she was safe.

But Jean was convinced that, if they both left Auckland, they'd never come back. She would lose her new life and be reduced to a helpless child again. It had been months since she'd even spoken to her family. The idea of slinking back home in pieces was humiliating. Going back to Christchurch would mean admitting that she wasn't capable of looking after herself her own way. Even if she and Ralph stayed with friends or found a place of their own, her family would remain nearby, gloating at the mess she'd become.

So she would stay behind in Auckland and wait for Ralph to come back. Brett promised to keep close watch on the situation with the Kingpins, ensuring that no harm would come to Jean. Ralph accepted Jean's decision unhappily, vowing to return quickly with enough money to move them into their own place and buy Jean a proper ring. He'd searched her face when he said it, trying to detect some sign that she would forgive him, that she still longed, as he did, for the rooftop wedding they'd begun planning only the week before. But Jean's face had remained blank, unmoved, until that moment in Caldwell's chair.

That was the moment she reconsidered: "I can extract the teeth with or without ether, but keep in mind, the ether can be rather dear."

Jean's fingernails bit Ralph's forearm, her chin wobbled under the shelf of her lips, and her eyebrows folded into a two-man pup tent.

Collapsing back on Caldwell's recliner, her tears slid down into her hair and her snot drained thick in her throat until she began choking and spitting and Ralph drew her up into his arms. Fighting to breathe normally, Jean watched Caldwell over Ralph's bony shoulder. He was twirling a loose thread round and round a button. She loathed him. She loathed all dentists. They were bloody sadists, as far as she could tell. Even her childhood dentist, a real dentist, had kept her still by holding a palm to her throat while he jabbed his sharpened hook at her six-year molars. And now here was this fake dentist, unlicensed, unsupervised, possibly a conman, who was proposing to wrench out her teeth without any fucking anesthetic. Jesus.

She'd been sure that nothing could drag her back home to her parents. Not poverty, not homesickness, not even Ralph. But the idea of Caldwell hovering over her in his op shop lab coat, humming with the radio as he wrapped pliers around her broken roots, all of this while she was conscious, feeling every nick of the tools and finally the wet, ripping squelch—Jean knew she would never let him do it. The blinding pain of biting the bar had been one thing, but to know what was coming and to wait for it was something else entirely. She teetered on the brink of hyperventilating. And then Brett spoke up.

"I'll pay for it. For the ether. You shouldn't be awake for it." Jean was vaguely aware that, while she'd been studying Caldwell and his frightening disinterest, Ralph had been looking toward Brett, probably pulling helpless, pathetic faces at him. Ralph immediately swore to a range of unrelated deities that he would pay his cousin back. Jean wondered later if either of them knew how close she'd come to ditching the whole thing and going home to her parents with their money and their real doctors.

So Ralph went south and Jean stayed in Kingsland with Brett. Caldwell put her out a few days later and pulled the teeth. No problem. He fit her for a bridge and things were pretty normal for a while. Jean's mouth healed and she went back to work. Ralph rang her almost every night. He reckoned he'd need about a month. But two things happened in that month. The first was inevitable. The second was poor engineering.

Ralph should have seen it coming. Everybody else saw it coming. And maybe Ralph did know what was happening, but he didn't know how to stop it. He didn't want to be the jealous boyfriend. He wanted to be broadminded and modern. So he told himself he was just being paranoid.

But he wasn't being paranoid. Exactly two weeks after he left, Jean and Brett had their first kiss. Her lips were a normal size again. Her partial fit. They were smoking on the back porch. There wasn't any full moon or shooting stars. Nothing particularly romantic or special. It could have been any night. It had been building for a year. They'd both known it, even if they would have denied it. So it was going to happen and it did. It was so unavoidable that it was almost casual. Jean was sitting on a low railing in short short cut-offs she kept having to pull out of her ass crack. Brett was barefoot in the grass. He stepped forward to pass her the joint, and he just took an extra step, so he was between her knees and an inch from her face. There was a second's pause and then they leaned into each other and kissed. Not hot and heavy, just natural, like something falling into its right place.

The hot and heavy came soon after. As I understand it, it was the weeks upon weeks of continuous sex, and I'm going to guess oral, in particular, that broke Jean's bridge. Though Caldwell's sheer incompetence might have had something to do with it.

In any case, Jean's bridge broke. They went back to see Caldwell, and in addition to the broken bridge, he found that the anchor teeth on either side were slightly loose. He'd stuffed up some calculation and they weren't strong enough to support the bridge. So he very calmly told Jean she could either go without her six front teeth entirely, or he could pull the rest of her top teeth and give her dentures, granny style. And Jean lost the plot. She palmed a tray of dental equipment over her shoulder like a waitress and threw it straight at Caldwell's face. The steel pokers bounced harmlessly off his glasses and mask, but Jean scooped them up again, shooting darts at his throat until Brett managed to wrestle her back into the chair. From there, she just cussed and spat through the gap in her teeth while Caldwell lounged in the corner, still cool as could be. Jean finally landed a nice gob of spit on his coat and watched it string its way down the white cotton as Brett marched her from the room.

She was still screeching and pounding Brett's leather arm for emphasis when they pulled up to the Kingsland flat. An unfamiliar bike was parked out front. Brett gripped Jean's thigh. "Stay here!" he ordered and sidled up to the window. Inside, Ralph was sprawled on the couch leafing through one of Brett's motorcycle magazines. "Don't worry," Brett called back to Jean. "It's only Ralph."

She crashed through the door, and Ralph sprang up, ready to embrace her. But Jean shoved him back down to the couch. "Ith only you. Ith only Rowf."

Her lisp just wound her up more. "Ith your fauwt I need denshursh. I'm barely eighteen and I need denshursh! You can fuck awfh back to Chrithchurch. I don' wanna see you."

Jean stalked off and Ralph got up to follow, but his cousin stood in his way. "Let me." Ralph listened through the closed door to Brett's bedroom. They squabbled and swore and made up.

When Brett and Jean emerged, Ralph smiled over the top of his magazine. Jean lifted his crossed legs and sat on the couch, his feet in her lap. "I'm sorry Rowf." He waited. "I ssouldn't haf said this was your fauwt." He kept waiting. "I need another shergery an' new denshursh, but I don' expec you to pay for it." She paused. "Brett will len' me the money." Ralph kept waiting, but she wasn't going to tell him. He felt his heart working much too fast, pumping blood to the back of his head, where it throbbed in triple-time, and to his whole torso, smothered inside his T-shirt.

Ralph drew back his legs and stood to put distance between Jean and the obvious moisture gathering all over his body. "No. This is my fault. I'll pay for it." Both Jean and Brett started to protest, but Ralph raised a hand to silence them. "Seriously. I've got this." The other two stopped arguing and wordlessly trudged off to work together, keeping well apart until they were out of sight of the flat.

Ralph rode past the shop on his way to see Caldwell. Brett had his clever fingers wrapped around Jean's bicep, laughing and comparing it to his own. When Ralph coasted into view, the pair leapt apart and Jean waved too enthusiastically and flashed him a gappy fake grin.

Ralph continued onward to Caldwell's office. He explained to the pseudo-dentist that Jean didn't care to speak to him or even see his face ever again. She just wanted this thing to be over with. Ralph paid in advance for the extraction the following day, and warned Caldwell not to stuff this one up.

That night, Jean slept with Ralph on the air mattress. They had sex just like before, but Jean cried this time, and then curled up away from him and wouldn't tell him what was wrong. He tried every leading question but the real one. He couldn't bring himself to ask and she couldn't bring herself to tell him.

The next morning, Brett took Jean to her appointment. Ralph promised them a delicious lunch of soft foods when they got home. Just as Jean requested, and perhaps for his own safety as well, Caldwell had his assistant put her out before he even entered the surgery. Brett waited in the next room, nodding off on a ratty old couch. The assistant tapped him awake an hour later with a sandwich bag full of teeth. He said the moulds and extractions were done and asked if Jean would be keeping the teeth, but Brett waved him away. Thirty minutes later, the same man returned to usher Brett into the recovery room with its sweetly nauseating stench of ether.

Jean was just resurfacing. The whole bottom half of her face was swollen and square. Cotton balls lined her lips, and as she woke and tried to swallow, she choked on the lack of saliva. Brett rushed to help her, sliding the water squirter between her lips. Caldwell had wandered off, but the assistant stood by with clean cotton balls. When Jean's throat was rehydrated, the assistant carefully rolled down her lower lip and began removing the blood-soaked cotton. Jean closed her eyes and seemed to drift off again, while Brett clasped her hand and watched the assistant place new cotton balls over her bleeding gums. A clean white row for the top. A clean white row for the bottom. The bottom ones seemed to be bleeding more heavily, which was strange, Brett thought, since gravity would...

It took him almost a full minute to catch on. The assistant's routine was so methodical it was mesmerizing.

When he did catch on, his face blanched. He carefully set Jean's hand back on the bed and tiptoed out of the recovery. As soon as he was clear, Brett's features darkened and he rampaged through the suite in search of Caldwell.

He found him out the back having a smoke. Brett rushed at Caldwell and lunged without stopping, ramming the man up against the wall by his throat. He raised him an inch off the ground and roared into his face: "You pulled them all!"

"Yeah?" said Caldwell, unruffled as ever.

"Why the fuck would you do that?"

"Her fiancé said that's what she wanted. Over and done with. Never have to worry about her teeth again."

"What?"

"He paid for it. I don't ask questions. He said that's what she wanted."

Brett threw Caldwell to the ground and kicked him once in the back.

Jean was waiting for him inside. Her eyes were open again and her eyebrows were drawn together. Brett didn't know if she was just confused generally, or if she'd already traced the amplified pain to her lower jaw. He watched her raise a finger, but she missed her gum, stabbing herself in the chin instead. The assistant shooed her hand away. Wetness ringed Jean's eyes as she looked up at Brett, but she seemed to change her mind about crying and, in another moment, was dozing again.

Brett dashed out to his motorcycle and roared away rehearsing a string of obscenities that weren't bad enough, that could never be bad enough. But when he got to Kingsland, Ralph was gone. His stuff was gone. His bike was gone. He hadn't left a note. He was just gone.

Contributor Biographies & Notes

Brandy Abraham's fiction and poetry have appeared in *Gambling the Aisle*, *Cardinal Sins*, *Squalorly*, *A Narrow Fellow*, and *Stone Highway Review*, among others. She is a native Michigander who is currently at work on a collection of short stories and a novel.

Comment on "Following the Encantado"—I have always been fascinated by lore and mythology—ever since I was a child growing up in the eerie, hard-harvested parts of Michigan. When the main character finds himself entranced by an Encantado, I too am entranced. This shape-shifting spirit that sings, much like a mermaid, lures men to their death. It reminded me of the times my parents and I would take trips on the Au Sable River in our beat-up canoe, and if you looked hard enough, listened hard enough, you could swear that there was more than fish under the water.

Richard A. Ballou is a former executive with an international information technology consulting firm who cashed in his stock options years ago to write literary fiction full time. He is currently working on *Mentalities*, a volume of loosely linked short stories that will complete a trilogy of short fiction collections exploring three facets of a common theme. Richard and his wife, Dee, live in Cary, North Carolina, where their home is a sanctuary of sorts to a certain flock of amazing children who regularly migrate to and from, along with an old and venerable itinerant cat (Jellicle by nature) drawn to the periodic magic and mayhem there.

Comment on "A Difficult Thing, a Beautiful Comfort"—The roots of this story go back over a dozen years to a brief conversation, five minutes at best, with a stranger. Unprompted, she shared how her grown son had disappeared without a trace while on a trip to South America. He had been traveling alone; years had passed, and he was presumed dead. I never saw her again, but the devastation of this mother's loss and her anxious and unsettled nature stuck with me. In time her pain coalesced with a son's longing, the isolations of the uniquely gifted, the search for solace, and the allure of Buenos Aires to become a short fiction. Perhaps sharing our stories with strangers makes us each more human.

Peyton Burgess teaches creative writing at Loyola University New Orleans and received his MFA in fiction from NYU. His work has appeared or is forthcoming in *Chicago Quarterly Review, Salon, Otis Nebula, Exquisite Corpse*, and *La Fovea.*

Comment on "Disaster Relief"—This was a story that I kept too close to me as I worked on it in the early stages. Some anger, heartache, and bitterness always got in the way of its crafting. There was a lot of unorganized shouting and screaming on the page. Eventually I gave up on it to focus on more experimental stuff, which was so liberating. I revisited the story about four months before submitting it to this anthology, maybe August 2013, and by then I think enough time had passed for me to release the story from my motives and allow it to exist a little bit more on its own terms.

A former secondary school and college teacher, **Joseph Cavano** is the author of *Half-past Nowhere* (CPCC Press, 2008) and *Love Songs in Minor Keys* (CPCC Press, 2009). His fiction has earned awards in contests such as the Doris Betts Fiction Prize and the Elizabeth Simpson Smith Short Story Contest, among others. His two most recent stories, "The Honey Wagon" and "Story Cloth," appeared in the Summer 2012 issue of *North Carolina Literary Review* and the Spring 2012 issue of *Potomac Review,* respectively. An accomplished jazz pianist, he often performs at his signings in order to illustrate the similarities in creating music and writing fiction.

Comment on "The Widow's Tale"—I first heard about the woman who would become the widow when I was a child. My grandparents lived downstairs from us then, and occasionally I'd hear them talking about their lives in Italy before they came to America in 1909. The story I heard my grandfather recount one night as I stood outside their door listening was not nearly as dramatic as the one I'd eventually write, but the two had much in common. Both featured a strong, determined woman and a large amount of money. Both ended poorly. In 1983, I visited relatives in "the old country" and discovered not only was the story true, but that much had been omitted. When I heard about my cousin Genaro and the August night he supposedly earned his questionable reputation, I understood why.

Jocelyn Cullity earned a PhD in Creative Writing from Florida State University. Her work has been published most recently in *The Writer's Chronicle, TWJ Magazine*, and *Blackbird*; her TV documentary about women teachers in China, *Going to the Sea*, aired nationally in Canada and Europe and continues to be purchased by libraries around the world. She teaches in the BFA program at Truman State University in Missouri.

Comment on "Visiting Chairman Mao"—This story came to me years after teaching in China in the 1990s—a time that changed my life. The character, Xiao Li, appeared before me one day while I was at my desk, and I realized she was standing in Tiananmen Square, one of my favorite places to go in Beijing. I immediately admired her for her tour-guide skills and I stayed with her while she took an American traveler through Mao's mausoleum. I hope readers come to love her as much as I do.

Rochelle Distelheim's work has been published in *The North American Review, Nimrod, StoryQuarterly, Other Voices, Confrontation, Salamander, Mississippi Valley Review,* and *The Chicago Tribune.* She has been awarded the William Faulkner–William Wisdom Society Gold Medal in Novel, the Katharine Anne Porter Prize, the *Salamander* Second Prize, Finalist Press 53 Open Awards, Finalist *Glimmer Train*, Illinois Arts Council Literary Awards and Fellowships, Ragdale Foundation Fellowships, Sewanee Writers' Conference Tennessee Williams Scholarship, and nominations for Best American Short Stories, 2013, and Pushcart Prize, 2015.

Comment on "Comfort Me with Apples" —I was in Jerusalem, trying the city on as I would a new coat. In my search for people who had emigrated to Israel from Russia, I wandered onto Ben Yehuda Mall, a lively collection of cafes and shops, and found a young couple performing. He alternately played the harmonica, clarinet, guitar. She, in a shredded silk something, danced and, from time to time, held out a man's cap to collect coins from the crowd. I looked around at the collection of people speaking at least six languages. Male and female soldiers, school boys, women, some in marriage wigs, others in sandals and sundresses, men in keepas and prayer shawls, all intent upon the dancing girl. Jerusalem, I thought, my spiritual home, but an impenetrable mystery. At any moment someone could open a paper bag, or a jacket, and detonate a bomb.

David Ebenbach is the author of two books of short stories—*Into the Wilderness* (Washington Writers' Publishing House) and *Between Camelots* (University of Pittsburgh Press)—plus a chapbook of poetry entitled *Autogeography* (Finishing Line Press), and a non-fiction guide to creativity called *The Artist's Torah* (Cascade Books). He has been awarded the Drue Heinz Literature Prize, fellowships to several artist colonies, and an Individual Excellence Award from the Ohio Arts Council. With a PhD in Psychology from the University of Wisconsin-Madison and an MFA in Writing from the Vermont College of Fine Arts, Ebenbach teaches Creative Writing at Georgetown University.

Comment on "Rue Rachel"—On a train to Montreal a few years ago I met a young woman, sort of like the character Rachel, prescription-drug hazy and traveling to see a sketchy boyfriend. She wouldn't leave me alone during the train ride. In fact, I couldn't get rid of her even after we'd arrived and she'd gone her way; her strange stories and her slippery-life philosophy and her shoes and her dubious immediate future all stayed in my head and made their predictable demand: *Write about me.* Then I stumbled across a street in Montreal called *Rue Rachel* and, although her name had not been Rachel, I acquiesced to the demand.

Jeff Fearnside lived and worked in Central Asia for four years, first as a U.S. Peace Corps volunteer and later as manager of the Muskie Graduate Fellowship Program in Kazakhstan and Kyrgyzstan. His writing on the region has appeared in many publications, including *Rosebud Magazine*, *Bayou Magazine*, *Crab Orchard Review*, *Permafrost*, *New Madrid*, *Potomac Review*, and the anthology *The Chalk Circle: Intercultural Prizewinning Essays*. His writing has been nominated for *Best New American Voices* and three times for a Pushcart Prize. He currently lives with his Kazakhstani wife Valentina and their two cats in Corvallis, Oregon.

Comment on "A Husband and Wife are One Satan"—The Russian language is rich in colorful colloquial expressions, something I was (and remain) fascinated with, and which I wanted to play with in a narrative, though in an exaggerated, stylized way—not to write a story strongly representative of a particular culture but rather, by blending show and reality, to use a particular culture's idioms and epithets to explore universal ideas regarding the overlap of what's considered public and private, relationships (between friends both male and female, couples both married and unmarried, and—in the case of the character Alikhan—an outsider and society), and the influence of language on our lives, particularly in how we use it to rationalize the choices we make.

Teresa Hudson is a lifelong resident of Powhatan, Virginia. She first became interested in Russia when she was twelve years old and saw *War and Peace* on television. She made her first trip to Leningrad (now St. Petersburg) in 1988, and has been a regular visitor to Russia since the early 1990s, volunteering for various arts organizations (including the State Hermitage Museum) as well as editing cultural publications. She holds both undergraduate and graduate degrees from the University of Richmond, and is currently pursuing an MFA in Creative Writing at Virginia Commonwealth University.

Comment on "The Art of Living"— I've worked as a volunteer at the State Hermitage Museum in St. Petersburg for many years. The idea for "The Art of Living" came to me after learning that a dear friend and guide there had been diagnosed with cancer. Not surprisingly, she continued to work until just before she died. I wanted to write something to honor both her dedication and passion for art, and her generous spirit.

Alden Jones's first book, *The Blind Masseuse: A Traveler's Memoir from Costa Rica to Cambodia*, was called "the best travel book of 2013" by *The Huffington Post* and was the winner of the Independent Publisher Book Award in Travel Essays. Her story collection, *Unaccompanied Minors*, won the 2013 New American Fiction Prize. She lives in Boston.

Comment on "Heathens"—When I was twenty-two, I spent a year in rural Costa Rica as a volunteer for WorldTeach. I struggled constantly with issues of class, nationality, and privilege. A fellow volunteer lived in a community similar to mine, and a group of teen American missionaries came to her town to help build a church. We spent a lot of time rolling our eyes at their cultural insensitivity. When I wrote "Heathens," I imagined the character of Lana, this hardcore anti-tourist, who tried to take an American like this to task. In some ways, Lana's heart is in the right place, but she doesn't have anyone to help her understand when she goes too far. I loved writing Lana, but I'm not sure I'd want her as a travel companion!

Jay Kauffmann holds an MFA from Vermont College and has taught at Randolph College, Vermont College, University of Virginia, and Miller School. Winner of the Andrew Grossbardt Memorial Prize and nominee for a Pushcart Prize, his work has appeared in *The Writer's Chronicle, Lumina, upstreet, CutBank, Storyglossia, Gulf Stream, Mid-American Review*, and elsewhere.

Comment on "In the German Garden"—I have an ex-girlfriend who lives in Berlin, within walking distance of the Grunewald, a vast and surprisingly wild place, where they really do have wild boars roaming the forest and wreaking havoc. The confluence in Berlin of old Nazi estates, an old American military base, a large transsexual community, my ex-girlfriend's teenage son, and a boar-terrorized park, all cried out to be made into a story.

Jennifer Lucy Martin is a fiction writer and aid worker. She holds a master's degree in international nutrition from Tufts University and is currently an MFA candidate in the creative writing program at UMASS-Boston. Before matriculating at UMASS, Jennifer worked for fifteen years in emergency and public health nutrition in Africa, Southeast Asia, and the Caribbean. She has been writing fiction since she was a child. Many of her short stories take place in the developing countries she has lived in as does her novel, a work in progress based on her experiences as an emergency nutritionist in South Sudan.

Comment on "International Women's Day"—I was inspired to write the story by the horror of a conflict brought on partly by the greed for Congo's natural resources. But I was specifically motivated by something I heard about a woman who prevented her daughter's rape by offering her own body to the soldier who was threatening them. I was struck by the impossible choice that woman faced and the sacrifice she made to protect her child. I was also struck by the monstrous entitlement of the soldier, an entitlement that runs beneath the surface of the war and the story—the U.S. and Europe are entitled to cell phones, regional countries are entitled to Congo's gold and diamonds, Congolese soldiers and rebels are entitled to power, men are entitled to sex.

Marc Nieson is a graduate of the Iowa Writers' Workshop and NYU Film School. His background includes children's theatre, cattle chores, and a season with a one-ring circus. His prose has earned two Pushcart Prize nominations, the Literal Latte Fiction Award, and Raymond Carver Short Story Award. Excerpts from his memoir, *Schoolhouse*, were noted in *Best American Essays 2012* and have appeared in *Literary Review, Iowa Review, Green Mountains Review,* and *Chautauqua.* Award-winning, feature-length screenplays include *Speed of Life, The Dream Catcher,* and *Bottomland.* An assistant professor in Chatham University's MFA program, he's working on a new novel, *Houdini's Heirs.*

Comment on "The Ring"—While living in Venice, Italy, I traveled to see a one-ring circus, *Circo di Budapest*, whose humble, green poster I'd spotted in passing. Soon I was captivated by a duet of acrobats, and their act kept spinning in my dreams that night. Come morning, I took the train back to Padova, but found the caravan had already packed up and departed. All that remained was a circle of tent-spike holes in the ground, and a handful of romping Roma gypsy children. I played with them instead, and somewhere between their migrant laughter and our dirty fingernails, "The Ring" was born.

Holly Painter is an MFA graduate of the University of Canterbury in Christchurch, New Zealand. Her fiction and poetry have been published in literary journals in the U.S., New Zealand, and Australia, including *Sport, Landfall, New Zealand Listener, Barrelhouse*, and *Cream City Review.* Holly is currently working on a novel set in contemporary Singapore and a collection of poetry about the people of Detroit. She lives with her wife in Singapore and writes love poems on behalf of besotted people around the world at adoptapoet. wordpress.com.

Comment on "Jean"—This story comes from *Undie*, an unpublished novel in stories set during the 2009 Undie 500 student road rally from Christchurch to Dunedin. On their way south, the characters hold a storytelling contest in the spirit of the Canterbury tales. In the novel, "Jean" is a story told by a young woman who will soon be facing up to a rapist in court. The seed for this story came with a visit to Detroit, where I came across an unlicensed dentistry clinic operated by a man with dubious qualifications but enormous enthusiasm for giving it a go. I did not allow him to touch my teeth.

Matthew Pitt is the author of *Attention Please Now*. Winner of the Autumn House Fiction Prize, this story collection later received Late Night Library's Debut-litzer Prize and was a finalist for the Writers League of Texas Book Award. Pitt's fiction appears widely in journals and anthologies including *Conjunctions, Oxford American, Epoch, The Southern Review* and *Best New American Voices*. An Assistant Professor at TCU, his work has been cited in several end-of-year anthologies, receiving honors and fellowships from the Mississippi Arts Commission, *St. Louis Post-Dispatch*, and the Bread Loaf, Sewanee and Taos Writers' Conferences.

Comment on "Au Lieu des Fleurs"—Set in France, and written in the U.S., this story's genesis came from The Netherlands. As the 20th Century came to a close, I won a fellowship to a peace conference in The Hague. While discussing child soldiers, landmine restrictions, and Milosevic's war crimes, I scanned an article about Mouna Aguigui's death. I'd never read such a buoyant obituary. It struck me that this anarchist prankster was, through madcap acts, working to illuminate the same injustices and absurdities we were. When I tackled a draft in earnest, a graduate professor revealed he knew Mouna, spilling stories that helped me better catch the voice. That instructor makes an unbilled cameo in this fiction, although, in the spirit of Mouna, I'm not saying where.

Midge Raymond's short-story collection, *Forgetting English,* received the Spokane Prize for Short Fiction and, according to the *Seattle Times*, "lights up the poetry-circuits of the brain." Originally published by Eastern Washington University Press in 2009, the book was reissued in an expanded edition by Press 53 in 2011. Midge is also the author of two books for writers: *Everyday Writing* and *Everyday Book Marketing*. Her work has appeared in *The Writer*, the *Los Angeles*

Times, TriQuarterly, American Literary Review, Ontario Review, Bellevue Literary Review, and others.

Comment on "The Ecstatic Cry"—This story was inspired by my own expedition to Antarctica many years ago, during which I realized that perhaps it's not such a good idea for this fragile environment to receive as many visitors as it now does—tourism in Antarctica has increased from a few thousand travelers a year in the 1990s to tens of thousands today. I channeled my anxiety about what's happening to the animals, the oceans, and the earth's climate into the story's narrator, making her a scientist on the forefront of what's happening at the bottom of the earth—and along the way she became so much more than a cranky biologist.

Tim Weed's fiction has appeared in *Colorado Review, Gulf Coast, Sixfold*, and many other journals and anthologies. He is the winner of a Writer's Digest Popular Fiction Award and a Best Travel Writing Solas Award, and his collected stories have been shortlisted for the New Rivers Press Many Voices Project, the Autumn House Fiction Prize, and the Lewis-Clark Press Discovery Award. Based in Vermont, Tim is a lecturer in the MFA Writing program at Western Connecticut State University and a featured expert for *National Geographic Expeditions* in Cuba, Spain, and Patagonia. *Will Poole's Island*, Tim's first novel, was published in 2014.

Comment on "The Money Pill"—One of the somber joys of being a fiction writer is that you can insert your characters into difficult and/or morally dubious situations without having to suffer or inflict the real-world consequences of their actions. "The Money Pill" grew out of a series of trips I made to the eastern part of Cuba in the earliest years of the twenty-first century. Writing it was, in part, a process of taking several jotted-down interactions and playing them out to their logical conclusions. On a deeper level—over the many drafts it took to get the story into an intelligible form—certain themes began to emerge that captured something essential, for me at least, about Cuba and the wealthy superpower that is its close and yet utterly estranged neighbor.

Jill Widner was born in Houston, Texas, and grew up in Indonesia, where her father was a petroleum engineer in the 1960s. Her novel in progress observes a subculture of expatriate children growing up in an oil camp in south Sumatra during the years before and following the Sukarno coup. Her fiction has appeared recently in *The Fiddlehead, Short Fiction*, and *Shenandoah*. She has been the recipient of a Hawthornden Fellowship, an Artist Trust/Washington State Arts Commission Fellowship, and she has been selected for residencies at Yaddo, the Virginia Center for the Creative Arts, and VCCA-France. She is a graduate of the Iowa Writers' Workshop and lives and teaches in Yakima, Washington.

Comment on "When Stars Fell Like Salt before the Revolution"—The story is set in Iran, where my father worked in the early 1970s, and is based partly on a road trip I took with my mother to Isfahan and Shiraz at the age of nineteen. Douglas Glover, who selected it as one of two honorable mentions in *The Fiddlehead's* 23rd annual fiction contest, calls it "a wonderful story about love, poetry, and translation set in Iran before the shah was deposed." It is one of the stories included in my collection, *A Green Raft on a Muddy Swell*, which was shortlisted for the 2013 Scott Prize (Salt Publishing, UK). For me it is a memory of how forthcoming young people can be and how easily they can overlook the chasms between their lives.

William Kelley Woolfitt teaches creative writing and American literature at Lee University in Cleveland, Tennessee. He is the author of a book of poetry, *Beauty Strip*, forthcoming from Texas Review Press. He is also the author of a fiction chapbook, *The Boy with Fire in His Mouth* (2014), and two poetry chapbooks, *The Salvager's Arts* (2013) and *Chorus Frog* (2014). His poems and stories appear in *Shenandoah, Michigan Quarterly Review, Threepenny Review, Tin House* online, *New Ohio Review, Appalachian Heritage, The Cincinnati Review, Hayden's Ferry Review, Ninth Letter, River Styx*, and elsewhere.

Comment on "The Boy with Fire in His Mouth"—Meredith Sue Willis advises writers to cut a third of the words from the first full draft because "trimming intensifies expression." As I look back at older drafts of "The Boy with Fire in His Mouth," I see that Willis's advice has served me well. In one early draft, "The Boy" was about 2,300 words long and included a mysterious nun, a bus trip to the equator, and more details about the narrator's rakish father and austere mother. That draft seems like a blabbermouth party guest, yammering for attention. Somehow, the leaner final version (about 1,000 words long) seems richer, more complete to me.

Susi Wyss served in the Peace Corps in the Central African Republic from 1990 to 1992, and subsequently worked on health programs in Africa for nearly two decades. Her first book of fiction, *The Civilized World* (Henry Holt, 2011), is inspired by her experiences in Africa. It received the 2012 Maria Thomas Fiction Award and was named a "Book to Pick Up Now" by *O, The Oprah Magazine*. Susi has a master's degree in fiction writing from Johns Hopkins University and is a two-time recipient of the Maryland State Arts Council's Artist Award.

Comment on "Eggs"—Ten years after my Peace Corps service, I returned to the Central African Republic to visit. While there, I ran across Sheila, a sixteen-year-old girl I'd known when she was a child. In the time since I'd seen her, she had lost her mother to AIDS and become a mother herself. "Eggs" was an attempt to give voice to girls like Sheila in the developing world whose potential is undermined by a lack of opportunities. After it was published by *Bellevue Literary Review*, I decided the character of Grace deserved a longer telling of her story and began working on a novel that expands on her life.

About the Editor

Clifford Garstang is the author of the novel in stories *What the Zhang Boys Know*, which won the 2013 Library of Virginia Award for Fiction, and a collection of linked stories, *In an Uncharted Country*, which won the 2010 Maria Thomas Fiction Award. Garstang, who served as a Peace Corps Volunteer in South Korea, practiced international law in Singapore, Chicago, and Los Angeles with one of America's largest law firms and with the World Bank in Washington, D.C., where he was Senior Counsel for East Asia. His work has appeared in *Bellevue Literary Review, Blackbird, Cream City Review, Virginia Quarterly Review*, and elsewhere. He is the co-founder and editor of *Prime Number Magazine*.

CPSIA information can be obtained at www.ICGtesting.com
Printed in the USA
LVOW10s1123260715
447684LV00006B/719/P